LIQUID COUGAR

Cover, interior, eBook design by The Book Cover Whisperer: OpenBookDesign.biz

979-8-9856363-0-7 Paperback
979-8-9856363-1-4 eBook

FIRST EDITION

C.N. FARGO

LIQUID
COUGAR

CHAPTER 1

The Travel Agency

Mark skipped out over lunch and stopped by his travel agent. While he wasn't a Luddite, he thought using a brick-and-mortar travel agent would help him keep the trip a secret from Stef, zero digital footprint. Everything was coming together, the five-year anniversary trip that he had planned was almost complete. He just had to finish the final touches.

As Mark entered the travel agency, the receptionist put a finger up but didn't look at Mark while typing on her computer, "Hold on honey, have a seat. All of our agents are busy, but you're next in line." The receptionist then glanced up and gave Mark a once-over, "Hey, you look like a smart guy…what is a country in North Africa that ends with an O and has seven letters?"

"Don't you work at a travel agency?" Mark replied. "Try Morocco."

"Oh yeah, sure enough, that works!" the receptionist cheerfully replied "Thank you!"

Mark had spent a couple months in Morocco last year, opening up an office for Kilimanjaro Risk, the company he worked for. This trip however was going to be different; this was all for fun. A two-week journey through Greece and the Greek Isles. Although he grew up traveling extensively through his mom's job (she was the partner of a global consultancy to sovereign wealth funds) he had never been to Greece. It was always something they had talked about but never pulled the trigger on.

He was pretty sure Stef had no idea. He had it all planned out: tonight they had reservations at their favorite restaurant, and he'd prepped the waiter in advance to bring the tickets on cue. They normally went out on Friday nights so this was nothing unusual. Stef was getting off work at two p.m. She had recently transitioned to part-time, in addition to experimenting with theater acting. It was going to be a great night of dinner and surprises.

"OK doll, you can go back now, Marcy is ready for you. She's the third gal on the left," the receptionist snapped.

Mark hopped up off his chair and bounced down the hall looking for Marcy. "Over here Mike, have a seat," he heard from his left.

"Oh hi, actually my name is Mark, but no worries. I called and spoke to someone. I think my trip should be all set up but wanted to come by to tie up any loose ends and get our tickets. It should be under Mark Coghlan, I'm taking my wife to Greece for our five-year anniversary," Mark said with some excitement in his voice. It was starting to seem real.

"Let's see Mr. Coghlan, here it is, two first-class tickets to Greece. First class…nice…I think your girlfriend is really going to like her birthday present."

Mark gave Marcy a bewildered look. "Umm, actually it's my wife, and like I said it is our five-year wedding anniversary, not her birthday."

Marcy, completely unaware of her error, responds, "That is fantastic, I have always wanted to see Greece. The Coliseum sounds amazing. I wish I had a job that allowed me to travel."

Mark, unsure of exactly how to respond and questioning his choice of travel agents, said, "Uh, you might be confused. I believe the Coliseum is in Rome. As a travel agent aren't you encouraged to...travel?"

"Exactly, you will love it," Marcy responded, not even looking up to acknowledge him. "OK, it looks like we have you flying into Athens three weeks from now and staying for two weeks, and you've upgraded to our special VIP island tour package...ooh, classy!" Marcy shouted and giggled awkwardly. She then looked off into the distance and said, "That reminds me, one of my ex-boyfriends used to call me Medusa. I think she was some sort of Greek goddess. Geez, I thought I'd marry him. I still can't believe he dumped me for not having enough career focus and ambition. If he could only see me now...guess I'm getting the last laugh. I hope that loser saw my Facebook post announcing I was employee of the month once last year." She snapped back to reality, picking up the travel documents and handing them over. "Hmm, OK, so back to your trip, you should be all set Mike. Here are your tickets!"

Mark, getting more frustrated but showing restraint, replied, "My name is Mark, and yes I think it's clear it was your ex-boyfriend's loss." Mark paused, contemplating whether or not to share with Marcy that Medusa was actually a monster with snakes on her head but decided it was best to move on. "I think this looks in order, we should be set."

As Mark stood up and thanked Marcy, he turned to walk out with the plane tickets in hand and Marcy shouted, "Make sure to take pictures of the Coliseum! I hear the pizza is great!" Mark smiled awkwardly and as he exited the office, he shook his head.

Mark quickly forgot the odd experience and started walking back to work. Now that he had the tickets, he was even more excited. He wondered what else should he do to make the night perfect? Should he get down on one knee like when he proposed? Should he say something funny, like the tickets really weren't to Greece but instead to a hedonistic clothing optional resort for swingers? How about a camping trip? Stef hated camping. Maybe a mission trip to Africa taking care of sick children? She also was never a big fan of kids. She did however always like his sense of humor. He knew there was no way he would be productive this afternoon. He had a couple conference calls, but he was now focused on surprising Stef and making the night perfect. Only five more hours until he met Stef for dinner and shared the surprise.

CHAPTER 2

The Dinner

It was a bit after five and Mark just wrapped up his last conference call. He raced out of his office, heading to the restaurant. He needed to get there in time to give the tickets to the waiter and make sure everything was set for the big night.

At 6:20, Mark was starting to wonder where Stef was. She knew reservations were at six and she only worked until two today. Why wasn't she responding to his texts? Hopefully everything was OK. *Oh well,* he thought, *surely she got caught up shopping somewhere or stuck in traffic.* She could have just been tied up with her friend Amy.

A few minutes later Stef stepped into the restaurant, several shopping bags in tow. Over the five years of their marriage Stef's spending habits had broadened. She seemed to shop more and work less, but Mark was always easygoing about it. He rationalized the behavior: why not spend money while you have it. He liked his job and didn't mind that Stef was becoming less career motivated. It was all about being happy in life, if that's what made her happy, then he would support it.

"I'm sorry Mark, Amy and I got caught up shopping and lost track of time. Jimmy Choo just got their new line in and the store was *swamped*," Stef flatly explained as she walked towards him. "I saw that you texted, but Amy and I were busy trying on shoes, I didn't want to be rude to the clerks and be typing on my phone."

"That's OK, Stef." Mark was just happy to see her and excited for the surprise night.

After the maître d' sat them at the table that Mark had pre-arranged, they started exchanging the normal catch-up about how their day was.

"I really think this job fits me better. I can relate to all of the clients that come into the center," said Stef. "I met a lady today who had been cursed by gypsies, actually her entire family going back several generations had been cursed. We used the negative energy in her spirit to chase the demons away and healed her with a crystal-laced steam bath. You could tell she was a different person after she left."

"Wow, that's...interesting," replied Mark who had become used to Stef's stories, but lately they seemed to be getting increasingly bizarre.

Mark and Stef met shortly after college. They both coincidentally lived in the same building. On the day he moved out, he was pulling out of the parking garage one last time after the movers had left, and in a rush, he backed into a car. Nobody was around, so he left a note with his phone number on the windshield and a day later got a call from Stef. He was relieved the person he hit wasn't too upset, she was easygoing. Once they talked and laughed about it, they also realized they'd seen each other in their building but never met. Mark offered to take Stef's car in to get it fixed so she didn't have to deal with it, and it was that act of chivalry that kick-started their relationship. They began dating, and a few years later they married.

After Stef graduated from college, she pursued careers in business, but nothing ever stuck. She then fell into random jobs, all of which centered around physical and mental health: yoga instructor, day spa sales, massage therapist, and now working in a spiritual healing center. This job was the most unusual. She had picked up this work about two months ago, and Mark noticed a slight change since then. Many of the stories she would come home with were hard to believe, and he had a difficult time relating to them or knowing what to say. He always thought to himself, *If the Stef he married were listening to these stories, she would have thought they were crazy, but now they were part of her normal day.* In any case, although the job didn't pay well and he was slightly annoyed by the shift in attitude, he wanted her to be happy. If this is what it took, so be it.

"So what does something like that cost, you know, to get rid of an evil gypsy curse and then take a bath in crystals?" Mark asked slightly tongue-in-cheek but partially because he was curious.

"Well, she was referred by one of the Sherpas we know, so it was only $129. Which by many standards is a steal, you can't even talk to a medical doctor for less than $1,000, much less be healed of an evil curse."

"True," Mark replied, thinking if it was anyone other than Stef he would have probably had a much more sarcastic and sharp-witted reply. He was eager to switch gears and change the subject. "I've been thinking…our five-year anniversary is getting closer. It's hard to believe we've been married that long!" Mark's voice was filled with excitement as he thought about sharing the news. "Have you thought about what you want to do?"

Stef paused and looked a little uncomfortable by the question, finally remarking, "We don't need to do anything, in fact Amy had been talking about doing a girls' weekend right around the time of our anniversary. She found a 'women in power' workshop that sounds interesting. The entire idea revolves around unleashing the predator power that is deep within a woman. The literature claims it will turn even the meekest into an 'alpha she-wolf' in one weekend."

Mark listened as Stef described it. Amy was one of Stef's best friends, but they couldn't have been more different. Stef was a fairly passive person, more of a follower and influenced by others. She rarely had strong opinions, but often would adopt the opinions of those she was closest to. Mark always felt that was one reason why there was an uncharacteristic appeal between the two. Amy was about as hardcore as they come, aggressive was an understatement. She would routinely put down all men and had zero filter when it came to holding back. Mark didn't know why she acted the way she did, but she was the oldest in a family of four sisters, and her dad left her mom for someone twenty years younger. Amy had been estranged from her dad ever since, and Mark always suspected her family situation molded her to be how she is today. She might have seen Stef as one of her sisters, someone to protect from all men, whether they were a threat or not. Stef seemed to value her dogmatic strength and opinions. Amy's heart was likely in the right place, but her actions were misguided and extreme.

This pattern started from the moment they met. When Stef moved into the city she decided to take a self-defense class, which happened to be taught by Amy. 'XX Domination,' a name that played off the chromosome genetic make-up of women, was an all-female self-defense class started by Amy. Stef ended up being one of her early students. She took an immediate liking to Amy; she was everything that Stef was not—assertive, dominant, and controlling. Amy viewed Stef as weak, and someone that needed protection but could also be molded. They started hanging out almost immediately.

"It sounds like Amy could teach a class like that. Does she really need to find her alpha she-wolf?"

"She's just opinionated, and men have a hard time with that," Stef replied in defense of Amy. There had always been some tension in their marriage because of Amy. Mark felt that some of Amy's anti-men/anti-marriage views had rubbed off on Stef over the years.

"You're right," Mark replied, knowing that he didn't want to start an argument, certainly not tonight. "In any event, getting back to our anniversary, I really want to do something big, this is a milestone." He paused, shifting in his seat a little. "It seems like it was just yesterday when we first met. I can clearly picture it. It was serendipitous to accidentally back into your car." Mark decided it was a good time to fill her in. "So, I know you like art and architecture, and I planned the perfect trip for us. Can you guess where that is?" Mark asked.

"Umm Mark," Stef replied, cutting into his point and shifting her demeanor. "There is something we should talk about, but can you hold on a second?"

"OK." Mark was confused and unsure what was going on, although it didn't seem good.

"I'll be right back." Stef walked away briskly.

What was probably a few seconds felt more like minutes as Mark was sitting at the table, still unsure what Stef was doing. He was intrigued. Maybe she had a gift for him and left it at the coat check. His train of thought was broken as he looked to the front of the room and saw Amy walking back with Stef to their table. Mark was confused, unsure what to say.

As Amy and Stef sat down, Stef nervously said, "I have something to talk with you about and Amy and I both thought it was a good idea if she were here. I've been doing quite a bit of thinking about us and my life, and I feel we are growing apart. I want to find myself, and the more I talk with Amy and my new co-workers, I need to chart a path of self-reflectiveness, a mind journey."

Mark, at first thinking this was a joke, started to laugh a bit. He soon realized it wasn't a joke, and his smile turned to concern and confusion. "Ooookkk, what exactly does that mean, and why is Amy here?"

"We both thought it was a good idea for her to be here. I want to spend some time figuring out what my greater purpose in life is, you know, what my destiny is."

Mark replied with a stammer in his voice, "What do you mean, I don't think I understand…" Before he could get the sentence out, Amy cut in.

"Look Mark, she's leaving you. The journey she is talking about doesn't include you. She's divorcing you, and she wanted me here for support because she didn't know how you would react. I told her to do this in a public place to avoid any violent outbursts from you. Go ahead and try something, I wouldn't mind giving you a beatdown in front of all the other diners."

Mark, almost in disbelief, was trying to catch up in his mind with the words being said. He stumbled a bit, but finally said, "Stef, I don't really know what to say or where to start, but don't you think this is something we should talk about a little more *on our own*." Mark continued, shifting to speak more from the heart. "I'm shocked. I guess I didn't see this coming. I think we should talk through it. This seems like a very rash decision, I'm having a hard time understanding it. Why on earth did you think I was going to be violent? I've never been violent to anyone, certainly not you. You aren't making any sense, none of this makes any sense."

Stef looked at Amy, then back at Mark and said somewhat flatly, "I'm going to stay at Amy's tonight. I've already packed a bag and I'll send someone to get more of my stuff later this week. Amy told me it's probably best if we keep this conversation short."

"What!?" Mark's confusion turned to anger. "At what point in our marriage did Amy start calling the shots and telling you what to think? Stef, this is our marriage, nobody else decides for us. Let's at least talk about it, consider counseling, take a vacation, or do whatever it takes.

I set up this dinner to tell you that I bought us tickets to Greece for our anniversary, that was my surprise!"

Stef looked blankly back at Mark and all of a sudden Amy piped in. "Stef, let's go." Amy snapped her fingers at the waiter who had been waiting on the sidelines to bring the tickets but now looked almost as confused at Mark. "Box this up for us and make it snappy. Also, throw in a couple orders of crème brûlée to go," Amy said, almost routinely like this was a normal conversation and part of her everyday life.

Amy and Stef quickly got up, while Mark stayed seated, staring into the abyss, dazed from what happened. He looked over to make a last-ditch attempt to talk to Stef, but they were already almost out the door. As he stood, the waiter came by and still looking confused said, "Sir, here is the bill, and I guess the tickets?" Mark quickly paid the bill and left, accidentally walking out the fire escape door and tripping the alarm which put the restaurant in a state of chaos, but Mark was oblivious to it all, flummoxed by what had just happened with Stef.

3 weeks later

Over the next few weeks, Mark's three best friends went out of their way to make sure they were there for their friend. They also tried to get him over some of the misconceptions Mark had about the divorce and to confront reality. Meanwhile, Stef was spending more time than ever with Amy, particularly now that she was living with her. At first Mark tried to engage Stef in texts and voicemails, but it became clear she wasn't reciprocating, and deep down he was starting to wonder if it just wasn't meant to be. Maybe they could still be friends he tried to convince himself.

As Mark and his friends sat down to grab dinner, Steve asked, "How are the discussions going with Stef so far? Have you guys talked about how you will divide things? What has she said about alimony or maintenance?"

"Stef doesn't want my money." Mark was out with his friends— Christian, Steve, and Ronald for a drink. "She just wants to find herself. I understand now we probably just weren't meant to be, I should have been better at picking up on signs of her and Amy spending so much time together."

"Listen, Captain Optimism," Christian said, "do you really think your soon to be ex-wife, the one who bought more Louis Vuitton handbags last year than most women do over a lifetime is *not* going to go after your money? She's going to SEAL Team Six your ass, and you won't have a clue what hit you. You'll be like Bin Laden sitting in your fancy man palace, thinking you're untouchable, and BAM!" Christian shouts, slamming his beer down on the table. "All of a sudden you'll have a wrath of femi-nazi fury rain down on you like Desert Storm. I'm telling you, she's lining up the tomahawk missiles as we speak, the weapons of mass destruction are being strategically aimed at your ass while you sulk in your mystical fantasyland of divorce bliss. You couldn't be an easier target, an up-and-coming executive who makes a lot of money versus a poor girl who can't fend for herself. I can write the script for how this story is going to end."

"OK enough of the war analogies, I think you're being a little cynical Christian, you don't know Stef the way I do. Plus, I don't think you're the guy who should be doling out advice on women, you've never been married and you have a new girlfriend every week. Which begs the question: who is the flavor of the day now? Jasmine the Pilates trainer again, or was that last week?" Mark, and all of the guys continuously give Christian a bad time for his revolving-door approach to girlfriends.

"She goes by Jazzy, not Jasmine. That's exactly why you should take advice from me, I understand women better than any of you fools. I've been getting into the psyche of women ever since I nailed my Spanish teacher, sophomore year. I understand women better than they understand themselves." Christian never lacked confidence.

"I think you should write a book Christian, just think what you could give back to the science community, contributing to the subject of rare venereal diseases. There are doctors around the world that would learn from all of the viruses you've contracted since your sophomore Spanish teacher," Steve quickly retorted. Steve was the complete opposite of Christian. Christian was the risk-taker in the bunch, a fast-talking sharp-tongued investment banker who claimed he would never get married. Steve was the conservative friend who avoided any kind of risk. After marrying his high school sweetheart and becoming a middle school math teacher, they settled down and had two kids. "Mark, I don't think you should take any advice from Christian."

"Hey guys, do you think that guy across the bar has been looking at me funny?" Ronald finally chimed in randomly after being quiet up until this point in the night. "I think he's following me."

"Who, the idiot in the Members Only jacket?" Christian asked, feeding into Ronald's usual bizarre questions.

"Yeah, that's the guy. I'm glad you see it too, he's totally watching me. He won't take his eyes off me."

Christian quickly retorted, "Ronald, the guy is looking at his beer right now. Despite that however, I'm sure you are being followed. In fact, I'm thinking the CIA might be investigating how you are manipulating the price of popcorn at the Howard Cineplex. I'm sure the story is going to be broken wide open by *20/20* very soon, probably the same guy who does those pedophile sting operations. You already know him, right?"

Although it was a little cutting, Ronald was the friend everyone made fun of, the easy target. He was in fact the assistant manager at the local movie theater and when he wasn't working, he spent most of his time smoking pot and researching conspiracy theories. He still lived with his mom, partially because he was convinced that as soon as he signed a lease or got a mortgage, he would be traceable. He had a bit of a messed-up childhood. He never met his dad, and all he really knew about him is that he was one-third Jamaican, one-third Japanese, and one-third Irish. His mom was Middle Eastern, which made Ronald his own diverse melting pot of greatness. He was slightly overweight and his facial and body hair grew uncontrollably. The blending of Jamaican, Japanese, Irish, and Middle Eastern gave him dark curly hair, which he normally grew out into a mini-Afro. At five feet eight, he was by far the shortest of the friend group. He was a short and hairy guy who had a bizarre but lovable personality. Although his friends were convinced he didn't have a credit card or bank account because he couldn't get one, he claimed he pays with cash for everything to avoid being tracked.

"Have you thought about an attorney yet?" Steve, largely ignoring the banter between Ronald and Christian, wanted to focus the discussion back on Mark.

"I have, actually. I'm leaning towards hiring some guy my admin recommended, one of her ex-boyfriends. She said he's been a little down on his luck, he could use the work."

"That sounds a little risky, do you know if he's any good?" Steve was skeptical but wanted to give Mark the benefit of the doubt.

"Well, I guess so, but I haven't asked much. She said he mainly does real estate work, but my divorce should be straight-forward. I just need someone to help me with the filing, and someone who can work with whoever Stef hires."

"Hey, professor dipshit, did you hear anything I said about five minutes ago?" Christian snapped. "I wish I was your ex-wife! Not only do you think she won't want your money, but now you're going to hire some mortgage guy to handle your divorce. Smart. You might as well shove your balls down the garbage disposal."

"Geez Christian, why don't you back off a bit, the guy just had his life turned upside down. I don't think he needs you laying into him." Steve was always defending Mark and usually taking the opposite side of Christian.

"Hey guys, I'm still sitting right here, and while I appreciate you all looking out for me, I can take care of myself. I've gotten this far, haven't I? Seriously though, I think this guy will be fine. I meet with him on Wednesday, how complicated can it be?"

"I think you need to be careful Mark, I know you feel that Stef will be reasonable, but there is a risk that you could be wrong. You have a lot at stake, literally tens of millions. Not just what you pull down at Kilimanjaro, but all of the money from your mom's consulting business which you're a shareholder of." Steve, trying to be the balance between Mark's and Christian's extremes. Mark's mom was still alive and well, but she had made Mark a shareholder of her consultancy for estate planning purposes.

All of a sudden Ronald piped in. "I just know if I was getting a divorce, I'd hire the dude that OJ had. Either that, or I'd represent myself. For starters I'd have an airtight prenup."

"Wow, where to start with that comment! The 'OJ guy' kicked the bucket years ago, but he would probably still do better from the grave than you would representing yourself. Not to mention he was a criminal defense attorney. Also, you are an assistant manager at a movie theater, what exactly are you protecting with a prenup!?" Christian was laughing as he was talking, both at his jokes and with Ronald. "You do realize that when I told you to not highlight on Tinder that you are a manager at a movie theater, it wasn't because I was concerned women would want you for your money, right?"

"Hey!" Ronald snapped, "my job has a lot of fringe benefits when you add up the free movies and jumbo pretzels. Not to mention I work with a lot of hot girls, I mean *a lot*. I'm also like the only hot guy there."

"Sure, you do work with a lot of girls, some of whom have a curfew of ten thirty, and hopefully will have their driver's license in the next year. Maybe you can go to prom?" Christian again with the sharp-witted comments. "Also, if by 'hot guy' you mean a guy who is five eight, in his mid-thirties, slightly overweight and rocks obnoxious body hair then yes, you are definitely the *only* hot guy."

At this point all four guys were laughing pretty hard, including Ronald even though he was the butt of the jokes.

The waitress came by. "Anyone for last call?"

"I think I'm going to call it a night," Mark quickly inserted. "I have a presentation tomorrow I still need to prep for."

All four guys decided to leave, except Christian. As usual he stuck around. He rarely ever left a bar alone, and worst-case he would give Jazzy or someone else a late-night booty call.

On Mark's walk home, he was thinking about how great the night was. It had been a while since he had laughed that hard. Although the four guys couldn't be more different, they were great friends, and had been for over twenty years—all growing up in the same small neighborhood. While their adult lives had taken them in different directions, they had the strongest of bonds. They had spent most of their waking adolescent minutes with each other, whether it was running a con against one of the bullies who lived near them to trade away his best baseball cards or helping pick up the pieces when one of the guys had girl problems. That early bond between the four had arched into the lifetime friend goals that everyone strived for. Although Christian could be an ass, Mark knew that when push came to shove, he'd always be there for him. The same went for the other guys. One good thing about the divorce, he could now spend more quality time with his friends.

CHAPTER 4

Across Town

Meanwhile, a similar situation took place with Stef and some of her friends on the other side of town, including Amy. Tonight was Amy's kickboxing class, and she had invited Stef. Amy had been talking to Stef quite a bit about the divorce, especially considering they had been living together temporarily. Amy had become an even more dominating force in Stef's life lately.

"I told you Stef, he makes a lot of money, he owes you. You earned it," Amy shouted as she gave the beefy male kicking post a roundhouse to the head. "Knowing Mark, he was probably hiding money from you all along. You should hire a forensic accountant to start digging through all of your accounts. A friend of mine got a divorce and found out her ex had hidden hundreds of thousands in hard-to-trace accounts and safe deposit boxes. He even started funneling it to others so they could hide it for him and give it back later."

"You really think he would do that?" Stef voiced a hint of concern and skepticism.

Amy planted another sharp roundhouse to the kick dummy and turned to Stef. "Are you kidding? Of course he would, he's a guy, they are selfish and will do anything to protect themselves. I told you the other day, I know a great attorney. The guy's a shark. You know with Mark's business connections and ties to the legal industry he will try to hire the best, and you need to do the same."

Amy's comments were starting to sink in for Stef. At first she was more focused on her self-proclaimed mind journey. She felt that Mark would be more than fair with the money. After all they had been married for five years and she felt she knew him better than anyone. Now as Amy was continuing to influence and mold her thoughts, Stef's goals were shifting. This was her future. Amy was right; she needed to look out for herself.

CHAPTER 5

Enter Tony

Over the next couple weeks, Mark poured himself into his work more than usual, it was a healthy distraction for him. Even his boss Tony, the CEO of Kilimanjaro Risk, was telling him to ease up and relax a bit. Tony was not a typical conservative executive. Professionally, Tony spent most of his time and had made most of his money from Kilimanjaro, but his latest side hustle, start-up venture called "Liquid Cougar" had vaulted him into the upper echelon of success. Liquid Cougar took the craze in energy drinks to the next level; it was like Red Bull on steroids. There were rumors that Tony had someone bribe the FDA to get final approval. He was one of the co-founders and significant shareholders when Liquid Cougar went public. Although he was chairman of the company, he left the day-to-day operations with the CEO and broader management team. Personally, Tony was divorced twice and now thrived on living the life of a hardcore bachelor.

When Liquid Cougar went public, Tony threw a massive party and hired Kanye West to perform. After consuming way too much Liquid Cougar—laced with vodka and Ambien—he ended up sleeping with one of his daughter's sorority sisters. It wasn't the first time it had happened and wouldn't be the last. Mark always described Tony as being like a bad car accident, you know it isn't good, but you can't take your eyes off of it. Although they were completely different, they had a mutual level of professional respect for the other. Tony had the relationships in the industry and was a consummate networker; Mark was the brains and operations wizard. They had worked together for eight years, and Mark would never minimize the fact that Tony plucked him fresh out of school to give him a chance. Despite their differences, they had worked very well together.

"For starters, I'm glad to see you're moving on and no longer wearing your wedding ring. Now you need to get laid, Mark. Let me set you up with a piece of tail that I banged a few weeks ago, her name is Darcy. I met her at an AA meeting."

Mark knew Tony wasn't an alcoholic or a member of AA. "What were you doing at AA, were you supporting a friend?"

"I just pretend to be an alcoholic. It's a great way to meet chicks that have hit rock bottom and are totally dependent on someone. It's classic, they are looking for a shoulder to cry on and some sympathy, and I can deliver on that. It's like shooting fish in a barrel. You should feel lucky, I normally don't let people in on my secrets like that, I'm opening the kimono for you, Mark."

"Tony, you opened the kimono long ago, against my will. I've seen the dark underbelly, and it's scary. Seriously Tony, that's even low for you." Mark had a somewhat serious tone, knowing that nothing he would say or do would ever influence Tony to change his ways. "Don't you have to take some kind of oath going to those meetings?"

"Everyone in life wants something Mark, it's all a game. Shareholders want returns, bald men want hair, recovering alcoholics want someone to talk to. I just want to share myself with twenty- and thirty-year-old women. Guest what Stef wants?"

"Save it Tony, I don't need another lecture from you. Between you and my friends it's all I hear about lately."

"There are many things in life that I'd take your advice on Mark, but divorce is one category I know much better than you."

"I just met with my attorney yesterday again and we feel good about our case. Although the mediation we had wasn't successful, we're confident going into trial."

Mark and Stef had a court-ordered mediation about a week ago, and it hadn't gone well. The delta between what Stef was expecting and what Mark was willing to give was too significant to close. Although the failed mediation had started to concern Mark, he still believed that he didn't have much to worry about.

"Oh right, the douchebag attorney your admin told you to hire. We have relationships with all of the top-tier law firms across the country, yet you hire a guy who has done two divorces prior to yours, and both were his own."

"It's divorce court, not complex litigation. Although Stef does seem to be a little more money motivated than I expected, the judge will be fair. He'll see that I'm the one who worked hard and earned all of the money, while Stef was never very motivated and only focused on spending our money. It's not as if she's going to be coming for blood. It's still pretty amicable."

"You're *way* more optimistic than I would be, Mark. IMO, you will look like the young, rich executive, who makes more money than the judge," Tony quickly interrupted.

"I know what I'm doing," retorted Mark. "You said it yourself Tony, I don't make bad decisions. Wait, I take that back, when I accepted your job offer out of college that was a bad decision, which led to many other bad decisions, all influenced by you. Outside of that my track record is solid."

"I guarantee your luck will turn around if you join me at the AA meeting tonight, Mark. In fact, a young good-looking prospect like you, your luck could turn around two or three times in one night. You can even borrow some of my Cialis. You mix that stuff with a few shots of Jäger and Liquid Cougar, you'll have a night for the books," Tony stood up and shouted. "We would be looking at the new and improved Mark Coghlan!" Tony laughed with his voice booming throughout the office.

As Mark drove home that night, he made his twice-daily stop at the Dog Den. Tyson, his five-year-old Boxer rescue, had been a frequent guest at the doggy daycare facility ever since Mark first picked him up at the rescue shelter two years ago. With Mark's busy life and Stef's overall lack of interest in having a dog, it was the only way it worked for them. Dogs were man's best friend for a reason, and the relationship that Tyson and Mark had was no exception. There was nothing that Tyson wouldn't do for Mark and vice versa. They were equally loyal to each other.

"Hey Mark," Katie, the manager of the Dog Den excitedly greeted him. "We'll get Tyson for you. He should be extra tired tonight, he was getting chased around and swooned by all his girlfriends even more than usual today. He's the Brad Pitt of dogs, a total lady's man!"

Mark laughed, Tyson always enjoyed being the center of attention.

As they waited for Tyson to come bounding through the gate, Katie said, "I know you keep a hectic work schedule, but some of us are getting together on Saturday with our dogs at the park on the east side. It's mainly employees but you and Tyson are welcome to join us."

"Sounds fun, we'll definitely keep it in mind."

"Perfect, here is my number if you decide to come. We aren't sure yet what time, but we usually get there early and make a morning of it."

Mark grabbed her number and said he would let her know. As he was leaving he wondered if Katie just asked him out.

CHAPTER 6

Dinner with Friends

The next few weeks flew by, Mark had been busy with work, and in his free time had started to work with his attorney preparing for trial. He had also started to get into more of a normal routine without Stef in his life. He was really reconnecting with his friends—Christian, Steve, and Ronald—and also had been spending more quality time with Tyson. His outlook was starting to improve. He even managed to get together with the Dog Den crew and Katie a couple times for those Saturday morning dog park meet-ups.

As Mark experienced more freedom from Stef, he realized that the divorce was a positive change in his life. Tony and his friends even commented how he seemed more relaxed and happier in general. Although Mark had reached out to Stef early on, shortly after the fateful dinner night, now he had basically cut all ties and didn't talk to her unless he had to. He was anxious for the trial to be behind him and move on to the next phase. As happy as he was that was the one thing that was still weighing on him. It was the night before the big trial, and Mark was out with his trio of friends. They thought it would be good for him to get his mind off things.

"So isn't this when we plan some big divorce party for you, get hookers and cocaine in Vegas, and stand on the Strip passing out pictures of Stef with her phone number and a message to call for free sex? Hell, why stop with flyers, you should put up a couple billboards. I have a buddy in the ad industry who could totally cut you a deal."

"Yeah Christian, I'm sure Mark's attorney would think that's a great idea the day before trial." Of course Steve had to bring the sarcasm down.

"Hey guys," Ronald said in an even more fidgety manner than usual, "I was going to wait until after the trial to say something, but since it's tomorrow and we're all out, I thought I'd break out the big news."

"What's that Ronald?" asked Mark.

"I did a little research on Stef's attorney, and he's going to be getting a surprise visitor at his office tomorrow morning before the trial."

All three guys looked at Ronald with concern, most notably Mark who at this point grew a little pale. Knowing Ronald, it was impossible to predict what was going to come out of his mouth next.

"I thought it would be funny to have a few tranny hookers show up at his office tomorrow morning right before the trial. They are going to bypass the receptionist and go straight into his office. When they get there, they will start shouting about how he didn't pay them for last night, and then one of them will bitch slap him. It's going to be so epic, that old fool won't know what hit him. He'll be completely thrown off for the trial. How could someone focus after that happens?"

At this point all of the guys were just staring at Ronald, their eyes widening and jaws dropping. "I wanted to surprise Mark, but it's just one of those secrets that's too good to hold in." Ronald was beaming with pride like a kid who scored straight As on his report card.

"Holy shit!" Christian laughed, at this point he had gotten off of his chair and was buckled over.

Steve piped in. "Oh my god, please tell us you're kidding Ronald."

Meanwhile, Mark's face went from pale, to the color right before throwing up.

"They get there at eight thirty tomorrow morning, just in time to throw him off his game before the trial." Ronald had a dead serious look on his face, slightly perplexed why his idea wasn't being received with more excitement.

"Ronald, you need to undo that *immediately*!" Steve shouted. "Do you realize what you have done?"

"What, it will be perfect. It will be a shit-storm. The old dude won't know what hit him. Christian even said we should do something to Stef's attorney a couple weeks ago, I took it upon myself to help out. You're proud of me, right Christian?"

Christian was still rolling at this point but managed to stop long enough to interject. "Dude, while I totally admire the idea and there is a big part of me that loves it, I don't think that's quite what I had in mind, and I didn't literally mean we should do it. Don't tie me to this decision!"

"It's not like I hired a hit-man. I mean I did think about it, but what good would that do. I'm sure Stef would just get another attorney." Ronald was still oblivious to everyone's concern, proud of his actions. "This is the best of both worlds, nobody dies, and Stef's attorney gets thrown off his game before trial."

At this point Mark still had not said anything, still looking like he was going to vomit. He eventually managed to regroup and calmly said, "Ronald, I know you were just looking out for me and while I *greatly* appreciate that, you need to call off the tranny hookers right now. Please tell me you can do that, *please*." Mark begged. "There are real people involved here, I don't think this is the best idea."

"Alright, I just don't understand what the big deal is, but I'll call them off," said a defeated Ronald.

All the guys were still a little bit in disbelief. They all knew Ronald meant well, but sometimes he just lacked common sense. At this point Ronald had his phone to his ear and had turned to the side. He was just loud enough so the others could hear him.

"Hey Chastity, what's up girlfriend," said Ronald, whose demeanor had changed from being totally deflated to now laughing as he was on the phone. "Remember that favor I asked you to do tomorrow morning, well I don't want you to do it anymore." There was a short pause, and then Ronald continued, "I know, it would have been good, but I just need you to not do it."

"Make her promise," Steve asserted loudly, "under no condition can that happen."

"No, I know," Ronald said, still talking with Chastity and ignoring Steve's comment, "even though you aren't doing it, it still counts as the favor you owe me, I get it." He then turned his head slightly away so the other guys couldn't hear him, whispered something and started laughing hard, then hung up shortly after that.

"OK, done, she's not going to show, I mean he won't show, umm, or I guess Chastity won't show up." Ronald corrected himself, unsure what pronoun to use.

"Hey Ronald, I'm going to ask the obvious, you mind explaining why a transvestite hooker named Chastity owed you a favor?" Christian was genuinely curious.

The guys were all well aware that Ronald had a track record of bizarre but very entertaining behavior. One night Christian got a call at two in the morning from Ronald. He was calling from a US Coast Guard holding cell. They had picked him up in a stolen canoe wearing nothing but swim goggles with a spear gun in his possession. He claimed to be doing some late-night fishing and wasn't hurting anyone. It was such a bizarre event that the Coast Guard let him off with a warning, even though he also had a small amount of pot in his possession. Christian was a master of influence, convincing the Coast Guard that Ronald had some pretty deep-rooted issues. He made up some story about his parents abandoning him when he was an infant and that Christian had basically adopted him like a brother. He also claimed Ronald had some rare disorder that resulted in him being obsessed with spears and having an allergy to clothes so he would often be naked out of a medical necessity. It was so bizarre the Coast Guard bought it.

"I met her at a Clay Aiken concert and helped her get out of an uncomfortable situation with one of her ex-lovers," replied Ronald very matter of fact. Like everything he just said was completely normal.

"You went to a Clay Aiken concert?" Steve had an amused look on his face.

"Is that really the most unusual part of the sentence to you, Steve?" Christian smirked.

"Guys, let's stop questioning Ronald so much. He called it off and that's what matters." Mark knew that oftentimes it was best to leave a little bit (or a lot) of the mystery about Ronald alone.

"So are you ready for the big day Mark?" Steve was also eager to change the subject.

"Definitely, it will be great to have it behind me. It's the last thing that needs to happen before I can have a fully normal life again."

All the guys were concerned for Mark. Although he seemed confident, they couldn't help but think he was being uncharacteristically naive about how the trial was going to go. That said, they hadn't brought it up much in the past week, knowing that the trial was approaching, and they were doing their best to be respectful and upbeat for their buddy.

"Kidding aside, we should do something when this is all done. We need to celebrate." Christian was always looking for a reason to party.

"I second that, let's do something…maybe a weekend guy's trip somewhere," Steve quickly chimed in. "Are you sure you don't want us there tomorrow? We all can get out of work and be there for moral support."

"No guys, I'm good, but thanks," commented Mark. "It isn't worth taking a day off for."

"Will you be on Judge Judy?" Ronald asked, completely serious. "I usually catch that in the afternoon before my shift at the movie theater. My mom and I love to watch it together."

"No Ronald, I don't think my case will make it on Judge Judy."

"That's too bad, she seems very fair, not to mention hot," Ronald said excitedly.

"Wait Ronald, you think Judge Judy is hot?"

"You can learn a lot from older women, Christian," Ronald retorted.

Mark raised his beer and said, "On that note, here's to Judge Judy being hot, and a great group of friends starting the next chapter in life. I couldn't have made it through this without all of your help—you guys are the best and we're lucky to have each other."

"Good night, everyone," Mark said as they stood outside waiting for separate Ubers to head home for the night, except for Christian, who was already on his phone presumably texting one of the lucky girls who managed to make it into his round robin of late-night calls.

CHAPTER 7

The Court Case

The next morning Mark woke up earlier than usual. He took Tyson out for a long run, which helped clear his mind. He felt focused and ready. He met his attorney at a coffee shop across from the courthouse about an hour before the trial so they could run through any last-minute things they needed to catch up on.

"How's it going Rudy, are we ready?"

"I was up all night watching *The Firm*. That Tom Cruise sure is a sharp dude. I think I picked up a few pointers!"

Mark had come to realize Rudy had a terrible sense of humor. He was one of those guys who tried really hard to be funny but picked the worst jokes at the worst times. He was a quirky guy, but Mark had gotten used to him.

"All kidding aside, I think we're ready, Mark. Just to recap everything. Both you and Stef will take the stand, I'll ask some questions and so will Stef's attorney. We'll present our exhibits and arguments, and then it will be up to the judge to render his decision. I've incorporated all the questions you wanted me to ask Stef in my notes, along with the questions we discussed to ask you. Let's head over," Rudy said.

As they crossed the street, they saw an older green Mercedes pull up; it was Stef's attorney. Mark had been studying him, between interacting with him in the mediation and just asking around, he knew what the guy was like. One of the more reputable divorce attorneys in the area, but at the end of the day he was still a divorce attorney. As her attorney got out of his Mercedes, Mark laughed to himself. He was a slight, bald, and older man, probably in his late sixties. Mark was convinced that if a transvestite had bitch slapped him early that morning, he may not have survived. *Dodged a bullet on that one*, Mark thought.

As they got inside the courthouse and turned the corner to find their room, he caught a glance of both Stef and Amy standing down at the other end of the hall. *Shocker*, Mark thought to himself. There was no way that Amy would have missed the opportunity to be here. Divorce court, a chance to watch a guy get ripped to shreds by his ex-wife, was like a pay-per-view event for her.

As he walked closer, he had played this moment out in his mind several times, wondering if it would be awkward seeing Stef at trial. He wasn't sure how he would feel, but now in the situation he felt calm. Emotionally he had moved on. He had come to realize he likely wasn't as invested in the relationship as he thought he was. The divorce proceeding at this point was more of a business transaction. He was confident the outcome would be fair, and this was the beginning of the next chapter for him.

Mark was enthusiastic, despite the uncertainty. As soon as Stef and Amy noticed him, Amy immediately shot him a stare that would have made Liam Neeson cower in fear. She then nodded to Stef and they walked inside the courtroom to sit down. Stef had avoided eye contact with Mark.

The courtroom was fairly empty, and this wasn't a jury trial, so the judge would make the decision. Everyone was seated and whispering quietly when he walked in, the bailiff giving the "all rise" command.

The judge ran through some of the procedural items in the case before turning it over to the plaintiff, which in this case was Stef.

While the judge was going through opening remarks and getting ready to hear from Stef's attorney, Mark couldn't help but think the judge looked familiar. He was generally pretty good with names and faces. While he knew from asking around that the judge was generally known to be conservative, he didn't know much else about him. Judge Paul Thomas sounds like a common name, but why did he look so familiar? Judge Thomas kept looking over in Mark's direction too, making direct eye contact with Mark. Maybe that was normal, but he seemed to be more interested in Mark than anyone else in the room. *Thomas, Thomas, Thomas, why does that name sound so familiar?* All of a sudden it came back to him…and it wasn't good. *Oh shit* he thought to himself. He looked familiar because he had seen Judge Thomas at his workplace a few years ago— storming into his boss's office, and after some shouting, abruptly storming out.

Mark vaguely started to recall the story—it was another one of Tony's many foolish decisions involving younger women. Not surprisingly, shortly after Tony's second divorce, he had a two-month fling with a very hot twenty-four-year-old NFL cheerleader. They'd met at a bar and she ended up going back to his condo for the night. Their relationship went on for a few months and started to involve bizarre role-playing. One day she invited him to the family lake home for the weekend. Tony eagerly accepted, but the weekend ended abruptly when her dad showed up unannounced at the lake house. As soon as her dad heard sounds from the master bedroom, he swung the door open, and a plume of marijuana smoke came pouring out of the room. Judge Paul Thomas was staring at his naked twenty-four-year-old daughter with Tony tied to the bed and wearing a Ronald Reagan mask. Like Tony had said, they got into some really weird role playing. Not surprisingly,

Judge Thomas went *ballistic*, and as soon as Tony was untied, he ran out of the house as fast as he could, jumping into his car half dressed. It was shortly after that Mark recalled her dad visiting the office to confront Tony, and lo and behold that was unfortunately how Mark now recognized Judge Thomas. Mark vaguely recalled talking to Tony about it at the time; her dad was indeed a judge. There were hundreds of judges in the state, Mark never even thought that it might be the same person. He felt a pit growing in his stomach—this was not good.

Immediately after Judge Thomas finished the procedural items, Stef's attorney stood up and gave his opening argument, stating the length of their marriage, their lavish lifestyle, and emphasizing Mark's position as Executive Managing Director at Kilimanjaro Risk, no doubt that name was a trigger for Judge Thomas. Sure enough, as soon as Stef's attorney mentioned it, the judge shot a look at Mark.

Stef was called first to the stand, and after some brief background questions, her attorney started probing about Mark's job. "At what point did you begin to notice that Mark was not completely supportive of your career goals?"

Mark almost fell off his chair as he heard the question. What the hell? First of all, it was a leading question and second of all, it was absurd. If Stef had career goals, she certainly hadn't told Mark about them.

"It was about two years into our marriage, and I told Mark I wanted to open my own yoga studio. I put together a business plan and had researched locations, finding a spot that would have been perfect. I talked to Mark about it and he wouldn't let me do it."

Mark couldn't believe what he was hearing. Although technically it was true that Stef had talked to Mark about opening a yoga studio and he had said he didn't think it was a good idea, Stef conveniently left out two fairly important points. The first was that she wanted to partner with a friend of hers who had just filed for bankruptcy after racking up $180,000 in credit card debt over a pyramid marketing scheme. The second was that they picked a location in the most expensive part of town. Stef's business plan failed to solve for the fact that rent was going to be so high they wouldn't break after ten years even if they were at max capacity and charging above market prices. Mark specifically told her that she should find a less expensive location and it could work, but of course Stef didn't want to.

"So if Mark had supported you, is it fair to say you might be in a position of running your own successful business, possibly even much larger than just one yoga studio?"

"I'd like to think so. That was always my dream, and a lot of my friends and family felt I'd be great at it, except for Mark."

"Your honor, I'd like to submit into evidence a proposal prepared by a reputable business valuation expert citing the 300 percent annual growth in the yoga industry over the past three years, and an estimate of the average revenue and income for yoga studios."

As he took the report to the judge, he handed a copy to Mark's attorney. Mark grabbed it, skimming the report. *Unreal*, he thought to himself. They were arguing that the average revenue for a yoga shop was over $500,000 a year and had profits of $225,000. Ridiculous numbers not to mention the fact the story was entirely one-sided and not true.

Moving onto the next topic, Stef's attorney asked, "Is it true that Mark traveled extensively for his job, many times being gone on international trips for weeks at a time? Was there ever a time that it was hard for you to support that, your husband being gone for long periods of time?"

"He did travel extensively," Stef replied. "Usually staying at five-star hotels and resorts. While he was gone I had to be responsible for maintaining the house, taking care of our dog, household chores, and laundry, and doing this all while working at the same time. Although it was difficult, I knew it was the best for Mark's career, and I always wanted the best for him. Even if that meant personally sacrificing my own career and life goals." Stef continued to avoid eye contact with Mark.

At this point Mark wasn't sure if he was going to explode with laughter or start throwing up in disgust. He couldn't believe what was coming out of Stef's mouth, clearly her theater work was paying off. It was almost as if she actually believed her life was so terrible. This had to be fed from Amy, there was no way Stef would have come up with this all on her own. As if taking care of a house and dog for a few weeks was that difficult. Some people work two jobs just to make a living, yet Stef was somehow making a charmed and easy life feel like time in prison.

"So, is it accurate to say that you put your life aside to make Mark's career a priority, and he may not have reached the level he had today if it hadn't been for your support?"

"Yes, I would say that is accurate."

At this point Mark was livid, but he had shifted into damage control mode. First off, he hoped the judge wasn't buying any of the bullshit, but he had started writing notes to Rudy, making sure he would ask good questions on his cross-examination.

"Stef, I know this will be difficult, but can you talk about the night you told Mark you had been thinking about divorce?" Stef's attorney asked. "You chose to do it at a restaurant, because you were worried how Mark was going to react. You thought he might be violent?"

"That's true." Stef's voice started to crackle slightly.

"That's a significant accusation, why did you think he might be violent?"

"Although I loved Mark, over the five years we were married I started to live in fear."

"Stef, can you tell us why you were afraid of your husband?"

Stef paused a little bit, "I'm sorry, I get a little nervous talking about it. Over the last two years Mark had developed a passion for guns. He knew that I hated them and it made me uncomfortable, but he still continued to collect them and he recently started to collect knives. He seemed almost obsessed with weaponry, and he even started subscribing to magazines and joined a gun enthusiast club."

What the fuck, Mark thought, *this is beyond ridiculous*. He collected antique guns and recently bought two WWI knives he found at a swap meet. He bought them thinking he would hold onto them for conversation pieces or sell them at a profit since he got such a great deal. He didn't even shoot the guns; he just stored them in a locked vault. He had always loved antique war memorabilia and his collection started when his great-grandfather, who had served in WWI, passed down a gun that he'd owned. The club he joined was a WWI club, and the magazines he subscribed to were the same. Stef was making it sound like he was collecting AK-47s and had a basement full of ammunition and machetes. There was no way the judge could be buying all of this.

"Stef, aside from Mark showing an unusually high interest in collecting weapons, was there anything else that made you feel he was going to be violent?" Her attorney's voice sounded confident, knowing this line of questioning was going well.

Stef paused and looked away for a moment. "Well, there was something else, but it's very hard to talk about." A tear started to drip down her face, those theater classes really paying off at this point.

"Take your time Stef."

"I didn't find this out until after we were married, but Mark's family had a history of domestic violence, his uncle had been arrested for assault." Tears were streaming down her face and her hands trembling at this point.

"I'm sorry Stef, I know this is hard. You're being very brave talking about this."

"The guns, the knives, the family violence. It was a difficult environment to live in and I never felt comfortable. When I first found out about his uncle, I didn't really worry, but then when he started becoming obsessed with weapons...I, I, just worried about what else was next. My friends even picked up on the dangerous situation."

During this entire time, Mark had been feverishly sharing notes and whispers with Rudy, wondering how the hell Stef could get away with this and why they couldn't object. The incident she was talking about with his uncle was ridiculous, it was his Uncle Jasper, and while he had been arrested eight years ago for assault, it was because his girlfriend was crazy. He woke up in the middle of the night with a pillow being shoved over his head; someone was trying to smother him. He swung his arms up punching towards the person. Turns out it was his girlfriend, and she was smothering him because she had a dream that he cheated on her. She woke up pissed off and decided she would try to kill him in retaliation for the dream she had.

In the tussle, Jasper had been flailing his arms trying to get up and he hit her. He said he had no idea who was even choking him since his face was covered by the pillow, and it was self-defense. When the cops arrived, she denied the pillow incident and it was her word against his; they charged him with assault.

Rudy seemed to be in over his head. He was reading Mark's notes but not really doing anything except staring in bewilderment. At one point he tried objecting but didn't state his premise for the objection, and the judge scolded him for it.

Rudy's face turned red in embarrassment and immediately sat down. It wasn't going well for Mark. Mark desperately wanted to do something but had little control over what was going on. At this point he was still holding onto hope that the judge must think this is ridiculous and clearly fabricated.

The remainder of Stef's testimony was equally damaging to Mark's chances. His attorney took full account of their standard of living, the numerous raises and promotions Mark received while Stef was "supporting his career," and the overall success Mark had achieved as a result of Stef's "unwavering support." This droned on for what felt like an eternity to Mark, all the time he had to sit on his hands and craft notes to his befuddled attorney. At one point, it was so bad when Stef was on the stand talking about her fear of violence the judge actually handed her a tissue. *Maybe the judge was actually believing this*, Mark thought.

After Stef's destructive testimony, it was now Rudy's turn to cross-examine. Although Mark knew it was all bullshit, he was immediately regretting hiring Rudy for the job. He never imagined Stef would concoct so many crazy stories that weren't true and entirely one-sided.

"Stef, you mentioned the yoga studio you wanted to start, didn't Mark ask you to look at other locations as options?" Rudy asked.

"I don't recall exactly, but I believe after he said no I begged and pleaded with him. He finally said maybe I should look at putting it in a cheap warehouse. I told him you can't put a yoga studio in a cheap warehouse. Mark controlled all the money in our household, I didn't have any say in those matters. I was trapped and controlled."

Rudy looked over at Mark, seeming unsure what to ask next. A million things were running through Mark's head. First off, why didn't Rudy be more specific and ask about the business plan like he suggested in the notes he passed earlier? Why did he allow Stef to respond to his question with more damaging testimony? The pit in Mark's stomach was growing as every minute ticked by. He was now fearing Rudy was not just unhelpful to him but actually more damaging.

"Was Mark ever violent towards you?" Rudy asked.

Stef paused, looked down for about five seconds without saying a word, then looked back up with tears streaming down her face. "I'm sorry, this is just very hard, can I have another tissue?" The judge had the tissue box on the side of his podium from earlier. Stef dabbed her eyes and tried to collect herself, finally responding. "Aside from collecting weapons which he knew scared me, he hadn't yet reacted to his genetic predisposition to be violent. You know, since it ran in his family, with his uncle."

Again, Rudy looked back at Mark. Mark wasn't even sure Rudy knew what genetic and predisposition meant. Shit he thought to himself, there was no way to salvage this, he was fucked.

The rest of the trial continued to go terribly for Mark. Once he had his chance to get on the stand, Rudy asked a few questions that should have helped in painting Stef as not being ambitious from a career perspective.

They talked about the guns being from the WWI era and cleared up some of the other items, which Mark thought would be somewhat helpful. That being said they were now in defense mode. The picture had been painted pretty clearly for the judge, and Rudy was in way over his head. Although most of what came up was total bullshit, the judge's perspective up to this point was that Mark was successful and had significant financial assets, they lived a fairly lavish lifestyle, he had squashed Stef's career ambitions while she did everything to support his, and on top of all that she lived in fear of him being violent. Even if the judge didn't buy the bullshit about the gun-toting family violence, there was enough testimony that made this Mark seem like a totally different person from the real Mark. Not to mention, Mark was fairly certain every time Judge Thomas looked at him he had flashbacks of seeing his twenty-four-year-old daughter on top of Tony. What

Mark thought was going to be a straight-forward trial was turning into Armageddon. He felt so defeated. Mark even noticed as he was testifying that Judge Thomas was scrolling through his phone smiling. The attorneys both wrapped up all their questioning and at this point the judge dismissed everyone for fifteen minutes, indicating that his verdict would come quick.

The next fifteen minutes felt like an eternity for Mark; he felt sick. As the minutes ticked by, he could hear Amy talking to Stef down the hall; she was laughing.

The bailiff called everyone back to the courtroom, Judge Thomas was returning. Mark was doing everything he could to keep himself upbeat. How bad could it be? Even if he had to give Stef half of his income for a couple years, he made a lot of money. He'd figure it out and make it work.

Judge Thomas started reading the judgment. "All assets will be divided evenly, and included in the valuation will be all of the Defendant's unvested employer stock and his ownership in his family's consulting business."

Ooooof, Mark thought. He originally believed worst case scenario he would have to only pay a percentage of his vested stock to Stef, after all the unvested wasn't even his yet. Not to mention the shares from his mom's business that were transferred to him were included in the valuation. He was quickly running numbers in his head, the only way that was going to work was if he liquidated the majority of his other assets and gave that to Stef.

"In terms of the Plaintiff's plea for spousal maintenance…" Judge Thomas was speaking slowly, as if to draw out the suspense. "The court awards the Plaintiff maintenance of $30,000 monthly for a period of ten years, and 70 percent of any bonuses received."

Mark thought he must have misheard, that equated to more than half of his salary and bonus for ten years. There was no way that could have been the real judgment; it must have been a mistake.

Judge Thomas continued to read the judgment. "This is a straight-forward case, and the judgment is based on the Defendant's significant income and earning potential in relation to the Plaintiff, and actions by the Defendant during the course of their marriage that prevented the Plaintiff from having a successful career. The court finds that if the Plaintiff had been supported by the Defendant in her career aspirations, she could have enjoyed the same or more success as the Defendant. This judgment is intended to offset the lack of investment in the Plaintiff's career during their marriage."

As Judge Thomas finished reading the verdict, he shot a quick terse look over to Mark, and he could have sworn he actually winked at him. It was like a message: tell your friend Tony I said hi.

Mark sat motionless in a catatonic state; it felt as if all the life had been sucked out of him. There was still part of him that felt he must have misheard or maybe this was really a dream.

"Mark. Mark. Hey Mark," Rudy said as he tapped him on his arm. "You OK buddy? Maybe we can appeal?"

Mark didn't want to talk to anyone right now, his mind was racing as he stared blankly off into space. Off to his side he heard Amy laughing with Stef. How could this happen he thought to himself. How could it be legal that he had to pay roughly 70 percent of his income to Stef, and for a period of ten years? Leading up to the case had talked with others and had researched case law, their entire marriage was only five years, worst-case scenario he thought it would only be three years of alimony. None of this made any sense. It was anything but fair. Mark said a few words to Rudy and started walking out of the courtroom, his head still in a fog. He knew appealing the verdict was a long shot at best, and probably not viable based on advice he had heard from others. He slowly walked outside and to his car, sitting in the driver's seat for at least twenty minutes staring into his windshield before even starting it. For the first time in his life, he wasn't sure what he was going to do.

CHAPTER 8

The Idea

About a week after the trial, the guys arrived at Mark's place, poker night was a recent development and an attempt by Mark's friends to cheer him up. It was working, he loved the event.

"I call your five dollars, and raise you with a movie voucher." Ronald had a very serious tone, wearing a pair of mirrored aviators and a baseball hat that read, My eyes are up here.

"How many times do we have to tell you, you can't bet movie tickets, keys to your mom's place, or dates with your fifteen-year-old sister." Christian as always, bringing the quick wit.

"Yeah, because aside from the fact she's underage, she has morals, she'd never date a man-whore like you Christian."

"Sure Steve, if by man-whore you mean someone who didn't make the fucked-up decision to marry his high school sweetheart, sleeping with only one woman for the rest of his life, then yes I'm definitely a man-whore. How are Jennie and the kids doing anyway? I'm surprised you could even make it out tonight. Shouldn't you be at home watching *Frozen* and getting ready for a weekend of binge-drinking wine out of a box in the cul-de-sac while complaining about the weather and rising property taxes?"

"Guys c'mon, let's focus on the game," Mark inserted, laughing to himself but also enjoying playing the role of mediator between his friends. Although Christian always gave Steve a bad time for marrying his high school sweetheart and having kids, everyone loved Jennie and Steve's family.

"Do you have to give 70 percent of your winnings tonight to Stef? Don't worry, we'll keep it on the DL so the judge doesn't find out."

"I should be safe Ronald, but thanks for thinking of me."

"Have you figured anything out yet? Are the options to appeal limited like you originally thought?"

"Unfortunately I have no chance of appeal, Steve. I would just be lining some attorney's pocket with billable hours. I don't think I have many options, I'm just going to have to try to make it work." The topic of Mark and his maintenance verdict had been discussed extensively since the trial. He had met with several attorneys asking about options and talking with anyone who would listen. There weren't any viable options.

"Maybe Tyson can get a job," Steve joked. "You should go back to the judge and ask for support for him, all of the Dog Den bills and his food add up." Tyson's ears perked up, he was sleeping underneath the poker table. He liked poker night as much as the guys. "I still can't believe you have to pay so much. It would be one thing if you had kids and you had to pay child support, but it's beyond comprehension how anyone would think that it was fair to make you pay more than 50 percent of your income for twice the length of your marriage!"

"It doesn't make sense, the judge just had it out for me, and although I could blame Tony for part of that, it's really my fault. I should have taken the trial more seriously and hired a good attorney. I was too nice to Stef and underestimated her hunger for money and greed. Now I'll pay for it. Unless she miraculously gets a very well-paying job or remarries, I'm stuck paying a lot of money for the next decade."

"I could get her a job at the movie theater. One of our concession girls just left and I need to fill the position. I usually look for girls that have nice racks, so Stef would fit in."

"What the hell dude, do you really think it is appropriate to talk about Stef's rack? You say the stupidest things." Steve often got annoyed with Ronald's unpredictable comments and genuinely cared for others' feelings.

"It's OK guys, I don't think Ronald meant anything bad by it. Although I like the idea, I don't think a job at the concession stand would sway the judge to amend the maintenance payment, unless Ronald can offer her more than $200,000 a year. I can tell you first hand that Stef's rack isn't worth that."

"Nice! Now that sounds like a side of Mark we haven't seen for a while," Christian immediately replied. "We'd like to see more of that guy."

"I'm still here, just hit a bump in the road." Mark was showing a slight smirk.

"It really isn't fair what happened to you, I still think the entire thing is a crock of shit. That judge should be disbarred." Christian was genuinely furious for his buddy. "Ronald, I think now you have permission to call up your harem of transvestite friends to lay a smackdown on the judge."

"Yeah, it sucks when bad things happen to good people. We all agree Mark, you didn't deserve this. Stef doesn't really deserve all that money." This was one of the few things that Steve would support Christian on, and not disagree.

"Thanks guys, I appreciate it."

"There is still a chance she'd get married before the ten years are up, you never know," Steve said, trying to find a silver lining for his friend.

"I'll do it for you Mark, I'll marry Stef," Ronald said very seriously. "Although her ass is a little bigger than I normally like, I'd do that for you. Just to save you from the high alimony payments."

"What the fuck Ronald, first you talk about her rack and then you start talking about her ass. Really, did your mom snort paint chips when she was pregnant with you?" Steve said, even more upset than the first time.

"Wait a minute Steve, Ronald may be onto something," Christian chimed in abruptly.

"Thank you Christian, I knew you'd support me. You can be my best man, it's official. I was going to go with Steve, but not anymore, and it would probably be too awkward to have Mark do it, being a recent deee-vorcee." Ronald said with extra emphasis, as he put up his hand to high-five Christian.

"Take it easy Captain Dipshit, Stef isn't marrying you," Christian said. "I meant your idea isn't that outlandish about someone marrying her."

"Guys, I'm pretty sure she's not even dating anyone," Mark chimed in. "It's not as if she's going to run into that perfect guy and just marry him in a few months, or even in a year for that matter."

"Hear me out," Christian interrupted. "How much do you have to pay her over the ten-year period?"

"You really think this is going to be therapeutic, having Mark add it all up?" Steve said, jumping into the conversation. "I don't know who is worse, Ronald talking about Stef's ass or you asking Mark to add up how much he has to shell out."

"It's a lot, I try not to think about it," Mark said. "Just ballparking, probably in the ten million range, give or take. By the way Christian, Steve is right, you are depressing me."

"OK, so let's say seven and a half million to be conservative. That's a lot of money," Christian said completely disregarding Mark's comment about being depressed.

"Are you getting to your point?" Steve said, annoyed at the conversation and concerned this was making Mark feel worse.

"Instead of Ronald marrying Stef, why don't we find someone else who will? Mark could easily make it worth their while."

"Wait, so are you saying we'd pay someone to marry Stef?" Mark was intrigued, clarifying what Christian meant.

"I know some male prostitutes," Ronald proudly interjected. "Although I think they prefer the term gigolo. I'm not sure what they would charge to marry someone, but a handy usually runs about fifty bucks."

"Gross, a fifty-dollar handy? Where do you come up with this stuff, and why do you know these people?"

"Well, Steve, I considered prostitution for a while, but then landed the management gig at the movie theater and the hours wouldn't have worked to do both. Gigolos typically service their clients in the evening, peak times being between seven p.m. and midnight. Although I could have easily pulled down a couple grand a night selling my body, I'd be stupid to pass up a job in management with full benefits."

Nothing that came out of Ronald's mouth seemed to surprise the guys at this point, his comments were too good to make up. "We should make a reality TV show out of your life Ronald," Steve said, coming with the quick wit now. "By the way, just doing the quick math, in order to pull down a couple grand as a male gigolo you'll need to give about eighty handies a night."

Even though all the guys were laughing, Ronald had a look of confusion on his face. That was the funniest part, despite the fact that most of the comments coming out of his mouth were utterly ridiculous, Ronald was stone serious. He actually thought he could pull down a couple grand a night being a gigolo. "Guys, while this is all very interesting could we get back to my idea about Stef? I'm serious about getting Mark off the hook this way."

"Christian, you can't just develop some scheme to have someone secretly marry Stef. Despite the fact you believe otherwise, you can't buy your way into or out of everything. Nobody would marry someone just to make a buck, and Stef isn't just going to magically fall for someone who wants to marry her," Steve said, passionately arguing against Christian's idea.

"I have to agree with Steve on this one, Christian. While I would love nothing more than for Stef to get remarried and get me out from under the less than fair alimony payments, I don't think we can just hire someone to marry her." Mark genuinely wanted to see it happen but was skeptical.

Christian listened to Steve and Mark argue against his idea. Then, leaning forward, he looked at Mark with a serious expression—unusual for Christian's constant sarcasm. "I have one question for you, Mark. At what point in your life did you decide to accept defeat? Maybe it won't work, maybe it is a bad idea and we wouldn't be able to find someone to marry Stef, but the Mark I know wouldn't just accept defeat and give up without a fight. Particularly when you know what happened to you wasn't right.

"Sure, maybe people would take issue with the idea, but do you think what happened to you was right? The legal system and case law had nothing to do with the verdict the judge gave you, it was personal and none of it was ethical. What did you do wrong? Do you really believe you held Stef's career back? Do you really feel that the judge was right? If you do, then you should just accept it and move on. You're right, this idea probably isn't for you. We're all your friends and will support whatever decision you make, but I think the Mark that all three of us know wouldn't just accept something that isn't right.

You have nothing to lose, post an anonymous ad on the personals site 'Megslist' to source guys – see if it works."

The room fell silent after Christian's brief but moving message. Even Tyson perked up under the table knowing something was going on. Although the idea was crazy, Christian had made a few points that were hard to argue against, and most importantly it was unlike Christian to be so serious about anything. It just made his message that much more powerful and thought-provoking. Finally breaking the silence Ronald looked at the guys, stood up, and shouted, "Yeahhhh, rise up my brothers! Let's take them all down—the judge, Stef, and anyone else who fucks with our friend Mark…woohoo!" He slammed his beer on the table and walked off with his arms raised above his head chanting, "Take them down, take them down, take them down!"

Despite Ronald doing a great job of breaking the silence, the rest of the night was a little quieter than usual. The guys were all pondering Christian's comments and wondering what Mark was thinking. Mark was in good spirits, but he was impacted by what Christian said. Just when all the guys thought the night was winding down, Mark, Steve, and Christian looked out onto Mark's terrace to see Ronald looking down from his third=floor loft with his shirt lifted up and rubbing his nipple. "I don't even want to know who is down on the street," Mark commented. "My neighbors used to like me."

"When he dies, I definitely think his brain needs to be donated to science," Steve said jokingly.

"Hey Romeo, can you come back inside, preferably with your shirt all the way on and not rubbing any part of your anatomy?" Christian shouted across the room.

Ronald winked at whoever was down on the street and came walking back into the condo. "I don't know what's more fun, taking money from you guys or picking up Mark's hot neighbors."

"Right, you wouldn't know, you can't do either. You're down sixty bucks, and I have a feeling whoever was down on the street is probably calling the special victim crimes unit right now to report that a nasty bearded man partially exposed himself to innocent bystanders," Christian remarked.

As Ronald came back to the table, it was becoming clear to everyone that they should probably call it a night soon. Not only was it getting late, but Christian's speech still had a lingering effect on everyone's mood. As the guys finished off the last hand and settled up with each other, Mark decided to walk out with them. He had to take Tyson out for a late night walk anyway.

"Adios muchachos," Ronald shouted as he walked down the street away from the guys. "I'm going to find those babes from earlier and continue the show I started."

The other guys just shook their head, laughing at the same time. Both Steve and Christian hopped in separate Ubers and Mark started walking with Tyson down to the park a couple blocks away. The walk was good for him, it was a perfect night and he would often take Tyson out for long walks or runs to clear his mind. He knew Christian was right about some things he said—Mark wasn't the type that just gave up. He agreed that the judge screwed him, the entire situation wasn't right. Tyson trotted happily along taking in the fresh air with Mark. Although he loved walks, he especially liked spending time with Mark no matter what they were doing; they were best buds.

Mark didn't sleep very well that night, continuing to ponder what Christian had said. As he got into the office that morning he had some down time, his morning was wide open. He was torn about the idea and still thought most of it was crazy—paying someone to marry Stef. He even wondered if there were laws he would be breaking. That said, he couldn't quite break free of the idea. He decided he would test fate. He would post an ad, something innocuous. If more than twenty people answered it over the course of two days, he would consider doing it; if fewer than twenty people answered, he would forget it was ever mentioned. For better or worse, he would let the users of Megslist personal ads decide. Even if more than twenty responded, he would still need to find the right person who could convince Stef to marry him and that seemed unlikely given all the reasons she had to stay single. The chances were so slim this would work, he convinced himself that if it did, it must be meant to be.

As he sat at his computer, he was pondering what to write. How would he place an ad that would attract guys interested in marrying his ex-wife, so he could get out of alimony payments? After editing and several rounds of wordsmithing, he came up with something he thought would work:

Seeking single males between the ages of 27–40 who would consider marrying an attractive 34-year-old blonde woman. Major $$$$ reward for the lucky winner. If interested, upload a two-minute video describing yourself to the private YouTube address listed below."

That's it, Mark thought. It was too easy to simply reply to an email. This way someone would have to actually submit a video. There was a deeper level of commitment. If he was going to test fate, he would do it fairly, requiring more than a simple "apply now" button. He stared at the screen, asking himself once more if he was ready to hit post. He was surprised, even just writing it out seemed to be therapeutic. Without further thought, he quickly tapped his mouse—it was now posted. No turning back, fate would be tested. He decided he wasn't going to tell anyone else yet, this was his secret for now.

After the posting, Mark immediately went about his day, mainly getting caught up answering emails from Europe and Asia that came in during the middle of the night. Mark loved the constant demands of his role. His afternoon was busy with back-to-back meetings, his team was launching a new Kidnap and Ransom insurance policy in Mexico, and they were interviewing the vendors who would ultimately negotiate with the kidnappers in the event there was an actual kidnapping event. Although he forgot about the ad during his busy day, placing it did seem to lift his spirits a bit and change his attitude.

CHAPTER 9

Stef's Celebration

Across town, Stef was still celebrating what she deemed to be a massive victory at the divorce hearing. Even her attorney was stunned at the landslide verdict. Over the last few weeks, Stef and Amy had become even closer. It was almost as if Amy had a sort of Stockholm Syndrome effect on Stef. While it wasn't abusive, it wasn't necessarily heathy from a two-way relationship perspective. Even though Amy had a visceral personality, Stef took a certain comfort in the strength of her "I don't give a fuck" attitude.

With the weight of the trial lifted and a clear picture of how much money she ended up getting, they celebrated with weekly shopping sprees. Stef had also just signed a lease on a condo that made their old place feel like a youth hostel. A high-rise with all the amenities one would expect: twenty-four-hour concierge, a spa and fitness center, and a huge rooftop pool/deck with amazing views of the city. Oddly enough, although Stef was taking full advantage of her newfound wealth, it was really Amy who had been driving the decisions and fueling Stef with ideas. She sought out the condo and convinced Stef to take a unit in one of the more prestigious buildings, despite the fact that Stef had already found something she liked that was about half the price. Today they were out car shopping. Even though Stef said she didn't need a car, Amy convinced her they should go check them out. There was a BMW dealership that was near where they had been shopping. As they walked into the showroom, a younger salesman came to greet them. He looked to be in his late twenties, shorter and very tan. He was dressed sharply.

"Hi ladies, my name is Alex, what brings you in today?"

Stef, worried that Amy would say something embarrassing, immediately piped in. "We were just in the neighborhood and thought we'd stop by to look, I'm considering getting a car."

"Well, we have a beautiful selection of our 2021 models I can show you. Were you looking for something for a family? We just came out with the new JX, it has a feature very popular with moms. You can get in and out of the third-row seat without having to remove the child safety seat in the second row." Although Alex was trying to be nice and helpful, he would soon regret those words.

"Are you married Alex?" Amy came across as if she might be flirting with him.

"No ma'am, I'm single," Alex responded eagerly.

Amy gave Alex a little smirk, acting a little shy. She started slowly walking towards Alex and running her finger along one of the spotless showroom vehicles. "I bet a guy like you could literally have your pick of women. Good looking, access to all kinds of sweet cars, how is it that a guy like you isn't taken yet?"

Stef noticed that Alex's demeanor shifted to confidence, she imagined he was thinking this was his lucky day. He shot a smirk back to Amy and responded with, "I guess I just haven't found the right woman yet."

By this time Amy was standing extremely close to Alex. She slowly lifted her hand up and brushed the side of his hair with her fingers.

The forwardness caught Alex off guard, and he wasn't sure what to do standing in the middle of the showroom floor. Nobody else was around, and his boss was back in his office out of sight. Despite being shocked, he was enjoying it, grinning from ear to ear. Amy leaned in so she was almost kissing his ear. Stef imagined at this point that Alex must be thinking this was his lucky day and likely wondered if Amy would start making out with him right there. Just as Stef notice that he closed his eyes briefly, likely anticipating a kiss on his neck, a surge of pain coursed through body.

"Listen you little prick," she whispered in his ear. "A little advice for you the next time a woman walks into the showroom. Instead of assuming we are just babymakers looking for a minivan, think of my kung fu death grip, and how it feels on your nuts. Fortunately for you, I'm going to let go of your tiny balls and my friend and I are going to walk out of here, but before we do that I need you to tell me what are you going to do the next time a woman walks into the showroom looking at vehicles?"

Alex was gasping for air, feeling as if the wind was knocked out of him, tears streaming down his cheeks. He faintly let out, "Aaaahhh, I won't assume they are moms," with the words barely escaping his mouth.

Just as Amy let go, Alex finally buckled over in pain. Stef, always embarrassed by Amy's antics, was already starting to leave. "Let's go Stef," Amy said.

As they were walking out Stef asked Amy, "Was that really necessary?"

"I did that kid a favor, think of it as feedback—like that radical candor shit."

"OK," Stef replied, still thinking to herself that she probably didn't need a car but going along with Amy's ideas like usual.

"It's almost four p.m. Let's get home and change so we can make it to kickboxing class in time. Tonight's the first session in the Brazilian jujitsu series. We can't miss it." Amy got out her phone to get an Uber.

"Brazilian jujitsu...sounds intense," Stef wearily replied as they hopped in the Uber and sped away.

CHAPTER 10

Mexico

The next day Mark arrived at work extra early; it was Friday and he had a million things to get done before the weekend. It was especially busy since next week he was going to be in Mexico for a couple days for the finalization of Kilimanjaro's Kidnap and Ransom product launch. Mexico had unfortunately turned into a hotbed for kidnappers, and Kilimanjaro had a solution. They partnered with the Mexican government for a product that would be offered and sold as individuals came into the country. It was a new approach that had taken Mark over a year to build. Although Mark had done most of the work, Tony had been instrumental in finalizing it. He had friends in high places, and even to Mark's surprise, some of them were in the Mexican government. Mark almost didn't want to know the background on those relationships. The entire concept was a little unusual. The Mexican government was going to entice people to purchase insurance on their smartphone that would pay the kidnappers in the event they were taken. The government's solution to kidnapping wasn't to crack down on the criminals, it was to offer insurance to travelers. There was also a tracking element through the person's phone, but Mark was skeptical the Mexican authorities would really crack down. Mark had slight concerns the project wasn't entirely on the up and up, suspecting the kidnappers were paying off the Mexican government at some levels for the deal.

"So are we good to go for the Mexico launch?" Tony asked as he walked into Mark's office.

"We should be. I just received the final sign-off from President Torres's team. Starting next week, the Mexican government will start to sell and distribute kidnap insurance to visitors."

"I have to hand it to you, I was skeptical of this working out but you've proved me wrong," Tony said in a rare flash of humility. "I still think it's a little bizarre, as tourists pass through customs, they will be asked if they would like to purchase a policy for forty bucks that will protect them and their family against kidnapping. You'd have to really hate your family to say no to that!"

"It's a great deal for us, we'll sell thousands of policies a month. We pay the government 20 percent on everything they sell, and they share in the risk if we incur a loss. The last part is critical since it is near impossible to trust the Mexican government." Mark was proud of the deal.

"Make sure to stay away from those Mexican churros when you're down there, that shit will mess you up. That's slang for drugs, Mark, in case you didn't know."

"Thanks Tony, seems like good advice!"

The rest of the hours flew by for Mark, prepping for the trip. As he was heading out for the day and getting ready to close his laptop, he remembered the Megslist ad. He had not even had a chance to check it since he posted it yesterday. He hesitated momentarily, a little nervous. What if nobody replied he thought? No time like the present to check, hopefully at a minimum he would have a few funny videos to watch and a good story to tell. As Mark typed in his YouTube password, his heart started to race, and he clicked his mouse to log in. Mark stared at his screen; he was in disbelief. There were 1,215 new videos. That must have been a mistake because there was no way this could be right. Mark read it again and started scanning through the page—over a thousand guys wanted to compete to marry his ex-wife? Video after video was listed, all new, and all tied to the Megslist ad. Mark was still convinced he must be missing something. There was no way that over a thousand people had responded to his ad. Maybe it went viral; there was no other rational explanation to it. As it started to sink in for Mark, his feeling of bewilderment and confusion changed to excitement. He had set his threshold at twenty, but never in his wildest dreams did he imagine that a thousand people would respond. Fate has spoken, in a very big way. He needed to share this with the guys. None of them even knew he placed an ad. A million things were racing through his mind, but one thing he knew for sure, he needed help. He immediately sent a group text, they needed to meet tonight.

Later that night, the guys were all at Mark's place, digesting the big news of the day.

"What I think I like most is that you took my advice, but just wouldn't admit it to anyone. You thought I was right, but afraid to admit it," Christian said.

"What do you want? Would you be happy if we all bowed to you and admit you were right?" Steve quickly replied.

"Taking out a full-page ad in *USA Today* admitting you were wrong would suffice," Christian replied with a wide smirk.

"We still don't know if it will work, just because a lot of people replied someone still needs to marry Stef," Steve argued.

"Guys, while I thought Christian's idea was a little bizarre to start, I warmed up to it. As shocking as it sounds, he made some valid points that night at poker. I didn't exactly get a fair shake at trial, that's a fact.

At the very least I wanted to leave it up to fate. I'd place the ad and if nobody replied we'd know that it wasn't meant to be. If I received more than twenty responses I'd take that as a sign that it may be worth pursuing. I clearly underestimated the potential!" Mark felt like he had to defend his actions to his friends, or perhaps still to himself a bit.

"Most importantly, have you watched any of the videos yet?" Christian asked.

"Not yet, at first I was in shock, and then I wanted us to do it together," Mark replied.

"I don't know why you guys are so surprised," Ronald said, jumping into the conversation. "I'd totally marry someone for money—and I'm more normal than most."

"Right, if by normal you mean a thirty-year-old movie theater manager who lives with his mom and thinks the government is out to get him. There have to be thousands of guys like you who decide it's a good idea to go late night spear gun fishing naked in a stolen canoe," Christian joked.

"Exactly," Ronald said in a serious tone. Once again not picking up on the sarcasm.

"OK guys, getting back to the topic at hand, I really want your opinion on what you think we should do. I'm excited to move forward, but we clearly need to think this through. Starting off with how we are going to screen over a thousand videos! We can't exactly tell a thousand guys to start pursuing Stef. I don't think the law of large numbers is going to help us here."

"This was your bright idea Christian, why don't you lay some more of your wisdom on us?" Steve said sarcastically.

"I'm the idea guy, I don't involve myself with the details. That's why I hire guys like you, Steve. I'm too busy coming up with great ideas to worry about the details."

Mark piped in, "Outside of the obvious next step to review the videos, I think we need to develop a screening process, narrowing the number down significantly from where it is today, and then have a couple of rounds of elimination until the final. How about we ultimately select three finalists? We can't reveal Stef's identity until that happens, otherwise any of the other guys could just chase her on their own. Once we have the final three, then we can share all the details about Stef: what food she likes and dislikes, her personality, any detail that will help them get a head start on getting to know Stef and fast track the dating process. We want Stef to have the impression that these relationships were meant to be, as if they have some kind of mysterious unexplainable connection. I still know Stef better than anyone. Let's use all of that information to our advantage. The guys will essentially have a playbook outlining everything they need to know—a full dossier on Stef."

"Can we vote them off the island, like on *Survivor*?" Ronald asked. "I'll put their torches out by peeing on them."

Everyone ignored Ronald's remark and Steve chimed in, a little surprised Mark was taking this seriously. "So you are really going to give this a try?"

"Why not? I hear you, it's a crazy idea. That said, the trial shouldn't have ended up the way that it did and I agree with Christian, why just give up? This is as much about principle as it is about the money. The legal system doesn't leave me many options for appeal, so I'm creating my own appeal process.

"The next step: we need to go through the videos and weed out all the guys who are just bat-shit crazy, dangerous, or clearly wouldn't be a good fit for Stef. I'm going to start ASAP. I'm on a flight next week to Mexico and can download a batch to watch, but I can't do them all. We can come up with a list of qualities and traits that we all think we need to look for, and then each of you can take a couple hundred, weeding out those who don't fit."

The guys spent the next thirty minutes debating what qualities were important. This actually turned out to be somewhat complicated, and very funny. Honesty was a trait they quickly threw out the window, realizing the obvious, that their ideal candidate would have to be adept at lying and deception. They all agreed that it would probably take someone with a more dominant personality, not only to pull the task off, but it would also be an attraction for Stef. One idea was to find a male version of Amy. The entire time Christian was fairly adamant that it should be someone just like him. He was convinced he could get the job done in ninety days; it was too bad Stef knew him. Ronald kept making jokes that it needed to be a guy who liked "big jugs," and other sexist comments about her that ended up pissing Steve off more than anything. In the end they determined there were a few important traits, but more than anything they should just focus on weeding out the guys who were certifiable, and there would be plenty of those given the qualities it would take in the first place for someone to respond to that ad.

"So here's the plan: I'll take the Megslist ad down since we have more than enough guys interested. I'll plan on watching the first half, and you guys divide the rest. That's twenty hours of videos for me to watch, but it's a six-hour flight each way to Mexico, and I'm going to get a jump on it this weekend before I leave too. Let's keep only the top 10 percent. If we set the bar high early, it will give us a more manageable number before the final three. If we get down to about one hundred guys, we can then compare those against each other, perhaps start doing some face-to-face interviews." Mark said, barely taking a breath as the words rolled off his tongue like he had been thinking about this for weeks.

"You're the boss," Ronald chimed in.

"Why don't we make it an auction? In other words, we get it down to the final twenty or twenty-five guys and one of the qualifying criteria is how much they would charge to do it?"

"Great idea, Christian—thinking like an investment banker!" Mark immediately said with excitement. "If it is too high we can negotiate with them. It almost makes it a competition then in two ways. First, do they have the skills to pull the task off and marry Stef? Second, do they also know they'll be competing on price against others?"

Ronald sat up straight and nodded to Mark, winking. "It was more me than Christian, don't you think?"

"Yes, of course Ronald, definitely more you. In fact I think Christian just stole your idea." Mark patted Ronald on the shoulder.

Ronald looked over beaming with pride and laughing at Christian, "You should take notes buddy."

"OK, so the game plan is set, how about we meet back up next week Thursday night? I get back Wednesday from Mexico. Is that enough time for everyone?"

Everyone nodded in agreement.

"One thing guys, we can't tell *anyone* about this. Steve, this includes Jennie. *Nobody* can know." Mark shifted to a serious tone. Just as he said it, everyone looked over at Ronald.

"What? You're looking at the Great Wall of Ronald here," he said as waved his fingers across his face. "Nothing gets in or out. How do you think I've avoided detection by the government for all of these years? Always one step ahead in a four-dimensional chess game. I'm impossible to crack. I don't care if they hook my nipples up to a car battery and stick toothpicks in my penis hole."

"What the hell dude, you are so fucking strange. Where do you come up with this stuff?" Christian asked rhetorically. "He does have a point though, he is super private. All we'd have to do is tell him the government is after the information and I don't think anyone would find out. OK we got it, nobody knows, it stays between the four of us." Christian finally got the conversation back on task.

"Sounds good, let's plan on regrouping next Thursday night. Remember, I'll take the first half and you guys divide up the rest. The goal is to weed out 90 percent," Mark said, somewhat skeptical that his friends were as focused and deadline-driven as him.

"I'm still not sold on this idea, I'm a little worried this is not going to end well." Steve said somewhat ominously as his words hung in the air for a bit.

The guys all left Mark's place shortly thereafter. They could all sense a renewed spark in Mark. Even if the idea didn't work they liked to see their best friend getting back to normal. Although Mark was tired from a hectic week, he had a hard time falling asleep that night. With all that was going on he had almost forgotten about his plans with Katie. Katie sat on the board of "Rescue Rover," a conglomerate of dog rescue shelters in the area. She had mentioned to him they were having their annual fundraising charity dinner and he agreed to buy a table for the entire Dog Den gang, courtesy of Kilimanjaro Risk. He was helping a great cause and thought it would be a fun night.

As Mark had expected, the weekend flew by and it was already Sunday morning, he was at the airport ready to board his flight to Mexico. The Rescue Rover event was a success, and they ended up raising over $46,000. Although it wasn't a date and most of the Dog Den crew was there, Mark had a great time with Katie. He still didn't know if it was going to evolve into anything more, but he didn't really care; he had fun hanging out with her.

As Mark boarded the plane, he was almost giddy in anticipation of watching the videos. He had downloaded over six hundred yesterday, but only had a chance to watch a few dozen. The flight was going to be perfect—six hours of uninterrupted viewing time. If the first dozen or so were any indication, it was going to be a wild flight.

Mark was laughing out loud by what he saw—crazy didn't even begin to describe it. Although he found some that were clear winners and should make it into his final fifty, most of the guys were straight off a Jerry Springer casting call. There was one guy who did the entire two-minute video in a panda suit, a self-described "furry." Safe to assume he wasn't going to be a fit for Stef. She didn't even want a dog, so Mark was confident she wasn't going to hook up with some dude in a fur costume who went by the name Panda-man! Another guy spent the entire two minutes talking about how he was a "sexsomniac," which was a new term to Mark. He explained that it was a rare disorder which causes him to perform sex acts in his sleep. He claimed to have given his ex-girlfriend six orgasms one night all while he was asleep, and he was very proud of it. Mark also realized it was a waste to simply delete the ones that were completely ridiculous; they were too entertaining to not keep. Maybe this would be his next business idea: sell the rights to all of this to be made into a movie.

Weeding through the crazy guys, Mark did start to run across several that he felt may be a good fit. One guy was a fitness instructor named Dexter "Thunderbolt Love" Adams. Dexter reminded him like a cooler version of Rex Kwon Do from the movie *Napoleon Dynamite*. He was intense but dressed a little better than Rex (no Zubaz pants), so for now Mark put him on the "maybe" list. He didn't say how he got the nickname Thunderbolt Love, but Mark was almost intrigued enough to keep him around just to find out.

There was another guy named Dalton who was a professional lobbyist, focusing on all the sin industries: gambling, firearms, smoking, and porn. Mark thought he was a perfect fit, anyone who could spend his entire day defending the merits of the industries that a lot of people hate must be an excellent spin artist. Mark really liked him.

Mark was so engrossed in the videos he didn't realize they were only about forty-five minutes outside of Mexico. He had plowed through about two hundred videos, and had only kept fifteen—right on target so far. As Mark closed his laptop in preparation for landing, his mind was racing with excitement. Although Mexico was an important trip for him and the product launch, after watching the videos he was now even more focused to get back.

As Mark spent the next couple of days in Mexico, the trip was turning out to be a success. Border patrol agents managed to sell over a thousand policies in the first two days, far surpassing even Mark's loftiest expectations. It was clear that the Mexican government had spent a significant amount of money to get their agents trained to sell. Mark called Tony and provided a full report as he waited at the airport. Tony was going to put together a briefing document for the board and a press release was ready to hit the newswires on Thursday when Mark returned to the US.

Mark had also sent a note to the three guys and was happy to hear that they had almost made it through the videos. Mark didn't get a lot of details, but it sounded like their experience was similar to his—plenty of crazies. Mark only had about fifty or so left to view on the flight home. He was feeling good about the guys he had selected so far and felt equally good about the ones that were eliminated. As he viewed them, he even felt a little sorry for women in general: this is the male dating pool in America. Mark boarded his flight enthusiastic and happy, he was anxious to meet up with the guys. The videos he had watched were crazy, so he was very curious what kind of weirdos they had uncovered.

CHAPTER 11

The Auditions

Mark got home from work Thursday evening after picking up Tyson, who was as enthusiastic as usual to see him. The day was a little more hectic for Mark than he thought, the Mexican Kidnap and Ransom product launch hit the newswires and he had received several requests for interviews. Surprisingly they even got a call from the White House.

One of the staffers from the Secretary of State's office called inquiring about the joint venture with Mexico. Although they didn't tell Mark what their concern was, reading into the somewhat cryptic questions the staffer asked he could glean that they didn't fully trust the Mexican government and felt they could have a hand in some of the kidnappings. Mark was amused by the call, but didn't really think it would amount to much.

The guys had just arrived at Mark's condo and started to discuss the videos.

"If nothing else this little exercise made me understand even better why it's so easy for me to pick up women. If the guys in these videos are a representation of my competition, I need to try even less," Christian said, starting off the conversation with something about him.

"They seemed normal to me," Ronald said with a serious tone.

"There it is, I rest my case, that confirms I don't need to try as hard." Ronald just looked at Christian with confusion.

"Before we get started I wanted to get something out on the table that I think you'll all find interesting," Mark said, getting everyone's attention. "Remember last Friday when you were all here and we talked about the game plan and came up with the idea to make this an auction, where the guys competitively bid for the chance at marrying Stef?"

The guys all nodded their heads in agreement. Ronald then interjected, "Yeah, that's when I had the idea or I mean Christian and I had the idea to make it an auction."

"Exactly Ronald," Mark replied. "Thinking back on that conversation it seemed to be Christian who had the idea, but it was prompted by Ronald asking what the ad said, right? Do you remember that Ronald?"

Ronald looked a little confused but nodded in acknowledgment.

"Well I was on the flight back from Mexico and I realized why Ronald asked about what the ad said. Ronald, would you like to share with the group how I realized that?"

Ronald still looked confused, then said, "Hey guys, I think we're running low on beer. I'm going to run to the liquor store and grab some. I'll be right back!"

As he said that he was starting to stand up, Mark interjected, "No Ronald, you can't make an emergency exit, I think you'll want to see this." Just as Ronald turned around, Mark had his laptop out and started showing a video to the guys. Sure enough, it was a two-minute video snippet of Ronald trying out!

"Hahaha, classic!" Christian snorted loudly. "Why didn't you just tell us that's why you asked what the ad said?"

"I didn't want you guys to think I'm weird," Ronald said

seriously. "I look through the personals on Megslist on a regular basis. It sounded like a great deal. I'd marry someone for money and it was ironic that we had just talked about it a couple days before. I thought it was fate!"

"First off, out of all the crazy shit you have done that would make us think you are weird, this doesn't even hit the radar. Second, did you not think it was unusual that we had just talked about the idea and magically you happened to notice a blind ad on Megslist about the exact idea we had a night or two before?" Christian asked, knowing that none of the guys knew that Mark had placed the ad, but any of them should have been able to put it together if they had read the ad after they had just talked about it.

"I thought it was fate," Ronald said defensively. As the guys were all laughing and giving Ronald a hard time, he interrupted. "Don't tell me now though."

All the guys looked at Ronald a little confused and finally Mark said, "Don't tell you what now?"

"You know, don't tell me, I want to be surprised at the end," Ronald again said

"What are you talking about?" Christian interjected.

"If I made the cut, I want to find out just like the rest of the guys," Ronald said.

"Are you serious?" Christian said perplexed. "You aren't getting selected to marry Stef!"

Mark, sometimes feeling a little bad for Ronald and how much they make fun of him then interjected, "but it is only because she knows you already and knows you are friends with me. We can't risk the chance of her finding out. Hands down though Ronald if that wasn't the case I would have selected your video. Definitely in the top five out of the ones I watched."

Christian just rolled his eyes, Steve was laughing, and Ronald sat there smirking, even blushing a little on the heels of Mark's comments. "Thanks, Mark," he replied.

"OK, so now getting back on point with the videos. I know I had you guys pick about 10 percent, but let's try to leave tonight with a group of forty for the next cut. It's seven p.m. It will take us about four hours or so to watch the top videos everyone selected, and as a group we can decide who is in and who is out. Grab whatever you want from the bar and kill the lights. This will be fun."

They were zipping through the videos one after another, making fun of every idiot that came onto the screen. One guy claimed he was the perfect choice because he had some weird disorder that gave him a permanent erection.

"It sounds like a curse. I had that condition when I was seven, no control whatsoever," Christian replied jokingly.

"Priapism is a serious disorder, don't make fun of it," Ronald said defensively.

"Huh?" Christian asked.

"Priapism. Having a constant woody," Ronald replied seriously. "It affects thousands of people. The name comes from the Greek god Priapus—he had a disproportionately large and constantly erect penis. Google it if you don't believe me."

The guys stared at Ronald for a few seconds until Christian finally jokingly looked under the table and said, "Nope, I don't see it—don't think you got it."

"I don't have it you idiots," Ronald said as he leaned in as if he was covering up his groin as Christian laughed and pointed. "He's my favorite Greek god, I had a poster of him in my room as a child."

"Let me get this straight, when you were a teenager, you had a picture of some old Greek dude with a giant erection on your bedroom wall?" Christian said.

"He was my hero!" Ronald shouted and slammed his fist against the table. "Stop mocking him!"

"I stand corrected then, let me clarify. When most boys had a poster of Bruce Lee or Spider-man on their wall as their hero, you had a picture of some old Greek dude with a giant erect cock? I'll save the obvious question of whether you think that is a little unusual since we all know you, but did your parents or any of your friends ever think that was a little odd?" Christian asked. Steve and Mark had been relatively quiet just staring at Ronald.

"Only the stupid people who don't appreciate how awesome he is would think it is odd."

"He does have a point Christian, it's pretty cool on its own to be a Greek god, but I don't know what could be better than being a Greek god *and* having a giant erect penis. Having a poster of him in your room may be a bit much, but I side with Ronald on this one, the dude sounds legendary," Mark said finally diving into the conversation and coming to Ronald's defense, albeit in a sarcastic tone and turning the tide on Christian.

"Me too," Steve said also jumping to Ronald's defense and in direct opposition to Christian. "Who needs Spider-man, we need a movie made for Priapus!"

"Whoa, holy shit...check it out!" Mark said loudly as he turned the computer to face the guys. As the guys were talking, he had googled a picture of the mythical Greek god.

"I told you," Ronald said with a proud look on his face.

"The dude is enormous. It's like another leg," Steve said as they were all laughing.

"One time a donkey betrayed him, so he killed it with his penis, bludgeoned it to death," Ronald said proudly with a big smile on his face. "I'd like to see him take on Thor with his hammer. My money would still be on Priapus."

"OK guys, this is all very interesting but can we get back to why we are here tonight?" Mark asked, trying to get the conversation back on track.

As the guys continued to vet the possible candidates, there was no shortage of funny stories and bizarre idiots. Mark was clearly enjoying the role of ringleader. Although it took the better part of the night, they finally managed to get the number down to forty candidates.

"Nice work guys, well done, I think we have a great cast of potential bachelors for Stef," Mark said.

"So what is the next step? How will we narrow the guys down from here?" Steve asked knowing Mark probably had a plan.

"The next phase is the auditions. We'll bring them all in and judge each one individually. One question, Ronald, do you think we could use one of the theaters?"

"Please, I pretty much run the place," Ronald said as if it was a stupid question. "Well, as long as we don't set up cameras in the bathrooms and stream it into the screens, if I do that again I think there is a good chance I'll be fired."

"Right, I forgot," Mark said, afraid to ask too many questions about his remark. "Thanks Ronald, I think the theater will be the perfect venue. I don't think we want to bring anyone into our homes or show them too much of our personal lives. Ronald, can you arrange for us to use the theater this weekend? I'm thinking we will either need to do it in the morning or really late at night. Would nine a.m. on Saturday work?"

"Consider it done amigo."

As the guys all left Mark's place, there was definitely a sense of excitement. Nobody knew what was going to happen next or if it was going to work, but they were all confident it was going to be fun and a story they would be able to laugh and talk about for years to come. None of them had any idea how true that really was.

CHAPTER 12

The Field Tests

Saturday morning came quickly, and although Mark had to rush to prepare for it, he was ready. The email had gone out from a blind address, all forty recipients were instructed to show up at the theater promptly at 8:30 a.m. They had been the fortunate chosen ones to reach the next step, but knew little about what to expect, which was exactly how Mark had wanted it to be. They were instructed to show up and tell no one else of what they were doing, violating that would result in immediate elimination. Obviously a big element of this being successful was the fact that it needed to be kept a secret, which would be a challenge.

Mark had asked Steve, Ronald, and Christian to all show up at the theater at eight a.m., so they could be prepped on what would take place. He was a little anxious, eager to share the plan with them.

"A debate?" Steve asked.

"Think of a debate but with unorthodox topics," Mark said as he began to explain what he had in store for today. "When the four of us talked through what attributes are going to be most important in the guys we select, we decided the ability to communicate and think on their feet is going to be key in winning over Stef in a short amount of time. Think about it, they are going to be walking into a situation where they know a tremendous amount about a person, but they can't share with them that they already know it, or why. To Stef, it all needs to come across as it was meant to be. We need someone who can not only manipulate and think on their feet quickly but also can influence masterfully. That's where the unorthodox topics come in. They are going to have to debate things that are completely irrational and likely things they don't believe in. Presumably they won't fall in love with Stef, but they must convince her that they are. We can see the guys in action, how competitive they are, how quickly they think on their feet, how creative, and how they perform under pressure. We will divide them up into four groups and each group will debate the topics for about forty-five minutes. The four of us will sit in the audience throwing out the topics and judging them. Think of it as a big improv show. Not dissimilar to how it will be with Stef, the one difference being they will know a lot of the facts going into the situation. We will not only rate their performance on debating skill, but also physical attributes."

"It actually sounds crazy enough to work!" Steve said excitedly. "What are the topics?"

As Mark ran through the list of topics, the guys were all laughing. They seemed to get more ridiculous the further into the list:

You are a talent agent for models and this bearded man in the audience is your client, i.e. Ronald. Convince us all that he is the next Tyson Beckford.

You are a lobbyist for the grocers association trying to pass a law that would make it legal for cart attendants to carry handguns and shoot customers on the spot for not corralling their carts. Convince us why it should be legal.

You are married with two kids, a boy who is twelve and a girl who is ten. You live down the street from Snoop Dogg and you need to convince your wife why you want to hire him to babysit the kids for a weekend.

You have to pick one or the other: you either give a handy to a homeless man in an alley and nobody finds out, or you get a handy from an eighty-year-old bearded woman and all of your friends find out. Which would you choose and why? (This one wasn't really a debate question, but Mark thought it was funny nonetheless.)

The list went on and on. Mark had put a lot of creative thought into it. They had no idea how some of them would even begin to debate the topics, but it was clear they would certainly find out who the gifted bullshitters in the group were. Not only did Mark think this would be very effective in getting the list down to the final ten, but equally important, it would be fun.

All but four ended up showing up to the audition, so they would have four groups of nine. A good amount for a healthy and competitive process. As Ronald escorted the first group in, it was clear this was going to be entertaining. They had no instruction on what they were in store for—a couple of the guys were wearing suits and one guy came dressed in a male cupid costume. No doubt he thought it was a brilliant idea at the time, but you could tell he was regretting it. Most of them walked in with a swagger, not lacking confidence. While Mark wasn't looking for someone overly arrogant, he felt like they needed a certain level of confidence to pull the task off. Mark had also given explicit instructions to Steve, Christian, and Ronald. The more they could knock these guys off of their game and test them the better.

Mark had put nine chairs on the stage. Each guy in the first group filed in and took their seats. Christian, Ronald, and Steve all sat down, and Mark stood up approaching the guys on stage. "Congratulations men, you all passed the first round of eliminations. I'm sure you're all wanting more details, but I have bad news: you aren't going to get it. What you know is that you are all here competing for a chance to marry a girl you've never met, and one of you will get paid very well to do so. That's about all you are going to find out at this point. Look around, this is your competition, and only 25 percent of you will make it to the final round.

"Today's test is going to be a debate of sorts. My friends and I put together a list of topics that you may find bizarre and some may find offensive, but your challenge is going to be to debate the topics as we list them for you. You have ten minutes to talk, and once your time is up we'll move onto the next topic. If you don't speak up you'll have missed your chance. If any of my friends or I think you are boring or off topic, you'll hear an air horn go off and that's your cue to stop talking and leave. If you decide to be a dipshit and give any of us an attitude you'll also be eliminated. On your way in you all signed a confidentiality agreement, if you speak of this after you leave, we will come after you."

As Mark was talking one of the guys on the end started laughing quietly and making fun of the guy in the cupid costume. Mark immediately jumped in, "Is there something you have to share with everyone?" he asked.

"No, I was just wondering if Cupid Boy gets extra credit for dressing like a dipshit," the guy remarked.

Always at least one in every crowd Mark thought. "First of all, did I say you could ask a question? Second, I'm glad you brought up how he is dressed, we are going to level the playing field. Take your pants off."

"What?" the guy responded with a somewhat nervous laughter.

"You heard me, take your pants off. Either that or come down and kiss this man on the lips." Mark pointed to Ronald. Ronald sat up looking a little shocked, but then shrugged his shoulders and closed his eyes, sticking his lips out.

"No way, I'm not taking my pants off or kissing that dude, you're nuts."

"Perfect, then get out of here, you're done." Mark replied, testing the guy to see what he was made of. "You either take your pants off and do the entire debate in your underwear, kiss the bearded man, or you leave."

Steve, Christian, and Ronald were all laughing, particularly Ronald who decided it was a good idea to weigh in with some color commentary of his own, taunting the guy by standing up and doing some bizarre dance and pretending to take his own pants off, licking his lips while he stared down the guy on stage.

"You guys are fucking nuts," the guy on stage responded. "I'm outta here, this is stupid anyway." He stood up and walked out of the theater.

"Perfect, one down and eight more of you to go. Did anyone else have anything to add?" Mark asked as the room fell silent. Mark had accomplished what he wanted to, first of all the guy was an arrogant asshole and didn't fit what they needed. He also set the tone and took control of the room.

Over the next forty-five minutes, the guys had a blast throwing out topic after topic and watching the contestants ramble, stammer, and to their surprise in some situations, articulately state their case. Ronald was a riot during the entire model debate, at one point he got up and walked back and forth pretending he was on a catwalk. Christian also really got into it. This was his environment, he was born with quick wit, and used sarcasm as a weapon. One guy seemed to be his ideal victim, Niles was the chubbiest one out of the bunch and Christian kept calling him by different disparaging nicknames. This included Crisco, pancake, blubber nugget, and fat-tits. Despite Christian's constant effort however he could not shake the guy. The guy wasn't quite as large as Christian made him out to be, but despite that, he kept taking it and wasn't knocked off his game. He seemed adept at ignoring Christian, it was like fuel for him. The more Christian would hurl insults, the more articulate he became. This drove Christian mad, pushing him to the next level.

Despite his best efforts, he could not shake him. The other guys picked up on this and not only did they make fun of Christian, but they thought Niles could definitely be a player despite the fact that he wasn't the best looking.

The guys worked through the first group and moved onto the second, third, and the fourth and final group. It was an entertaining morning to say the least. They seemed to have more fun with each group. The level of craziness also continued to escalate. During the third group, Ronald thought it would be a good idea to walk right up to one of the guys as he was trying to debate one of the topics and dropped his drawers, standing about six inches away from the guy sitting on the chair. Despite Mark shouting for Ronald to immediately put his pants on and sit back down, the guys were sure the poor dude would never fully recover from trying to unsee that.

As the fourth group left the stage, all of the contestants had departed the theater.

"I've done some crazy shit, but this has to be right up there. I have no idea if we found Stef's future husband, but that was the most fun I've had in a long time." Christian said.

"Agreed, I have to admit I was skeptical of how this was going to go and didn't really know what to expect with today, but this was a blast." Steve said uncharacteristically agreeing with Christian. "So what's the next step?"

"We just need to talk through the guys and narrow it down to a final ten, I'd like to get that done before we leave today."

As the guys talked through all the candidates and replayed the crazy scenes in their head, they started to get it narrowed down. In the end it turned out to be a little more difficult than they thought. There were some clear winners. They all agreed Dexter "Thunderbolt Love" Adams, the fitness trainer, was in.

With the exception of Christian they all really liked Niles, the slightly chubby but extremely articulate guy that Christian couldn't rattle. Overall Mark felt like it was a successful day, and they had finally narrowed it down to the final ten guys who they all agreed had a legitimate shot at marrying Stef.

"I assume none of you have plans for tonight that you can't cancel?" Mark asked.

"Clay Aiken is on Celebrity Apprentice, but I suppose I could have Mom DVR it," Ronald said in a somewhat disappointed tone.

"I could probably make it work, although Jennie is going to be upset I didn't give her more of a heads-up," Steve said in a somber tone.

"For Christ's sake, grow a pair. Do you mean to say that Jennie is going to be pissed that you didn't ask for permission thirty days in advance to leave the house for something other than going to work or going to the grocery store to buy tampons?" Christian said, still on a role from the insults rolling off his tongue this morning.

"I realize this is short notice, but for what I have planned next we need to do it on a Saturday night, and I don't want to wait until next week. We need the element of surprise on our side," Mark said, ignoring the banter between Christian and Steve.

"I'll give you all the details later, but you need to be at Club Sabre at eight p.m.," Mark said, not letting on to what else was in store for the night.

Club Sabre was the quintessential place to be seen and had a reputation of being a magnet for hot girls who had no intention of going home with a guy.

"Think of tonight as the field test. Today they had the stage audition, but it's the real thing. We're preparing the troops for battle." Mark was grinning.

"Nice, it's smart," Christian replied with a big smirk. The guys were starting to witness their friend go through a transformation. The Mark today was not the same Mark they saw even a week ago. He was gaining confidence every step of the way and having fun.

"OK, see you guys at Sabre, eight p.m."

Before Mark called the final ten, he had one other call to make first. He stepped outside of the theater, "Hey boss, I need your help."

Later that night, the guys all made it to Sabre on time. Mark had arrived twenty minutes early and was already waiting for them, even securing a special VIP room reserved with private waitresses and bottle service."

"The Liquid Cougar and vodkas are on me," Mark said as he leaned back on the plush red couch.

"OK, I have to ask, I was impressed that the stooge bouncer had my name and let me in right away instead of the two-hour wait. How did you arrange all this on a moment's notice? This place is impossible to get into, and you not only got us in, but presumably ten other guys and a private room with bottle service. Who are you and what have you done with our boring insurance friend Mark? I only want to know because you should tell the other Mark to stay where he is, we much prefer this guy!" Christian shouted over the music thumping in the background.

Mark, grinning with his hands up by his side, thought about telling the guys it was Tony but decided against it. Tony was a regular at Sabre. He made one call and Mark was set for the night.

"So what's the plan, where are the guys?" Steve asked. It was evident that Steve was the old married guy in the bunch, showing up at the nightclub in a pair of off-white linen pants, a bright polo shirt, and boat shoes with no socks.

"Hey Gilligan, it's great to see you could make it off the island," Christian said as he pointed at Steve and then snapped his finger at the waitress. "Excuse me miss, my friend here would like something in a coconut, can you make that happen? Also, can you tell the DJ to put on something by the Beach Boys? We didn't realize it was "dress like your favorite *Loveboat*" character night." The waitress laughed as she walked away, with Christian turning his attention back on Steve. "Seriously, how is it that you're even married? I take back all of those criticizing remarks about being married to one woman the rest of your life, it's a good thing you are because there is no way you would even stand a chance if you were single. Even Ronald dressed better than you."

"Thanks Christian, I'm glad you noticed!" Ronald said, not picking up on the backhanded insult. "I only break out this shirt for special occasions." He turned around pointing to the back of his black dress shirt that had a picture of a horse rearing up with the words Take a ride on the Italian Stallion across the top. "Get it, hahaha, Italian Stallion?" Ronald said laughing, looking at the rest of the guys who just kind of stared at him blankly.

"It is beyond ironic that you are a blend of multiple great ethnicities, none of which are Italian," Christian joked.

"What, this isn't that bad?" Steve said, pointing at his outfit and not letting go of the fact that Christian was making fun of it. "Jennie and I went on a cruise two years ago, I bought it especially for that occasion and she couldn't keep her hands off me."

"Well then, I don't know what I was thinking. Clearly if you can pick your own wife up when you're on vacation after she's been boozing all day, then I'm sure you're right! As a matter of fact, I'm going to order that outfit from Walmart tomorrow so I can have sex with your wife too."

"Easy guys, can we get back to what we are here for tonight?" Mark asked rhetorically. "Christian, save the passion for the festivities tonight. We need your sharp wit."

"On that note, when do our ten dudes get here?" Christian asked, following Mark's instructions and letting Steve's outfit go.

"They should be here in twenty minutes or so. I wanted us to get here first so I could lay out the game plan with all of you. First off, I think we need to start the night off with a toast and officially kick off our project: 'The Megslist Husband.'" Mark said as he poured shots of vodka in all of the glasses. The guys all smiled and stood up, raising their glasses. "Here's to the best group of friends a guy could ask for, although individually we're all a little messed up, somehow we magically just seem to make it work together. No matter what happens tonight or with getting Stef married, let's commit to each other, we're always here to help each other."

All the guys clinked their glasses and agreed. They made a great team.

"And most of all let's totally mess with these idiots tonight. Blubber Nugget is going down!" Christian said laughing, referring of course to his nemesis Niles.

All the guys leaned in so they could hear Mark over the music. "I told the guys to be here at eight thirty, but they don't know what to expect. Once they get here, the objective will be simple: they have until two a.m. to score with as many girls as possible. That being said, they can't leave the bar. They need to stay here so we can observe and watch how they do. Each of us will act as spotters, we'll take mental notes of how the guys perform. We can even throw out challenges. If we see a girl who is already with a guy, we can tell them they'll get bonus points if they can get the girl to ditch the guy and hang with them. Although there is no clear scoring method, they will get points for both quality and quantity. We don't want the guy who hits on one girl and stays with her the entire night, they need to keep moving and working the room.

"Nice, what do you need from us?" Steve asked.

"Like I said, for starters you can hurl challenges at any of the guys, and be spotters. You're my eyes and ears."

Mark could see the enthusiasm and excitement on all of the guys' faces. Christian in particular looked deep in thought, no doubt thinking about the many ways he could totally mess with Niles. As they were plotting various ways they were going to challenge the guys, Steve nodded to the door, the first participant had arrived.

Dalton, the silver-tongued lobbyist came walking through the door, oozing confidence. Although the bar was already packed every-one seemed to look his way. Christian was right, he did seem to be the total package.

Standing about six two with olive complexion and wavy salt-and-pepper hair, he caught the attention of several girls right away. Dalton looked like a *GQ* model. Designer shoes with tailored pants and shirt, he was clearly ready for action. He immediately noticed the guys sit-ting in the VIP room and Mark waived him over. He poured Dalton a drink and told him to wait, the other guys should be here shortly.

Over the next few minutes, the guys came pouring in. Christian, who was like a kid at Christmas and too impatient to wait, looked over at Niles and said, "Hey slim, did you miss me?"

Again Niles ignored Christian and just grinned back, and then deflected by telling everyone a funny joke and in no way related to what Christian just said. Christian wanted some kind of reaction out of him, but Niles was adept at ignoring him. At that moment the last guy arrived and Mark stood up, motioning the guys to lean in so they could hear him.

Mark ran through the objective: this was their field-test, and they wanted to see the guys in action. No more simple interview questions or debates, this was the real deal and tonight they would pick three out of the ten who would make the final cut and have the chance for the money. For the seven who didn't do well tonight this would be the final stop, they wouldn't see them again. Mark outlined the one basic rule: hit on as many women as you can, but if you leave the bar you're disqualified. Everything else was essentially on the table Mark explained. They needed to pull out all the stops if they were going to win.

As Mark was talking, the guys were paying close attention but also occasionally glancing at each other, sizing up the competition. Dexter "Thunderbolt Love" Adams was the most buff of the bunch, rocking a tight black V-neck T-shirt with his arms bulging. He looked like he could be on the cover of *Men's Fitness*. His extra short hair and several days of not shaving made him look like a badass assassin. They had earlier found out he was a former Navy SEAL so he both looked and played the part. Despite the fact that Niles was not in the best physical shape, it was clear that he came prepared for action. What he lacked in physical appearance he made up in confidence, attitude, and personality. There was also a little more mystery to Niles. He didn't seem to fit the mold of a player.

Each of the guys had their own unique qualities, it was like an episode of the *Bachelorette*. Tyler was the quintessential musician, a bartender by day to pay the bills, and guitarist for a struggling band at night. The "artist type" would be attractive to Stef, which was one of the reasons why Tyler made the cut. Alex was a reporter, writing for several leading magazines. Zander, another one of the finalists, was a different type of artist, a painter and sculptor, who in Mark's opinion must have been struggling for work based on how desperate he came across, offering to marry Stef for $150,000—half of what most of the guys wanted. The reverse auction approach turned out to be a good decision. Even Dalton was only asking for $300,000, which was less than what Mark originally thought he'd have to shell out. Mark had guessed that most of the guys just viewed this as a quick marriage, get divorced in less than a year. There wouldn't be any issues over dividing up assets or risk of them losing money.

There were a few questions from the guys to make sure they understood the rules, but Mark was ready to cut them loose. Mark looked at his friends. "What do you think? Are they ready?" he asked.

"Remember Niles, the objective is to hit on the girls, not eat them. If I were the other guys I'd just throw a few Philly cheesesteaks your way as a diversion tactic," Christian said, again relentless on the attack against Niles. He just wasn't giving up.

"On that note, best of luck to everyone. May the best men win!" Mark said, knowing their success was his success. The interests were perfectly aligned: he wanted the three that would give him the best shot at marrying Stef, and they were all influenced by the cash.

Mark had asked that Christian hold off on any challenges for the first half hour or so. It would give everyone a chance to figure out their game plan.

He actually liked the idea of giving them a chance to first develop a plan, then throw challenges at them to see who could adjust. Some of the guys started to immediately go in for the kill, working the room like politicians at a town hall meeting. It was also evident that Dalton was no stranger to Sabre. He seemed to know at least 30 percent of the people there, if not more. That would be an advantage for him, but it also meant some of the challenges were going to need to involve people he didn't know.

After the first half hour passed, it seemed that Dalton, Dexter, and Tyler were off to an early lead. That said, the night was young and they hadn't even started with the challenges yet. With that in mind, Christian glanced over at Mark as if to ask if it was time, and Mark nodded to give the green light on challenges.

Christian could hardly contain his excitement. Mark was convinced he only managed to get about half a nod in and Christian was up off the chair and off to his first victim. Surprisingly though it wasn't Niles…at least not yet.

Christian approached Dalton as he seemed to be hitting it off with two blondes, he slapped him on the back and proclaimed, "Dalt-dog, what's up?" Dalton turned to give him a WTF look.

"Hey…yeah, what's up?" Dalton responded wearily, not sure what to do about Christian.

"Aren't you going to introduce me? Who are these two fine specimens? Are you working it with twins again? You dog! You should try triplets," Christian said, trying to put the kibosh on Dalton's pursuit.

Dalton paused and tried to read the reaction of the girls, then all of a sudden started laughing. "Hahaha, you are such a dick. Ladies, this is my cousin Victor. He does this occasionally, goes out of his way to embarrass me. There is this one time growing up…well, maybe I shouldn't tell this, it is a little embarrassing," Dalton said, trying to dig his way out but then pausing for effect as if he didn't want to say anything.

"Tell us," one of the girls said, still trying to get a feel for what was going on with the interaction.

"OK, I guess I might as well throw it out here, but you will think it is pathetic and cheesy. In junior high I used to keep a diary, I would use it to put my thoughts down and would even write poetry occasionally. It would all go in my diary."

"Ohhhh, that's sweet," one of the girls replied, both of them smiling in an endearing way towards Dalton.

"Stop it, I get embarrassed talking about it," Dalton said grinning sheepishly, knowing his story was working. "Well one day old cousin Victor here got a hold of it and thought it would be funny to write in it that I was in a romantic relationship with my teacher. He copied my handwriting and started a journal entry, then left it out on the kitchen table for my parents to find. Remember that Victor?" Dalton asked, glancing at Christian, not really waiting for a response. "Well his plan backfired. My parents freaked out, but instead of asking me about it they immediately contacted the school board and superintendent. The entire incident blew up as you can imagine. Victor ended up getting suspended for a month."

"What a jerk!" one of the girls said to Christian as she shot a stern look of disappointment his way and slapped him on the shoulder. "I hope you learned your lesson." Meanwhile, Christian was laughing inside and also impressed by Dalton's quick thinking. He passed with flying colors.

Across the bar the other guys were working up challenges, Ronald had entered the mix. He had corned Tyler, who was talking to a freakishly tall brunette. Ronald had worked his way into the conversation subtly at first, pretending to be friends with Tyler. So far Ronald was being well behaved, although that was quickly about to change. Tyler was going to face his first test.

Ronald looked at the girl, who at this point seemed to be into Tyler, and Ronald coming over was helping. Even though it was Ronald, girls tended to be more open to a guy if he was with friends and not roaming the bar creepily by himself. "You know my friend Tyler here is quite the genius, most of what I know I owe to him." Tyler looked at Ronald and smirked. Then Ronald looked at the girl and said, "Let me ask you a question. Have you ever been on a flight and had to sit next to a crying baby? Isn't that the worst?"

The girl looked back at Ronald and Tyler and nodded in agreement, "Yeah, that's never fun, but sometimes I just feel bad for the parents…"

"Oh yeah, totally, I agree. *I do too*!" Ronald said, which seemed to resonate well with the tall girl. "Well this brilliant guy here came up with the perfect way to get out of the situation, and I used it on a flight last week. It worked flawlessly. Do you want to tell or should I?" Ronald asked enthusiastically, looking at Tyler. Tyler just looked back and deferred to Ronald. He had no idea where this was going, but so far it was working out well.

"Ummm, you can go ahead and tell it." Tyler said, nodding to Ronald.

"Ok, well this baby next to me started wailing, so I called the flight attendant over and thanks to Tyler's idea I got moved to a seat in First class." Ronald said, leaving the story hanging a bit.

"What did you do?" the girl asked Ronald, starting to sound curious.

"I had the flight attendant lean in closely and then in a medium-whisper said, 'Excuse me ma'am, I'm a registered sex offender and can't be within twenty-five feet of this cute little baby next to me, so the only safe place for everyone is if I moved to first class.' *Brilliant*!" Ronald shouted as he slapped Tyler on the shoulder, while Tyler's face immediately changed to a look of rage.

"Isn't this guy a genius?" Ronald said as he looked at the girl who at this point had a look of complete shock. "I still remember when he told me he does that on flights and it works every time. What did you say exactly…oh yeah, I remember…'It gets you away from the crying little runts!'"

"That's sick, you do realize that's a real problem? Pedophilia is a disgusting issue, why would you even think it's OK to joke about something like that? You're gross," she said as she looked at Tyler with disgust and disappointment.

"Uhhh, yeah. I'm aware of that." Tyler said in a defeated tone as he now glared at Ronald. He knew whatever chances he had with this girl were completely shot.

"OK, I'm going to leave you kids to talk, good to see you again Tyler," Ronald said as he patted Tyler on the back and walked away. While Ronald was oblivious to the fact that most women did not think he was charming, tonight was actually the first night ever where that trait would come in handy.

As Mark and team continued to indulge in the VIP room, taking full advantage of the bottle service, the challenges seemed to escalate as the night progressed. They moved from trying to throw the guys off their game to more outright challenges, having the guys interrupt each other or hit on the same women at once to see who would win. They were clearly having a blast, treating the guys like ten-year-olds they could dare into any situation.

The best part was that most of the time the guys would do it and accept the challenge, sometimes failing miserably. As the night wound down, Mark and team told the guys the exercise was done; they would be contacted if they made the final three.

"Let's grab breakfast and decide on the final three," Mark said. "There is a place down the street."

As they sat down at the diner they couldn't help but laugh at all the stories from the night. Since the majority of the night they individually mingled amongst the guys, they didn't even know what the others were up to. To no surprise, Christian was clearly the most aggressive, and they all shook their heads at some of his stories. At one point he explained he thought Dexter was going to punch him, which probably wouldn't have ended well for Christian. The guys spent the first hour just laughing at all of the stories, one of the best nights in a long time, they all thought.

Once they finally got around to talking about which guys were making the cut, it was clear that Dalton was a shoo-in. The guy showed remarkable charisma and they could almost never shake him no matter what was thrown his way. The guy had skills, every woman was interested in him. Even Christian was impressed. Although the other guys showed some skills, Dalton seemed to be in a different league. The rest were still on the junior varsity squad compared to him.

"I kind of like Dexter, although he doesn't seem to be in the same league as Dalton he brings different skills to the table, which could be attractive to Stef," Steve said.

"I agree, I'm leaning towards including him. He's definitely a health nut and I could see Stef clicking with that," Mark said.

"He makes me nervous, the guy is ex-military, how can we be sure he isn't working with the government, undercover? I've watched *Rambo*, they call these guys out of retirement for black-ops shit. You know, secret missions. He could be trying to take our entire operation down or even worse, he could have been sent to infiltrate our group and turn us against each other," Ronald said in a serious tone.

"I did notice he was looking at you funny, Ronald," Christian said jokingly. "I bet you are right, he will probably take you hostage and go all Jack Bauer on your ass, tearing your teeth out one by one until you tell them where you hid all of those *National Geographic* magazines you stole from the library in '92."

"I didn't steal the entire magazine, I just tore pictures out!" he responded defensively. "And I should mention it was for a very important school project."

"Right…a school project," Christian said as he made a masturbation hand gesture toward Ronald. "Actually since the guy's nickname is 'Thunderbolt Love' maybe he won't rip your teeth out one by one, maybe he'll give you a dose of the 'Thunder,'" Christian said in air quotes as he was laughing at Ronald.

"Getting back on topic, what about Niles?" Mark asked

"I like him," Ronald said, I think he's a keeper.

"All you fatties stick together," Christian said, laughing at his own joke.

"What do you think Steve?" Mark asked.

"Tough call, I could see keeping him, but not sure. What do you think, Mark?"

"Although I hate to do it, I think we need to cut him. I liked the idea of him being the underdog, and particularly since it would piss Christian off so much I'd like to keep him, but I don't think he'll be what Stef is looking for. We have better options."

"Are you thinking Tyler?" Steve asked Mark.

"He's ok, but I maybe like Zander, the starving artist," Mark said.

"No way. Bad choice. He's lame," Christian said decisively.

"I oddly have to side with Christian on this one," Steve said. "What did you like about him? He seemed fairly unimpressive."

"There are a couple things that point me to him. First off, he's desperate. While that isn't normally a positive attribute, I want someone who is hungry, someone who needs this. They have an extra incentive to win. Zander seems like he needs this," Mark said.

"Ok, I guess I can see that," Steve said. "What else?"

"He's completely different from Dalton and Dexter in every way, and I like the idea of throwing him into the mix. He's a guy who follows his passion. Stef is still a little bit of a lost soul. She may gravitate towards someone who is a free spirit and perhaps a little lost himself. Lastly, he's pretty different than me, and you know what they say, you typically end up with someone opposite of your ex." Mark said.

"I sure as hell hope that's true if you remarry, you'll actually end up with someone pretty great if she's opposite of Stef," Christian replied quickly.

"A really fun girl with small tits!" Ronald said laughing as he high fived Christian. "Get it, small tits is the opposite of Stef?"

"Classic Ronald, yes we get it. You can't really let that go can you, can you?" Steve said, shaking his head.

"So it's decided, the starting line-up is Dalton, Dexter, and Zander," Mark said getting the conversation back on topic. Next step is to get them all together and tell them more about the mission. I need to head home to let Tyson out."

The guys all agreed it was late, even Christian said he was spent and planned to go directly home. The guys made a few final comments about how amazing the night turned out and agreed they should sell the movie rights once this is all finished.

"Remember, six p.m., my place, tomorrow night!" Mark shouted as they all got into Ubers and headed home for the night.

CHAPTER 13

The Stef Playbook

The guys arrived at Mark's house as scheduled the next night and Tyson happily greeted them at the door. Tyson had more energy than usual; given the late night before, Mark had slept in and didn't get out for his normal run. He spent most of the day preparing for the night ahead.

He had summarized everything about Stef he could think of, basically a full dossier of insider knowledge. Her favorite color, how she liked her coffee with one sugar cube in the milk while frothing, attending private school, the bond with her grandparents, how her parents passed away, what makes her laugh, what makes her cry—everything that anyone could possibly want to know about Stef. All of this information was aimed at giving the trio an advantage, an insider's ability to set the hook and move things along quickly. The only way this would work is if Stef felt that it was meant to be—she would meet someone who would know so much about her, but it could never be too obvious otherwise she would realize something was up and it would blow Mark's entire plan. He had to be certain the guys were aware of this, so they didn't do anything that could lead Stef to give her the impression it was a setup. Although it would be questionable whether or not she would have any legal recourse if she found out Mark was trying this, at the very least it would push her to never get married until she had extracted the last dime she could from him.

As Dexter, Dalton, and Zander all arrived, it became apparent how interesting this was going to be. These guys were each very different. Dalton made Christian look like a virgin altar boy. Wiki the word "player," and there should be a big picture of Dalton with pearly white teeth and olive skin. They knew guys like Dalton, who seemed to live a charmed life, always coming out on top. He was the perfect guy for this assignment.

On the other hand, Dexter was good looking but in a very different way. If they were magazine cover boys, Dalton would be *GQ* and Dexter would be *Men's Health*. Although a few inches shorter than Dalton's six feet two stature, he made up for his lack of height in pure muscle-bound testosterone. Although he wasn't the smooth talker that Dalton was, he seemed to exude more of a quiet confidence, almost a little mystery as to what he was thinking. If he didn't have anything productive to say, he might as well just stand there and look pretty.

Zander was still the odd man out. Although Mark seemed convinced he was a good pick, the other guys had reservations. Using the magazine analogy, Zander didn't fit anything—he was very unassuming and normal. He didn't dress incredibly sharp, and although he was skinny, it was apparent that it wasn't from working out. He seemed to be more of a free spirit, the kind of guy who would wear flip-flops every day and never be too upset about not being able to hold down a steady job. That said, there was something that seemed to be oddly motivating him to pursue this. It was clear with Dexter and Dalton, they were competitive spirits and wanted the money. With Zander it seemed to be a little less clear. It didn't seem like he had much money, but he also didn't seem like the type of guy that was motivated by it.

As the guys all sat down, Mark started explaining why they were all here and what they were going to be competing for. Although they all knew they may need to marry someone, this was the first time they were finding out specifics. Mark walked them through the divorce, the subsequent beating he took in court, and his ultimate solution—one of them marrying Stef. They were his sole option for appeal. Not only did they have to convince her to marry one of them, they had to do so in six months or less. Mark knew that was ambitious, but in his mind having a deadline was critical—key for motivation. Time was money for him, and the longer he paid Stef alimony, the less of a reason there was for him to pay one of them. He could always re-evaluate in six months. He explained he would share every little detail about Stef to them, so they had a huge head start. Watching the guys' body language as Mark explained the rules was interesting. Dalton seemed to look disinterested, almost as if this was beneath him to be competing against such inferior mortals like Dexter and Zander. Dexter was stoic, not interested or disinterested—just cool and controlled. The guys imagined this was probably how Dexter was the majority of the time, the guy appeared to have the patience of a sniper and might have been one as a Navy SEAL. Zander on the other hand seemed very interested and hanging on Mark's every word, feverishly taking notes.

Mark spent the next three hours poring over every detail about Stef. He dove deep into her likes and dislikes, and even joked about intimate sexual details. It was clear nothing was off limits and Mark's only interest was successfully getting Stef married.

All the guys were of course very anxious to see her picture. Although they were in it for the money, it would certainly be a bonus if she was hot. When they got to the point of showing them a picture, Christian set it up by saying, "Now not surprisingly she's gained a little weight since the divorce, but this is still a pretty accurate representation of what she looks like. Not too shabby, we all still wonder why Mark dumped her!" As Christian was talking he pulled out an 8" x 10" picture of a girl he had pulled out of a magazine and framed earlier that night in anticipation of this moment. The lady in the picture was a haggard late fifties heavy-set woman wearing an outfit that was two sizes too small. Dalton just stared at the picture with a stunned look. He couldn't stop staring. The shock was also enough to jolt Dexter's normally stoic look, he actually let out a quick, "Jeez, shit," and then realized he probably meant to say that to himself instead of out loud.

"Hey! What the hell, that's my mom you asshole!" Steve saw the picture, smacking Christian's shoulder and realizing he was clearly not in on the joke.

The guys all heaved a sigh of relief and laughed, particularly Dalton. They weren't even sure if he had taken a breath for the minute or so they had him fooled.

As the night continued, Mark was also clear about how critical it was that Stef could never know what was going on. If any of them ran into each other, they had to pretend they didn't know each other, even if Stef wasn't around. There was no room for error, he explained. One wrong move and not only would Stef know something was up, but it would kill the deal for everyone, and nobody would get paid. On one hand they were going to be fierce competitors, but on the other hand the overall mission took priority. A super playboy, a Navy SEAL, and a wildcard mysterious starving artist—all vying for the same girl. The more Mark thought about it, the more he was convinced this was a movie in the making!

Mark wrapped up the discussion with an important detail: how he was going to be updated and could coach the guys between dates. Although somewhat frequent updates were important and Mark wanted to stay apprised of the guys' progress, he also had to be cognizant to not jeopardize the mission. They would have a neutral meeting place, most importantly someplace that Stef would never be. Although Mark himself had never been there, he knew Liquid Cougar had a large distribution facility in the warehouse district. It was perfect, off the beaten path and isolated. On top of that, Mark thought meeting in an old warehouse would add a little mystique and intrigue to the mission. He was certain Tony wouldn't mind.

As the guys were walking out, Christian couldn't resist giving one last shout out. "Hey guys, one more thing about Stef that Mark forgot to mention, and this is important. Mark is always embarrassed to mention it, but I don't think it is fair to not tell you given the circumstances." All the guys stopped and turned their attention to Christian, curious to hear what this was. "She can be a little unconventional in the bedroom, she loved using strap-ons on him."

"You didn't tell me that Mark. We could have shared stories!" Ronald chimed in with excitement, oblivious that Christian was joking.

Dalton and Zander just shook their heads laughing, and Dexter just seemed to ignore Christian's antics.

"On that note, I think it's time to go," Mark said. "Game time, guys."

After the guys left, Mark and his friends chatted about the night, they all agreed it was a success. Even Steve, who had been and continued to be the most skeptical, had increased enthusiasm about the project. On top of that, they thought the competition between the guys was going to get insane, which would no doubt lead to more entertainment and stories in the days and weeks to come. After talking for a bit, they all decided to call it a night. It had been a long but productive weekend, but their adrenaline was starting to wane. They didn't mind being sleep deprived; it was worth it. This had been a weekend they would never forget.

CHAPTER 14

Stef Meets the Guys

The next day when Stef arrived at work at the Divine Mind spiritual center around ten a.m., her boss Savannah was already there.

"Someone called here asking if you were working today?" Savannah said. "But he didn't leave a name."

"He?" Stef questioned. "That's unusual, I rarely get calls at work, normally my friends just call my cell. Did he say anything else?"

"No. I told him you were scheduled to work today, but after I hung up I thought maybe I shouldn't have said. Who knows, there are a lot of crazies out there! Especially now that you are single, you need to be careful." Savannah said in a cautionary mom-like tone.

"It was probably just a client," Stef said. "Come to think of it, Ross said he may come in this week to see me, he sounded depressed." Ross was one of her regulars.

"You're probably right Stef, but just be careful," Savannah said. "Here, try this new essential oil that just came in. It's supposed to ward off evil spirits. I've also found that it really attracts cats though too."

It was a typical slow day at the Divine Mind, a few customers trickling in. One guy came in claiming that he was worried his ex-girlfriend put a spell on his dog. Ever since they broke up a week ago, his dog had explosive diarrhea. They ended up selling him a self-help CD, both for the dog and him. They also suggested taking the dog to the vet. Although they would always try to help whomever walked into the door, some cases were just beyond spiritual help. Later that afternoon a guy wandered into the store, appearing to look around as he walked in. Savannah was in the back office, so Stef went over to try and help him.

"Is there anything I can help you with?"

"I'm not sure, I hope so but I've never been here before. What types of problems do you help people with?" he said in a somewhat meek and uneasy voice.

"Our goal is to help you help yourself. We all have the power within us to solve any problem, we just help people realize that," Stef said empathetically.

"That's the problem, I haven't been able to help myself."

"Then you came to the perfect place!" Stef said excitedly as she noticed the guy seemed nice and down to earth. In addition, pretty cute too.

"Well, I lost someone close to me recently. I'm an artist, and this person was the inspiration for a lot of my art. She was the reason I became an artist, and ever since she passed, I haven't been able to work. I've tried repeatedly, and it always ends the same. I just keep thinking about her. It's almost like my creative mind died with her."

"Oh my gosh, I'm very sorry to hear that," Stef said. "Can I ask who it was?" Thinking it was likely his wife or a girlfriend.

"It was my grandma," he said. "It probably sounds a little silly that I was that inspired by my grandma, but she's the reason I became an artist."

"It doesn't sound silly at all," Stef said, a little surprised by his response. "I completely understand, actually better than you may think. I too was close with my grandma, she was a big inspiration in my life. When she passed away it was like a part of me died with her. Even though it was over five years ago, I still have a hard time with it."

"I'm so sorry, I had no idea," he said. "I didn't mean to bring back those feelings."

"Oh no," Stef said. "It is healthy to talk with someone who understands. People always assume grandmas and grandpas pass away and that's part of life, but it's different when you have a close relationship." As Stef spoke, she was starting to choke up a bit. "I'm sorry, you came in here to talk about your problems and feelings, not mine. I'm being selfish."

"Actually this is the most helpful that anyone has been so far. This probably sounds a little funny, but I was hesitant to come in here. That said, there was something that kept pulling me, it was almost as if a voice in my head was telling me to do it. I've always felt that every little moment in life happens for a reason. You can have the smallest minute detail of your life that at the time seems inconsequential, but later turns out to be very impactful." The man paused, looking down as if he was sorry he had just said all that. "There I go, talking about voices in my head and things that are meant to be, you must think I'm nuts."

"Not at all! I feel exactly the same way, in fact I have used those exact words before. I couldn't agree more with what you just said."

"So how did you move on? You clearly have your life together and look great despite losing your grandma," he said, slipping in the "look great" comment subtly. "What was your secret? Is there something I can buy here that will help?"

Stef thought about his question for a moment then looked back at him. She was thinking that Mark was fairly helpful for her, but didn't want to say that. "Time and friendship were probably the two things that carried me on. Oh, and reading. I think I read more books during that period than any other time in my life. It was helpful to lose myself in stories."

"I agree, I've read my favorite book at least six times since she passed. It's strange, I just want to keep rereading it. I'd recommend it if you're looking for something. It's called *Moments in Time.*"

Stef quickly picked up her head and looked back at him, staring but not saying anything.

"Are you OK?" he asked.

"Yeah, I was just shocked you said that. I love that book. It is one of my favorites as well!" she said with a big smile.

"You're kidding, what are the odds?" he asked. "I just love how the author, Richardson, is able to relate everything that has happened in his life, no matter how inconsequential, to who he is today. It's brilliant and so true," he said pausing slightly. "I'm sorry, I'm taking up all your time and I'm sure you have better things to do. I should let you get back to work."

"It's OK, this actually is my job you know. You came in here as a customer," she said smiling cutely.

Looking down at his watch, he said, "Well, I should get going anyway, I have to be on the other end of the city in twenty minutes and I'll already be late as it is. I really appreciate your help. This might sound crazy, but this is the best I've felt in months, just to talk to someone who understands where I am coming from." He seemed somewhat hurried now to leave and started walking towards the door. As he was walking he stopped, turned around and came back towards Stef. "I'm sorry, I apparently completely lost my manners. I was so wrapped up in our discussion I forgot to introduce myself. I'm Zander," he said shaking Stef's hand and smiling at her.

Stef smiled back. "I'm Stef," she said blushing slightly.

"I can see that." He pointed to her nametag. "At least I'll have a good excuse for being late!" he said as he walked out the door smiling.

Zander walked down the street to the train station, grinning to himself. The initial meeting went better than he had even hoped. Just enough to set the hook, he hoped Stef would be pondering that run-in in the days to come. His quick exit was all part of the plan, just enough mystery to keep her wondering and wanting more. The story was partially accurate. He had in fact lost his grandma last year, and she had been the person who originally got him interested in art. It wasn't entirely true that he had lost inspiration. He had never really had success as an artist, even prior to his grandma passing away. Zander knew he was going to have to walk a fine line between lies and truth if he was going to get close enough to Stef to marry her.

Back at Divine Mind, Stef was in a cheery mood on the heels of meeting with Zander. A little giddy, she went back into Savannah's office to tell her all about it. Amy was really her only good friend, and although part of her wanted to text her about it, she knew better. Amy would only come back with some man-hating diatribe. For now, it would have to be good enough to just share with Savannah.

Although Zander had gotten an early jump on the competition, Dexter and Dalton were each eagerly planning their own chance encounters. For Dexter, it was simple. He knew exactly how he would meet Stef. He grabbed his gym bag and ran outside to catch a cab. "East Bay Gym," he told the cabbie. Kick-boxing class started in an hour, and he wasn't going to be late.

Dexter was one of the first to arrive at the gym, exactly how he planned. His prior military training always conditioned him to have a solid understanding of the combat zone and terrain. Although Dexter "Thunderbolt Love" Adams was a civilian now, he could never escape his military training. It was part of how he lived, ingrained in his psyche. He viewed this as a mission, treating it like one of the many combat missions he had been part of. There was no way he was going to let some fancy playboy beat him and certainly not a struggling artist who wouldn't be able to survive a minute in even the easiest day of his Navy SEAL training. Although he thought Dalton was a viable threat, Dexter was completely confident in his abilities. He would succeed no matter what it took.

Stef and Amy showed up at kick-boxing class on schedule, Dexter immediately recognized Stef from the pictures and moved over to a spot near them. Fortunately it was a small class, so getting to know them shouldn't be difficult. Although everyone was in great shape, Dexter still stood out in the crowd, his muscles were rippling through his tight workout shirt. The class was evenly split between girls and guys, and he caught a few of the ladies already checking him out. When he made his way over to a spot near them he shot a smile to Stef. She was kind of cute. "Is this spot taken?" he asked Stef.

"No, help yourself," she said.

Amy immediately noticed Dexter, although she was impressed by his physique it didn't stop her from making a smart-ass comment. "Hope you can keep up, big guy..."

"Take it easy on me," Dexter said coyly, looking back at Amy and grinning. Perfect he thought, already connecting with them.

Although Dexter had never been to a kick-boxing class, he was a Navy SEAL and a personal trainer, he didn't think this was going to even be much of a workout. He had been casually joking around with both Amy and Stef as class went on, and in true form Amy kept taunting him.

Amy was the ball-busting friend that Dexter heard about from Mark. He was starting to realize that definition seemed to fit. As soon as the instructor asked everyone to divide up in groups of two for sparring, he asked Stef and Amy if he could just join them. Looking around the class it seemed that everyone was already paired up, so it worked perfectly. They could just take turns he told them. He pointed to Stef and suggested that she spar with him first to start off.

"Nice kick," Dexter said to Stef. "You have great form, it's clear you practice a lot."

Stef laughed inside thinking that it was only because her friend Amy would drag her here that she took up kick-boxing, but she played along. "Thanks, I'm only a novice, my friend is the real expert. You look like you know your way around a gym, although I don't recall seeing you here before," Stef said as she was practicing her high kicks on Dexter while he blocked with the gloves.

"My first time taking kickboxing class, coincidentally one of my friends suggested it," Dexter said, thinking that actually wasn't too far from the truth.

"OK, let's switch," Amy said, crouching down in front of Dexter as if she was ready to pounce, moving into the spot that Stef was in as Stef stepped away. "I heard it's your first time. I should probably take it easy on you."

"Haha, I'll do my best to manage," Dexter retorted, laughing at first but then barely getting the words out of his mouth as Amy was launching a flurry of kicks. Dexter was caught a little off guard trying to block them and working to regain his footing. Amy was launching kick after kick, some aimed at Dexter's head and others at his midsection. The velocity and frequency of kicks seemed to only increase. *Holy shit*, he was thinking to himself. She was no joke, a total bad-ass.

The class continued, and despite Dexter being in great shape, he was having a difficult time keeping up with Amy. They would alternate back and forth, but when he would finally get to spar back with Stef, he was fairly winded and shaken up from sparring with Amy that he wasn't entirely on his game. He thought this was going to be a fairly leisurely workout but it was only half done and already he was dripping with sweat. Amy was like a machine, she didn't let up. Though he did feel like he was making some progress with Stef, she seemed a little into him. Either that or she was just getting a kick out of watching Amy work him over.

"OK, last round, five minutes left," the instructor said as Stef was sparring with Dexter.

"My turn, I got one last crack at GI Joe," Amy said, interrupting Stef mid-kick. *Damn-it*, Dexter thought, *this is getting a little annoying.*

"Sounds good, I was starting to miss you," Dexter said jokingly, trying not to let on that she was clearly getting on his nerves.

Amy was letting it all out, Dexter was certain the power behind her kicks actually got stronger as the class went on. The kicks just kept coming, and Dexter was doing all that he could to block them. *Only a minute or two left*, he thought to himself. The flurry of kicks just wasn't stopping.

"OK, time's up," the instructor said. "Good workout everyone, see you on Thursday."

Just as the instructor said that, Dexter thought, *Finally*, and dropped his arms to his side, when all of a sudden he felt a crack on the side of his head and everything went black as he fell to the floor.

"What the fuck!" he yelled, grabbing the side of his head. Amy had just planted a high kick to the side of Dexter's skull.

"Whoops, I was so focused on kicking you I didn't realize the instructor told us to stop," she said. Dexter could already feel the side of his face and his eye swelling up.

"I'm aware of that," Dexter said still holding the side of his face. "Does your friend always treat new guys this way?" he asked Stef as he turned to look at her.

"I'm sorry, she does have a reputation," Stef said. "That looks like it hurts, I can run and get you some ice."

Dexter quickly played through the situation in his mind, should he take her up on the ice and keep the conversation going, or be a man and just tough it out? Which would impress Stef more?

"Ah, it isn't too bad, just caught me a little off guard. Probably not a bad idea to ice it though so it doesn't swell." He was fairly sure he'd have a black eye out of the ordeal.

Stef came back with some ice in short order and gave it to Dexter. They started chatting, although he knew so much about her and he was pretending he knew nothing at all. Amy had walked over to the corner and was doing push-ups and sit-ups, so Dexter was taking advantage of the alone time. Stef seemed to be a little flattered that Dexter had taken an interest in her. As they were talking about all of the usual first meeting items, Dexter thought he was going to need to act fast, no doubt Amy would return fairly soon.

"Say, normally I'm not this forward and I'm guessing there is already a lucky guy out there who you call your boyfriend, but would you have dinner with me sometime?"

Stef was a little taken aback, almost questioning to herself why this guy would ask her out, and be so forward? Not only was he by far the buffest guy in class and great looking, but her friend had just given him a roundhouse to the cranium that would leave a mark. She paused a little longer and then finally said she would, but warned him she was just getting over a long-term relationship and wasn't really looking for anything serious. Dexter immediately acknowledged that and said that coincidentally he too was just getting over a relationship and repeated that he normally didn't do this but there was just something about her.

Stef was surprised, and although it seemed a little forward and she did just get a divorce, she couldn't in her right mind turn a guy down like Dexter. Although she didn't feel an immediate connection, she didn't know if that was more from the fact she was surprised he asked her or if it was truly because there wasn't a connection. *Oh well* she thought, *one date is fairly harmless and Dexter seems like a nice enough sincere guy*. As they exchanged numbers and parted ways, Dexter thought that the other guys didn't stand a chance. Even the super playboy Dalton was no match for his Navy SEAL training.

Shortly after Dexter left, Amy walked back over. She had seen Stef talking to Dalton typing on their phones, and she was curious what had transpired.

"What did Hulk Hogan want?" Amy asked sarcastically.

Stef paused a little bit before answering, knowing she was going to tell Amy, but also anticipating some kind of man-hating response. "He asked me out on a date, believe it or not."

"I hope you told him that he was apparently kicked in the head a little too hard if he thinks some girl he just met is going to fawn all over him because he's wearing a tight T-shirt at the gym. Guys are just idiots, so predictable," Amy said as she was shaking her head.

"I didn't think it would hurt to go out on one date. He seemed nice," Stef responded somewhat meekly.

"Don't expect sex, he probably has testicles the size of peas from steroids."

Stef quickly diverted the conversation back to talking about their workout, knowing it was a no-win proposition trying to get Amy excited about her dating Dexter. Wasn't going to happen. Her tactic was effective, the only thing Amy seemed to like talking about more than hating men was working out. Within a matter of seconds, they were chatting about the next class. Stef had successfully steered Amy away from further disparagement and condescension.

As Amy and Stef walked out of the gym to Amy's car, neither of them noticed the sleek black BMW parked down the street and the guy inside watching them walk away. Not that it mattered, since neither of them knew the person at this point, but it was good that Dexter hadn't noticed the car either. Dalton had parked just far enough away to not get noticed. Just as he suspected, Dexter came walking out minutes before with a grin on his face looking at his phone. *Humans are so predictable* Dalton thought. He knew plenty of Dexter-types, and had a good idea what to expect. In Dalton's mind, Dexter was a thirtysomething version of a high school quarterback, confident he could win any girl over by flashing his muscles. Dalton laughed to himself as he raced away from the parking spot. This was going to be easier than he thought. As he drove away, he called his buddy, the plan was a go just like they discussed.

A little bit later that night, Stef was walking home from Amy's place. It was dark and almost ten p.m., but she liked the fresh air and it was only about a mile. She typically walked home when Amy drove to kick-boxing class.

Tonight she thought the walk would be good, it was an opportunity to clear her mind. She was still thinking about her run-in with Zander earlier this morning, how bizarre and a little mysterious it was. The episode definitely stuck with her. On top of that she was still a little surprised about Dexter asking her out. As she was walking and thinking about everything that happened today, she heard footsteps coming up behind her.

She kept walking but the footsteps were getting closer and closer, and Stef started to get nervous that someone was following her. She tried to look behind her but didn't want to be too obvious, and it was too dark to see. It seemed the faster she walked, the closer the footsteps behind her became. Was someone following her? There weren't really any stores she could pop into, and she didn't see anyone else around at all. As she was walking faster and faster, thinking through the options she now could tell the footsteps sounded like they were right behind her, literally inches. She immediately turned around hoping to find someone jogging, but instead came face to face with a strange man. She stood stone-faced, too shook up to say anything or even scream.

"I thought I recognized you," the man said loudly. "Remember me?"

"I don't think I know you," Stef said, her voice crackling a bit out of fear.

"Yeah, remember. I ran into you one night in a bar, how have you been?" he said, now stepping on the outside of Stef and cornering her a bit.

"I think you have me confused with someone else," Stef said nervously. "I really need to get going."

"Wait, don't go yet," he said, grabbing her arm. "You must remember. Your name is Stef, right?"

"How do you know my name?" Now Stef was second guessing herself, she was still freaked out by the situation, but she didn't know how this guy could know her name.

"I'm sorry, I really don't think I know you. I need to get going now," she said, trying to step around him but he quickly moved to block her. "Hey, let me go," she shouted. Stef was really nervous now, but in too much shock to respond with any kick-boxing tactics, plus she couldn't be sure if she had actually met the guy before.

"I'm not going anywhere," the guy said firmly, all of a sudden grinning. Immediately Stef knew this was not a good situation. As he went to grab her arm, a tall man darted over to them from across the street.

"Is there a problem here?" he said. Is this guy bothering you?"

"Mind your own business dipshit," the guy who claimed to know Stef said in response. "This is a friend of mine, we're catching up."

"Is that true?" the new guy said, turning to Stef. "Do you know this guy?"

"No, I don't think I know him," she said, her voice still crackling in fear.

"You heard her, she doesn't know you. Get lost buddy."

"Listen, I told you to mind your own business asshole, the girl and I are old friends and just catching up."

"Maybe I'm not being clear," the new guy said as he raised his voice. All of a sudden he grabbed the guy by the collar and shoved him up against the wall, slamming him so hard his head hit. "Let me be crystal clear. You can stay and get the beat down of your life or when I let go of your collar you can walk away and never give this girl any trouble ever again. Not just tonight, but ever." As he said that, the guy's expression immediately changed to a look of fear.

"Look, hey, I'm sorry, I don't want any trouble," the guy said, now his voice cracking. "I promise, I won't ever talk to her again. Please just let me go."

"That's what I thought. Now get out of here," the guy said as he let go of the man's collar. The guy ran away, not looking back.

"Are you OK?" the tall man asked as he looked at Stef and made sure the other guy was still running down the street.

"I think so," Stef responded. "That was really strange, I don't think I knew that guy, but he knew my name. He was really creepy."

"I thought something was up when I noticed the two of you talking from across the street. I normally wouldn't have interfered, but you looked scared."

"I can't thank you enough, I didn't know what I was going to do," Stef said, her voice still shaking from the incident. "Where did you come from anyway, I didn't think anyone was around?"

"I just happened to be walking by. My car is parked down the street. I'm a volunteer and was dropping off a prescription for one of our clients that lives in the area, Mrs. Peppercorn. She lives down the street. I always feel bad for her, she doesn't have family and is lonely. We aren't supposed to stay, but I'm not really a rule follower when it comes to helping people. She invited me in so we played checkers together for a couple hours." He did not volunteer for any such organization, nor did he know anyone by the name of Mrs. Peppercorn. He just knew what it would take to push all of Stef's buttons.

"I can't even imagine what could have happened if you didn't happen to be across the street and decide to intervene. It was like you were my guardian angel," Stef said relieved. She started to realize the gravity of the situation and just how critical it was that he was walking by.

"You can thank Mrs. Peppercorn. She wouldn't let me leave, despite beating me into submission six games to one. She's quite the checker ace," he joked with his pearly white grin. "By the way, it is late and dark out, why were you walking by yourself?"

"I was just walking home from a friend's house. I usually take this way and never have any problems. I guess I should probably be more careful."

"There are a lot of bad guys out there. Just to be on the safe side I'll walk you the rest of the way home."

"Oh no, that's OK, you definitely don't need to do that," Stef said, trying to sound confident but secretly still feeling startled and hoping he would walk her home. Now that Stef's nerves started to settle down a bit, she was beginning to notice the mystery guy who just saved her life was also tall, dark, and very good looking.

"I won't take no for an answer. I can be very convincing, just ask the idiot who ran off a few minutes ago!" he said as he smirked. "Do you really want to argue with me?"

Stef giggled, feeling calmer after the ordeal. The man had a calming sense about him, very confident and charismatic.

"By the way, where are my manners?" he asked. "My name is Dalton."

"I'm Stef," she said as she stretched out her hand to meet Dalton's. He had a very comforting way about him, even his touch instilled confidence and security.

As they started walking, Dalton poured on the wit and charm. He was about as charismatic as they came, and almost no girl could resist his irresistible good looks and equally matched silver tongue. He knew exactly what to say at exactly the right time. Being a lobbyist was the perfect profession, and that night he was clearly pulling out all the stops.

"This may sound a little crazy, but let's take a left at the next block. I have an idea, you're just going to have to trust me on this one." Dalton said, giving Stef his signature grin.

"I don't know, it's a little late and I should get home."

"You won't regret it, I promise. Plus, it's the least you can do—I did save your life."

"You do have a point," Stef replied. *It would be impossible to resist someone like Dalton*, she thought. "You could at least tell me where you are taking me. How do I know *you* aren't some freak too, maybe you set this all up?"

"Fair enough," Dalton said, laughing inside, knowing that her joke about him setting this all up was startlingly true, but she had no idea. "I know just what will cheer you up and take your mind off the night. There is a great little mom-and-pop ice cream shop down a few blocks around the corner. They have the best caramel swirl ice cream, I think they lace it with crack. I'm completely addicted. It is literally one of my favorite things in the world," Dalton said.

As he said that, Stef stopped and looked at him. "The Ice Cream Vault? I *love* that place," she said enthusiastically. "I've been going there for years, and the caramel swirl is my favorite! Now you are kind of creeping me out. Have you been reading my Facebook page and secretly stalking me?"

Funny, Dalton thought, *she has no idea.* "You caught me. Tonight I came home from work and searched Facebook for 'cute, funny, and charming girl who needs a knight in shining armor and also shares my love for caramel swirl ice cream.' Lo and behold your picture came up," he said as he grinned and winked at Stef while she started to blush a little.

The two walked through the dark and quiet streets and Dalton was in the zone. Every other comment he would drop some little tidbit that he knew would trigger something that he already knew about Stef. He was balancing perfectly the idea of keeping her amazed at how much they have in common with not coming across as being too obvious. He already knew every detail about her. It was almost like he was the Superman of the dating world, except nobody had figured out what his kryptonite was. Stef was eating it up, although slightly shy and intimidated by Dalton's charismatic charm and good looks.

At that point she had pretty much forgotten about the run-in with the crazy guy, who unbeknownst to her was an old coworker of Dalton's who owed him a favor. Someone he probably wouldn't see again, ultimately safe to pull off the stunt since Stef could never know he was an acquaintance. By the time they got to the Ice Cream Vault and sat down with their cones, it was like they had known each other for months. Dalton ever so eloquently continued to lay on the charm. Although he was adept at hitting on girls and had successfully been doing it since high school, this was the first time he could actually make money at it. There was only one thing that trumped his love for women and that was his love for winning. He had a hyper-competitive personality, and normally he never had to compete for women since his skills were unmatched. This was a different situation. This time it wasn't just to hook up. He actually had to get a girl to agree to marriage in a very short time frame.

Stef and Dalton had lost track of time, the owner of the Ice Cream Vault had to come over and tell them they were locking up for the night. As they were getting up to leave, Dalton of course immediately said he would walk Stef home.

"This may sound a little corny, but do you think everything in life happens for a reason?" Dalton asked in a serious tone, but full well knowing what Stef's answer would be.

"Absolutely, I've always felt that way. That's one of the things that draws me to my work at the spiritual center."

"I think it is great what you are doing, it must be so fulfilling to spend your days knowing you've helped people who in many cases are in desperate need. That's what life is about in my mind, helping people." Dalton didn't believe a word of what he just said, but it sounded good to him and he knew Stef would eat it up.

"That's very kind of you to say Dalton, not everyone appreciates my work," Stef said, thinking about how Mark used to somewhat support her, but deep down she knew he was always disappointed and not believing what she was doing made a difference. "Not surprising you think that way though, it takes an extraordinary and giving person to volunteer the way you do helping older people. That's a great organization, and people like you make a huge difference. Mrs. Peppercorn is lucky to have you," Stef said as started to open up a bit more than her usual shy tendencies.

"I'm lucky to have Mrs. Peppercorn, if not for her I probably wouldn't have met you, and even worse who knows what would have happened if I didn't come across that guy bothering you. To quote the great John Lennon, 'There's nowhere you can be that isn't where you're meant to be.'"

"Of course you would say that, I love the Beatles! I swear, you did read my Facebook page!" Stef said playfully.

"All you need is love, love...love is all you need," Dalton sang as he grinned at Stef. His eyes had this ability to pierce through any girl's soul and take her breath away. Although Dalton had been confident the night was going to go well, this had surpassed even his lofty expectations. *Game, set, match*, he thought. Dexter and art-boy stood no chance against the mighty Dalton. Tonight he was oozing with even more confidence than he normally had.

"Well, here is my place," Stef said, sounding a little disappointed the walk had gone so fast. "I don't know how I can ever thank you. Not only for saving me, but you somehow managed to get my mind off of what happened and set me at complete ease."

"The pleasure is all mine," Dalton responded with his trademark grin. "I'm just thinking, this may sound a bit forward, but if you really want to thank me how about you let me take you out for dinner," Dalton asked. "I promise not to sing anymore, and you can pick the place. We can even go for ice cream afterwards."

Stef was caught a little off guard. Although she had a fantastic time with Dalton, he still seemed like a guy that would be out of her league. Surely he had a girlfriend, or more than likely several girlfriends he would juggle at once. What could he want with her? She paused a little bit longer and realized there was no way she could say no. How could she turn down a guy like Dalton? After all he did rescue her. "That sounds great, I'd love to. Also, I really don't mind you singing, especially when it is the Beatles!"

They agreed to go out two nights from now. Although at first he said she could pick the place, he recanted and said that he had an idea for where to go. He would pick her up at 6:30 p.m. and the rest was a surprise. Stef happily agreed and said she was completely fine leaving it up to him, after all he somehow seemed to have a keen radar for knowing all of her likes in life anyway. The two exchanged phone numbers and they said their goodbyes. And as Stef was walking into the front door of her apartment building, Dalton was walking down the stairs singing, "We all live in a yellow submarine," further exploiting the Beatles connection and making Stef shake her head laughing as she walked into the building.

As Dalton walked down the street to his Beemer parked about a mile away, he was silently high fiving himself. Definitely a successful night, he wasn't sure what could have happened that would have made it any better. Although he was used to ending most of his nights a little differently than a walk to the girl's door, this was perfect. Certainly a risky move to have his acquaintance pretend to assault her on the street. Any number of things could have happened, someone else could have intervened or even worse the cops could have gotten involved. This was a game of high risk and high reward. As he got into his car, he pulled out his phone and sent his friend a "100" emoji, the altercation really was perfect.

As Stef got inside, her mind was racing from the day's activities. Although she was still wrapped up thinking about Dalton, it was bizarre to think that in one day she had met three guys who all seemed fantastic. There were also serendipitous connections with each. Although Zander didn't ask her out, she was still thinking about meeting him. Then there was Dexter at the gym, asking her out on the spot despite getting knocked out by Amy. As if that wasn't enough, her night capped off with a guy cut straight from the *Bachelor*, who would rescue her off the streets from some crazy assailant. What are the odds of that happening in one day she asked herself? Life was certainly turning around, and maybe she deserved it. The divorce was final; she should get out there and start dating again. Everything in life happened for a reason she told herself.

CHAPTER 15

Tracking the Progress

A couple days later, Mark was in the office early after his daily drop-off of Tyson at the Dog Den. There was a call he had been anticipating, and he was even more anxious to get into work than usual. His phone rang promptly at 7:30 a.m., right on schedule.

"Did you get the pictures I emailed you?" the voice on the other end of the phone asked.

"I did, they were perfect," Mark responded. "Seems like the plan is in full swing?"

The voice on the other end of the phone proceeded to explain everything that transpired over the last few days. How the guys had met Stef, when they approached her and where. Because everything was riding on this plan and he could leave nothing to chance, Mark hired a private investigator to tail Stef and provide updates to him on how the operation was progressing. Although he was going to get updates from the guys when they met, he didn't want to rely solely on that. Jason was an old friend who owed him a favor, and Mark thought now was as good of time as any to take him up on it. Hopefully this was the first and only time he would need a PI. As Jason described the details, Mark was pleased. It sounded as if all the meetings went well, and Jason confirmed all three guys had made contact. He laughed out loud when he heard the story about Dexter at the gym getting a swift round house from Amy. Although he was hiding out in a dark car when Dalton met her and couldn't hear the conversations at the ice cream shop, he was pretty sure the assault set-up worked well. He wasn't sure what had transpired with Zander since he was parked across the street and saw him go into the store, but he knew they had at least met and Zander left smiling.

Just as Mark was wrapping up the conversation with Jason, Tony walked into his office. He sat in the chair across the desk from Mark and waited for him to finish talking. Mark had Jason on speakerphone and Tony seemed a little perplexed at the conversation, wondering who he was talking to.

"I realize I just caught the end of that conversation, but who is the guy on the other end of the phone talking about following your ex-wife and why do you seem so happy?"

Mark paused, although he hadn't shared any of what was going on with Tony he knew he needed to. He trusted Tony implicitly and was all but certain Tony would have helpful ideas. Although Tony was well liked by many, he didn't get to where he was professionally without screwing many people along the way. Add in his sordid personal life, and this was a man who was experienced and versed at just about every bizarre situation imaginable. It was time for Mark to fill him in.

Mark laid out the entire scenario to Tony, going into detail about how the idea came to be, how he selected the final three guys and giving an overview of their personalities. This was his own personal appeal process he explained. Get his ex-wife married and he wouldn't have to pay the insane windfall the judge had awarded her. Although he conceded it was a long shot, it was one worth taking. It wasn't really going to cost him much to try, and there was significant upside if it worked. There was a slight risk that Stef would find out and then he would surely be stuck paying the entire sum of spousal maintenance, but there was a risk of that happening anyway.

"It is a long shot, but I don't really see I have anything to lose."

Tony listened quietly to Mark explain before finally exclaiming, "I've always known you were brilliant Mark, but this honestly takes you up a notch in my book. It is without a doubt the most ballsy move you have ever made! Well done, I don't think I've ever been so proud." Tony rapped his knuckles on Mark's desk.

"Thanks Tony, that's what I love about you. I do something that many people would question, and you are beaming with pride and approval. I knew I could count on you."

"I just wish I would have had that idea. It took years before my two ex-wives remarried. They took me for millions. It's a win-win, not only do you get out of paying alimony, but you also get the satisfaction of knowing Stef is going to fall head over heels for some guy only to be dumped on her ass months later. Clearly brilliant. How can I help?"

"You already did. By the way, I owe you for the night at Sabre. I think they charged everything to your house account since we were in the VIP room and you arranged it. It had to be a couple thousand dollars. I'll Venmo you."

"Nonsense, consider it a gift. At first I thought you were using the room to get laid, which I was of course proud to subsidize, but this is honestly even better. I'll do whatever I can to help, just name it."

"Thanks Tony, I'll keep that in mind. For now I think I'm good but I'm sure something will come up."

The conversation ended with Tony walking out of Mark's office, again insisting on his offer to help and pleading for more updates.

CHAPTER 16

Zander

Across town that morning, Stef was on her way to work, just getting off the train and walking to her favorite coffee shop a few blocks away. She had her date tonight with Dalton and had also gotten a call from Dexter about meeting for a picnic in the park tomorrow over lunch. She felt like the prettiest girl at the ball, two fantastic guys pursuing her at the same time. Her dreams did get kicked in the gut a bit after she filled Amy in on the stories of how she met each of them. Amy of course proceeded to tell Stef she didn't need a man, and getting a divorce was the best thing that had ever happened to her. Getting involved in a relationship now would essentially undo all of the forward progress she had made since the night with Mark at the restaurant. Stef found herself torn, although she felt excited and giddy about meeting Dalton and Dexter, she also trusted Amy's opinion. She started to question herself, maybe it was too soon.

Zander had set up his artistic canvas in what he thought was the perfect spot. He knew that Stef took the same route to work every morning, making a detour once she got off the train to her favorite coffee shop a few blocks in the opposite direction of Divine Mind. He had gone there the previous day to get a start on his canvas, just so it wasn't obvious that he had only started. To Zander it was all about chance meetings and fate. Stef obviously would have no idea that he was actually waiting for her that morning instead of just randomly there working on his next painting. It was the perfect spot—the street he had started to paint was scenic and quaint and the centerpiece of his painting would be Stef's favorite coffee shop. The awnings and architecture of the old buildings would make for a beautiful picture of the tree-lined street. Zander thought the idea was flawless, a perfect second meeting. A few days had passed since their first meeting and that was the optimum time, a chance visit now will be the perfect blend of mystery and intrigue. How coincidental would it be that he just happened to be painting her favorite coffee shop.

At first Stef didn't notice him, he had his back to her as she walked by.

"Stef?!"

Stef turned around, not sure who to expect. Stef immediately recognized him. "Zander? What are you doing here?" Stef was surprised and caught off guard, her mind had been focused on her upcoming dates with Dalton and Dexter.

Zander gave her a funny smirk, after all he was standing in front of a canvas holding a paintbrush. It seemed fairly obvious what he was doing, and after realizing it, she was a little embarrassed. "OK, I guess it is a little obvious *what* you are doing, but what are you doing here?" she asked laughing.

"The other day before I met you I walked on this street and was immediately taken by the beauty of it."

Stef took a look at Zander's painting. "Well it looks great, I really like it so far." she said excitedly, happy and a bit surprised she ran into Zander again.

"I'm only about half done, but I have you to thank."

"Me to thank, what do you mean?"

"This may sound a little crazy, but when I left Divine Mind, I felt better than I had in months. Our conversation changed my perspective. I played through our chance meeting in my head several times, thinking about you and your grandma, knowing that someone else in this world could relate to what I was feeling. I know it was a brief meeting and you have people like that come in every day, but what you said had an impact on me. It seemed like it was meant to be, and I wanted to come back here. I'm sorry, this all probably sounds crazy to you. I thought about coming back into the store to thank you but figured I better not, you'd think I was some psycho stalker!"

Stef was overwhelmed, taking in all of what Zander said. She of course wouldn't have thought he was psycho; she too was taken by their conversation. To know that he felt the same way and it actually inspired him to get back into being an artist was wonderful. How fortuitous that she ran into him again, not to mention he was painting the street that her favorite coffee shop was on. "It doesn't sound crazy at all. I really enjoyed our conversation. I'm just a little surprised to run into you. I was on my way to work, but I always come over this way. That's my favorite coffee shop over there on the right." Stef said, motioning down the street.

"You mean the one I'm painting a picture of?"

"Exactly." Stef too caught the coincidence of it all, laughing.

"Oddly enough, I had never been on this street before that day I met you. I don't even live in this neighborhood. I just started walking that day and managed to find my way over here, then over to your store. I live on the south side and almost never come up here. I felt stuck in a rut, and that day I woke up thinking that I should change my routine, and this is where I ended up. Funny how life works."

Stef listened intently to Zander. He seemed like such a sweet guy.

To think their paths crossed unexpectedly, and now all of a sudden, she was his inspiration to get back into art. It sounded like a romantic movie. "Life is all about chance and the smallest of details can end up being the most impactful, just like we talked about the day you came into the store. I really enjoyed meeting you, and I'd be lying if I said I hadn't thought about our conversation since. I thought we had a lot in common and share many of the same values." Stef instantly felt as if she may have shared too much in saying all of that, but it was true.

No big surprise, Zander thought. His plan was working. "I'm sorry, I'm probably keeping you from getting to work." Zander didn't want to be overly aggressive in his tactics, he knew Dalton and Dexter would be and that could come back to be a fatal mistake.

"I'm good. My manager is there and it's usually slow. She won't mind if I'm late. I have an idea. If it doesn't bother you, can I watch you paint for a bit? I understand if it's too hard to concentrate or focus with someone watching you."

"Not at all, in fact having the person who inspired me to get back into art watch me create my first piece seems fitting! I don't know how exciting it will be, watching me paint is about as dull as dishwater."

Stef paused, her grandma used to use that phrase "dull as dishwater" all the time. What were the odds that Zander would use it? "How about I run and get us a couple coffees?" she said with a big smile. She came back shortly with two lattes and watched Zander paint for the next twenty minutes. It was relaxing to watch him work, and she felt a sense of ownership since she was the person who inspired him to get back into painting.

"My grandma used to tell me that art is the truest form of expressing one's emotions or feelings. A person can look at a painting and tell what the artist was thinking or feeling when they painted it. Still to this day I am amazed at how she could look at something I painted and tell me exactly what I had been thinking. She claimed the painting told a story about the artist."

Stef just listened to Zander. She was moved by how close he must have been with his grandma, and it made her think of her own grandma and how much she missed her. "Your grandma sounds like an amazing lady."

"I think you would have liked her, and I know she would have liked you."

"What makes you say that? How do you know she would have liked me?"

"For starters she was a very spiritual person. She believed that people had the strength within them to get through anything, no matter how difficult. She was also a kind and compassionate person, always selfless in her acts of helping people. My grandpa passed away before she did, after a two-year battle with cancer. She wouldn't leave his side, even during the last six months when he was hospitalized. They wouldn't let her stay in his room so she would get up every morning, making her way to the hospital to be by his side as soon as visitor hours started. The staff had to kick her out every night. He passed away quietly one day holding her hand."

Stef found herself tearing up listening to the story, it was moving and reminded her a lot of her grandma. "She sounds like an amazing lady, and your description of her reminds me a lot of my grandma. I lost my grandpa to cancer too, and my grandma was the rock that kept him fighting."

Stef looked at her watch. Although she could be late to work, she had already stayed well past the twenty minutes. Although she didn't want to, she needed to get going. "I should probably get going, my boss is going to start worrying about me if I don't show up soon."

"No worries, you don't want Savannah to worry about you more than she already does. You can tell her that you were catching up with a client that you helped." Zander turned around, smiling at Stef. "I'm not sure if you'd be interested, but I'd love to show this to you when I'm finished. Would you be interested in seeing it?"

Stef paused. "How did you know my boss was named Savannah?" She examined Zander with a genuine look of confusion.

"Oh, I thought you mentioned her name earlier," Zander stammered, kicking himself for the error.

"I don't think I did." Stef's look of confusion started to turn to slight concern, as if Zander wasn't being honest with her.

"Oh wait, you're right. You know what, I must have just remembered it from being in the store the other day and seeing her nametag." Zander said, trying to think on his feet, recalling that Stef had had a nametag.

"Oh, you're right. For a second I was wondering if you were some weird stalker!" Stef recalled what Savannah had mentioned to her about being careful. "Wait though, I thought Savannah was in the back room when you stopped by?"

Another slip-up, Zander thought, *Shit, this isn't good*. "Oh, you're right again, she *was* in the back room. I remember now what it was, there is an article about how she started the store that is taped to the front window. I read that before stopping in." Zander remembered seeing an article, but hadn't read it. It was a long shot, but he had painted himself into a corner. "Sorry, I don't know why I didn't make that connection right away, I'm such a dunce."

"That's right, the article in the *Tribune*. Savannah was so thrilled when they did that profile on her!"

Zander sighed inside—that was way too close. That slip-up could have botched the entire plan. He was eager to change the subject before Stef started asking questions about the article. "So, back to getting together, I should be done by sundown. Maybe you could swing by after work?"

Stef hesitated, all of a sudden remembering that she has a date with Dalton later today, she was going to have to hurry home and change. He was picking her up at 6:30. She stammered a bit and then told Zander that tonight wouldn't work, but maybe tomorrow night.

Zander immediately wondered why tonight wouldn't work, assuming that Dexter or Dalton were probably taking her out. He played it smooth, keeping those thoughts to himself. "Sure, tomorrow night is great. Let's plan on it. I'm open to meeting somewhere, I can come to your place or if you're interested you can come to my place. My apartment is also my art studio, so you can see everything."

"I would love to see that. It sounds perfect."

"Great, you can come by any time after five p.m."

Stef took his address and they exchanged numbers. After they said their goodbyes, Stef turned and walked down the street, finally on her way to work. Savannah may be a little upset since she was late, but it was worth it. Her mind was racing, the coincidence with their grandmas, running into each other the way they did, and learning she was his inspiration to get back into art. Straight out of a romantic movie. She was already a little overwhelmed with both Dalton and Dexter, now she had a possible third guy in the mix. It was crazy and good all at the same time—each of the guys possessing qualities she found attractive. Before she married Mark, she never really dated more than one guy at a time, she wasn't sure how to handle three. That being said, she didn't really see a choice. At this point she couldn't turn any of the guys down. It seemed too good to be true, and she felt like she had to pinch herself to make sure it wasn't a dream.

Zander kept painting as Stef walked away. He couldn't stop thinking about the mistake he made about saying Savannah's name. That was way too close, he needed to be more careful. He knew he could win as long as he didn't mess it up with a stupid blunder like that. Dexter may have been rippling with muscles and Dalton was a playboy, but neither were a match for his strategy. In his mind, Zander was playing three-dimensional chess. Both Dexter and Dalton would likely go in for the kill too quickly, relying on looks alone. That may work for getting laid, but they are going to need to connect with her emotionally for marriage.

Later that night, after Stef finished her day at Divine Mind, Dalton pulled up in his black BMW. He hopped out, catching the attention of a few girls who happened to be waiting in the lobby of Stef's building. In traditional Dalton fashion, he was dressed like he had just stepped out of an Armani dressing room. His clothes were always perfectly pressed and tailor-made for his body.

Stef came down shortly after he arrived wearing a yellow sundress that accentuated her body well. She wanted to look good for her date with Dalton.

"I would strongly advise against you walking alone on the streets, especially looking like that." Dalton said as he opened the door for her. She did look good, he thought. Probably not someone he would seek out in a crowd, but he was the legendary Dalton. He would rarely seek out girls; he let them come to him.

"Trust me, I learned my lesson the hard way," Stef said as she slipped into Dalton's car with him holding the door. The interior smelled new she thought as she sunk into the stitched leather seats. As she sat down she noticed a few Harlequin romance novels on the floorboard beneath her feet. She reached down, grabbing one of them and turned to Dalton laughing. "Interesting choice of reading material. I had you pegged for more of a boring non-fiction business book reader but way to be unpredictable!"

"Ooops, I'm sorry, let me move that," Dalton said grinning. "Well, that's an embarrassing way to start off a date. Those are actually Mrs. Peppercorn's books, and I'm returning them to the library."

"Sure, likely story…blame poor old Mrs. Peppercorn as a cover to your perverted reading habits."

"It's true, I promise!"

"Riiiggghhht. Let's see what we have here." Stef proceeded to open the book to a random page and started reading. "'Gustav ran his finger slowly down from Penelope's cheek while kissing her lips, down the front of her chest, slowly unbuttoning the top button to her dress. Her bare breasts were heaving through the sundress, moist from the sweltering heat. Penelope felt her body trembling from his gentle touch. Gustav reached down and moved his other hand up her leg slowly until reaching the inner part of her thigh, realizing she had nothing on under the dress. She was already wet with anticipation as he gently stroked her, causing Penelope to let out a moan. Gustav proceeded to kiss her neck while continuing to penetrate her underneath the dress with his finger' Whoa! Mrs. Peppercorn is a perv!" Stef screamed, not expecting the book to be that R-rated. Her face was bright red in embarrassment.

Hilarious, Dalton thought. Although he was just expecting Stef to see the books and get more points for his fictitious volunteer job of helping the elderly, it was an added bonus she actually read an erotic part of the book. Perfect way to start the date. "I think she has them for a few more days if you'd like to borrow them. I doubt she would mind," Dalton said as he flashed his trademark grin. "You seem to be getting into a bit, and I'm certain you're curious to see how the Gustav and Penelope story ends."

"Haha, that's very thoughtful of you. I'm pretty certain I already know how it ends for both of them!"

"Maybe you and Mrs. Peppercorn should start an erotica book club. She would love that."

Stef was laughing at Dalton's witty comments. "Only if it means you still go to the library to check out Harlequin romance novels. Then it is worth it for me. The librarian must think you are a total perv!"

"She did give me a strange look the first couple times. I thought about telling her what I was doing but decided against it. Why ruin a good story for her? Librarians likely don't get a lot of excitement in their work lives. I'm certain she tells her librarian friends about the mysterious guy who comes in and only checks out Harlequin romance novels. If I told her about Mrs. Peppercorn, it would be far less interesting."

How sweet, Stef thought. Most guys would be embarrassed to go to the library and check out those books, and even if they did, they would immediately tell the librarian they were picking them up for someone else. Dalton on the other hand would not only go to the library to get the books for Mrs. Peppercorn and risk getting embarrassed, but he actually relished it. Making fun of himself for the benefit of others, definitely a good quality.

As Dalton sped through the traffic, he continued to ooze natural charm and magnetic appeal. Stef immediately picked up on the music, he of course had the Beatles's greatest hits playing in the background as a call back to their first encounter. He explained to Stef that he was taking her to a restaurant that was off the beaten path and not known by many, but it was one of his favorites. Dalton thought it would be a little too much to take her to a restaurant that was one of her favorites, too much of a coincidence. He already scored big with the Beatles reference and the Ice Cream Vault, he didn't want to risk having her really believe that he had been Facebook stalking her. That said, he was confident the restaurant they were going to would score the same amount of points as one of her favorites. Dalton was Italian, and his uncle and aunt owned a small Italian restaurant called Trattoria Matera, named after the town his uncle grew up in. It was true ethnic Italian; they had both immigrated here from Italy in their twenties and had been successfully running it for the past thirty-five years. Not only was it a great place, but Stef loved Italian food and Dalton knew that she would appreciate the family connection. Stef's parents had both died in an accident several years ago, and her extended family lived in other areas of the country. According to Mark, she always missed having family around. Dalton's family's restaurant was going to be perfect. It would show that he was close to his family and they all loved Dalton. When he went there, they treated him like royalty.

As expected, they arrived at the restaurant and Stef loved it. Dalton told her how he would come to the restaurant often but would never bring any girls. That of course made Stef beam. She was still a little skeptical, wondering why he was showering her with so much attention immediately, but for now she was going to go with it. It was true that Dalton would never bring girls by the restaurant, there was no reason to. He never let girls get too close to him. Dinner went as planned, Dalton was flawless in his execution. The ambiance was second to none. Once they stepped into the restaurant, they felt like they were in an Italian village. At one point Dalton's uncle even came over and started singing an Italian ballad. Stef had all but forgotten about her run-in with Zander earlier in the day. Her emotions were like a leaf in a tornado, constantly changing directions, constantly erratic and unpredictable. Although she was completely moved by Zander just a few hours ago, she now found herself immersed into her date with Dalton and wondering if life with Dalton would be like this all the time. It would be a difficult proposition to turn down. Dalton was like an addictive drug, slightly dangerous, but the moment she tried it she couldn't help but want more. They ended up spending the entire night at the restaurant, well past closing time. Dalton's uncle and aunt joined them and shared more great Italian wine and told stories in their thick Italian accents about Dalton when he was a little "bambino," about how he used to go back into the kitchen pretending to be a chef and toss the pizza crusts in the air, and about how he would try to speak Italian but always mess up the words. Stef loved it and Dalton played it well, showing his humble and emotional side.

The night concluded and despite his normal conditioning of going in for the kill, Dalton was a true gentleman. He walked her to her door, slowly put his hand up to her cheek, and gave her a gentle and warm kiss. He told her he had a fantastic time, and that the next date couldn't come soon enough. The wine had eased Stef's nerves, otherwise she would have probably been much more nervous. With Dalton driving off, Stef walked into her building almost in a trance, she wasn't sure if it was from the wine or the night—probably a little of both. She went upstairs and passed out, dreaming about what life would be like with Dalton.

As Dalton drove off, he knew the night was a success. He contemplated going into her apartment, but knew it wasn't a good play for the long term. Girls have a radar for guys like Dalton. They know they are players and expect them to be in it solely for sex. Although the date went as well as it could have, he had his other goal in mind. Stef was still recently divorced and coming off of a long-term relationship. There were plenty of girls he could call up right now for a late-night booty call if he wanted to get laid. He wasn't going to let sex with Stef get in the way of his goal. Plus he knew he had a busy day. Based on his intel, tomorrow was Stef's date with Dexter, and Dalton had a little surprise planned.

The next morning Stef woke up still feeling like she was on cloud nine, the night before with Dalton almost seemed more like a fairy-tale dream than reality. Everything about the night was perfect. When it came to physical appearance, Dalton was every girl's dream. In addition, he was witty, charismatic, and to Stef's surprise, he could also be humble and emotional. She still couldn't understand how he didn't already have a girlfriend or several. As she was making her coffee, the doorman called. Amy was on her way up. It wasn't unusual for Amy to just pop by unexpectedly, and she knew about the date last night and as a result was anticipating a barrage of questions along with condescending remarks. *Ugh*, Stef thought. She didn't want this right now, but since Amy was already there, she couldn't do much to stop it.

"Good morning Amy, awful early for a drop-by, isn't it?"

"I only have a few minutes, I'm on my way to Tae Bo and thought I'd pop by to see how the big night with Dextron went."

"His name is Dalton, not Dextron. The other guy's name is Dexter."

"Haha, that's pretty funny, I think you should just start combining their names and call them both Dextron. Tell them it is Latin for 'bro loser.'"

"Thanks Amy, excellent advice. I'll consider it. The date was good, we had a great time. He's quite a bit different than I thought he would be. Much more of a gentleman." Stef was guarded with her comments, she didn't want to gush too much. Amy would pounce on it and come back with an even stronger reaction.

"Riiight, different." Amy said sarcastically. "Wait a minute, this is the guy who is cut straight from *GQ*? Looks like a player, dresses like one too?"

"He dresses well and is good looking if that's what you're asking."

"If he dresses like a player and looks like a player, guess what Stef, he's a player. You need to wake up and realize all men are the same. Sex-driven Neanderthals who want to stick their semen trucks in anything that moves."

"We didn't have sex; he didn't even try." Stef's tone was defensive.

"It was the first date, just wait. Let me ask you this, did you talk about his personal life, girlfriends, if he has other relationships? If the guy is so hot, how do you know he isn't just dating different women each night? This extremely hot guy just randomly runs into you on the street and you magically fall into a relationship. Does that sound suspicious?"

"It could happen. We didn't talk much about relationships. I told him that I was just getting over a divorce and he said he hadn't been married before. I guess he could be dating other women, but he treated me well. We went to his family's restaurant, and he never brings girls there."

"Right, like I'm sure he just meets you on the street and decides to take you to his family restaurant that he 'never brings girls' to on date number one. Every guy has their go-to move. I'm guessing you are one of twenty who has been to the restaurant and they just tell you he never does that."

"I don't think so Amy. He seems very nice, and his uncle and aunt were nice too."

"Whatever, don't say I didn't warn you. I'm a little disappointed in you Stef. The divorce was a big move for you in a positive direction. It's like one step forward, two steps back."

Stef never wanted to disappoint anyone, particularly Amy since her rebuke was so harsh. "It's just a date Amy, I didn't say I was getting married to him or anything."

"You're better than this Stef. Don't you have your other date today, a picnic in the park? So cliché, 'oh dear, let's go sip rosé in the park, and feed each other grapes,'"

Amy said in a high-pitched tone. "WTF, gag. I gotta go, class starts in a few and I'm going to be late. Have fun with Dextron."

Just like that Amy was off, darting out the door and heading to class. Although Amy was the extreme of extremes, her comments still stung and left Stef wondering. Was Dalton just using her? Did he have other girlfriends? Was it stupid for her to be dating so soon after the divorce? Was this really a step backwards? Stef had this constant struggle for confidence, just as soon as she started to gain it, Amy would rip it from her. It was a cycle that continuously repeated itself. Maybe she should take it slow with Dalton, and who knew about Dexter. Then there was Zander, and she was going to see him later today. Stef was feeling conflicted and overwhelmed, three guys interested in her versus her best friend who she never wanted to disappoint. There didn't seem to be a right answer. For now she thought she'd take it day by day and see how things went, but based on Amy's comments, she felt like she should be very cautious. She was going to get a workout in and then headed off to her date with Dexter.

Dexter arrived at the park about thirty minutes early, he wanted everything to be perfect. He told Stef he would handle the details. He had picked out all of her favorites: spinach salad, an assortment of meats and cheeses, and peanut butter and jelly sandwiches—Stef's all-time favorite. She would surely be wowed, presumably 'guessing' all of her favorite foods. The weather was ideal for a picnic—seventy-five degrees and just a hint of clouds and light breeze. To wash it all down, he had picked out a vintage bottle of Pinot Grigio, again Stef's favorite. He laid down a large blanket and relaxed next to the picnic basket, waiting for Stef.

As Stef walked up she laughed to herself because he looked a little out of place. There weren't many guys who looked like Dexter hanging out by themselves in the park with a dainty picnic basket. Most women would kill for a guy who could pull off the rugged manly man look yet invite his girl to a picnic in the park, planning all the little details. Stef thought that it must have been funny to watch him get everything set up.

The initial meeting was a bit awkward. Dexter seemed slightly nervous and out of character versus when they spoke at the gym. Not surprising that this was out of his element, but Stef didn't mind. It was cute that he planned it all. As they caught up and got the awkward first few moments out of the way, both of them started to relax a little bit.

"Nice call on the peanut butter and jelly sandwiches. I'm not sure how you knew, but they are my favorite."

"I lived off of those in boot camp and throughout my time in the military. I consider them a delicacy, it was one of the better things I ate during that time. Living off the land in remote jungles, I've definitely eaten things most people wouldn't want to touch."

"I can only imagine."

The conversation was going well, Dexter seemed very interested in learning about Stef. After a bit, they started talking about her relationship with Amy.

"I think I would rather face a black ops mission in Central Africa than another kick-boxing class with her. She is intense!"

"She is an attorney by day, but her true passion is kick-boxing and self-defense or fighting in general. She has gotten more and more into it over the last two years. It's an obsession."

"It's great to have passions in life." Deep down Dexter was still a little upset about the entire kick-boxing episode, but he knew he had to let it go and focus on the mission, getting Stef.

Stef liked that Dexter seemed to not say anything bad about Amy, despite their first interaction. It always bothered her that Mark would say mean things about Amy, and he refused to respect her for who she was.

As the date progressed, Stef was finding herself increasingly captivated with Dexter. He seemed like a genuinely nice guy. It was difficult not to try and compare him to Dalton, since she had just been out with him the night before. The one aspect she liked about Dexter is that he seemed a little more down to earth than Dalton. Everything about Dalton was fantastic but almost too fantastic. He was drop-dead gorgeous, knew exactly what to say at exactly the right time, dressed impeccably, and was a gentleman. It was difficult to find any flaws, and it was that playboy image that scared Stef the most. With Dexter it seemed like she knew what she was getting. He struck Stef as being the type to be very protective, loyal, and trustworthy. A guy she could depend on, and his natural instinct was to protect.

Dexter had asked Stef about her childhood, which also impressed Stef. He seemed genuinely interested in her. He of course knew most of what she had been talking about from what Mark had shared, and every once in a while, he would drop a tidbit about something that ended up being a 'coincidence.' For example, Dexter knew that Stef's parents had passed away in an accident, and Dexter thought it was a good opportunity to share his background. He actually never met his Dad. Dexter was born while his father had been sent to fight in in Afghanistan, and his father ended up dying in battle. That's ultimately what inspired him to get into the military and become a SEAL. He talked about how every day he was enlisted he thought about his dad and the sacrifices he made for his family and his country. Stef was moved as he told the story. It was very touching, and she could see that Dexter told it from his heart.

As they continued talking and enjoying each other's company, Dexter spotted a tall and attractive blonde woman in hot pink workout gear walking quickly towards them. It seemed as if she was walking fast and with a purpose. Dexter didn't think much of it since he didn't recognize her, but Stef noticed him looking at something and turned around to see the woman walking towards them. Stef stayed turned around for a couple seconds, and to both her and Dexter's surprise, the woman stopped when she got to them. It was clear she was pissed about something and staring straight at Dexter.

"Can we help you?" Dexter had a perplexed look on his face. At first he thought maybe it was someone that Stef knew.

"Oh, can *we* help you?" the lady said, using a decisive and terse tone. "I think *you* helped me enough, isn't that right Dexter?"

"I'm sorry, do I know you?" Dexter looked even more confused as he observed the lady.

"You seemed to *know* me pretty well two weeks ago. You actually made it a point to *know* me for hours. In the kitchen, in the bedroom, in the living room, the bathroom. Should I go on, is any of this getting inside your thick fucking jarhead?"

Dexter's face turned bright red. He had no idea what this lady was talking about; he had never seen her before. "You must have me confused with someone else. I've never seen you before." Dexter was agitated, and veins started to sprout out in his neck. Stef just sat motionless looking back and forth between Dexter and the mystery lady. She was still trying to comprehend the entire situation.

All of a sudden the lady looked at Stef. "Let me play this out for you. Navy boy is going to be a gentleman. He'll take you on this nice picnic and you'll be enamored with his good looks and chiseled body. Then you'll sleep with him and he'll ghost you. He won't return phone calls, text messages, or emails."

"Hey lady, I have never met you before in my life and have no idea who put you up to this but you need to leave *now*!" Dexter was doing the best he could to control his anger. Although he still had no idea who this lady was, it was clear someone put her up to it, and he suspected it was Dalton or Zander. There was no other explanation. Those fuckers, he would literally kill them.

The lady just looked at both of them and laughed. "Don't say I didn't warn you," she said directly to Stef as she turned and walked away, storming off as quickly as she had arrived.

The silence in the seconds after she left were deafening. Dexter knew he had to come up with some type of explanation. Stef was shell-shocked, not moving. She looked equally confused as she did sick.

"I swear to you, I have no idea who that lady was. I promise I have never seen her in my life and certainly did not sleep with her." Dexter knew this was going to be a hole that was very hard to dig out of, but he had to try.

"She seemed to know you." Stef's response was curt. She wasn't really sure what to say.

"She did, and I think I have an explanation." Dexter paused for a moment, knowing he had just said he had an explanation, and now he had to come up with something.

"I'm listening."

"Someone must have set me up. That's the only logical explanation. That's how she knew my name."

"Seems like a fairly twisted practical joke. You have some bizarre friends if that's what they think is funny." Stef wasn't buying why would someone set him up.

"I don't think it is one of my friends."

"Then who?"

"My ex-girlfriend Angela. She has pulled this kind of stuff before."

"I'm still listening."

"We dated for about a year, it was quite a while ago. I noticed throughout our relationship she was the jealous type. Every time I would talk to a girl or even mention someone I met at the gym or at work, she would accuse me of cheating on her.

"It got to the point where she was obsessing about it, and I never did nor ever have cheated on anyone. I finally called it off, but she kept trying to get back together with me. She now stalks me on Facebook, and a couple months ago she heard I was dating someone and tracked the girl down and told her to stay away. I wasn't even dating the girl, she was just a friend. She told me about the run-in, and I called Angela and told her she needed to stay away. That may have spurned her on even more." Dexter was making it up as he went, but it sounded believable. As he was talking, he was wondering whether or not Stef would buy it, and also if she would be interested in a guy who had a psycho ex-girlfriend. It was a risky move, but at this point it was all Dexter had.

"How would she know you are here?"

"I'm not sure, possibly Facebook." Dexter knew he hadn't posted anything as to where he was going, but he didn't feel like he had to be extremely specific with Stef to make it somewhat plausible. "Who knows, I did tell a few friends that I met you and had a date and that I was very excited about it. It could have gotten back to her somehow. I'm really sorry, I feel terrible. I totally understand if you never want to talk to me again." It was a risky statement, but Dexter thought a little reverse psychology might be effective.

Stef pondered what he just said. He did seem like a nice guy, but it was a bizarre situation and he have made everything up. She agreed he seemed to be caught off guard. Stef thought if he knew the lady he would have probably squirmed more or reacted differently when he saw her walking up. "Your ex sounds pretty psycho."

Perfect, Dexter thought. She might be buying it or at least considering it was true. "She was a nice girl, but I honestly think she had some true mental problems. I know she was getting counseling and I was trying to help her, but I'm not sure it worked." Dexter was even starting to believe what he was saying. The real Angela was not psycho, but this explanation made him sound more like the concerned boyfriend, compassionate despite her shortcomings. "It's kind of sad."

"That is sad." Stef didn't really know whether or not to believe Dexter yet, but part of her wanted to. He seemed genuine.

Not surprisingly the date seemed to lose most of the steam after that; it was impossible to recover the momentum. It didn't end up being a horrific train wreck, but it didn't go the way either of them thought it would.

On the drive home, Dexter was playing through in his mind how he would pulverize either Dalton or Zander, whoever was responsible for this. Dexter was not a guy to piss off, and someone was going to learn that the hard way. He thought he had averted a crisis and that Stef would likely go out with him again, but he knew he'd be treading on thin ice. That was fine, the guys wanted a war and that was what they were going to get. Certainly some little impish artist wasn't going to be a match for him, and Dalton was all looks. He had already started strategically playing out in his mind the next steps. This was going to be a battle, a little different than ones he had fought numerous times before in the Navy, but the objective was the same: take out the enemy.

Stef on the other hand was thinking about whether or not she would see Dexter again. In the back of her mind she kept wondering that maybe Amy was right all along, guys were the same. It was hard to disregard what she said. On the flipside, she was starting to feed on all of the attention she was getting. That's something she hadn't been used to in the past. In only a few hours, she was going to see Zander again. This was uncharted territory for Stef. In less than twenty-four hours she had three dates with three very different but fantastic guys. She should have gotten a divorce a while ago she thought to herself. If these guys thought she was so great, she realized that Mark took her for granted and didn't appreciate what a catch she was.

Not long after the park incident, Dalton received a call from his accomplice.

"Project Picnic was definitely a success. You should have seen the look on both of their faces, they had no idea what happened. I hid from a distance for a while and watched as the guy tried to squirm out of it after I left, but we dug him in pretty deep. The girl seemed shell shocked; she was speechless."

"Perfect, you can consider us even now. I appreciate the favor."

"What is it that you have against that guy anyway Dalton? He must have really pissed you off to do something like that. The dude is pretty big too. I'd watch out."

"Thanks again for the favor, we'll talk soon." Dalton hung up the phone, not answering the question. Poor Dexter he thought, he would have loved to have been there to see the look on his face.

A few hours later Zander was at home getting ready for Stef's arrival. He had been preparing all afternoon. Over the last couple of days, he had rearranged his apartment and gallery to show off pieces that he thought Stef would like. He knew she loved to travel, particularly to Europe. He had some paintings that he had done over the years that were of European landmarks; the Eiffel Tower, the Parthenon, and others. He had enough to make Stef think Europe was one of his passions. He was ready. He was even thinking he would give her the picture he had been painting of her favorite coffee shop. It was the least he could do since she thought she was his inspiration to get back into art.

Stef arrived on time and as soon as she walked into Zander's apartment she was taken aback. For starters, he had a fairly cool loft apartment that was perfect for an aspiring artist. It was essentially one large room on the main level with a flight of stairs in the corner that walked up to a small loft that was his bedroom. It was the quintessential artist getaway, paintings and canvas covered the floor and walls. There were several areas that appeared to be under development, half-finished projects. It was sensory overload, she just kept looking from corner to corner trying to take it all in.

"This is amazing. I had no idea you would have so much art, it's all very beautiful. Did you do all of these?"

"I did. Wait, I take that back, except for these. I have to give my nephew credit for them." Zander pointed to the fridge. There were a few drawings of Barney he had up on magnets. "Although it's obvious we're family, we have the same artistic style."

Stef laughed and smiled warmly.

"Sorry I tried to clean but it is still a little messy," he said. "I don't invite many people over."

"Why not? This is amazing. I wouldn't call it messy, it's just your working area. It makes it more real than some snooty art gallery. You can actually see the work in process, the paint, the canvas."

"You're exactly right, I appreciate it much more here than hanging in some gallery. I can actually enjoy it. It serves as inspiration. I'm a fairly private person, particularly with my art. Only people who actually appreciate art are allowed to come in and see it."

"I feel flattered to make the list!" Stef smiled at Zander. "So where is the painting you started the other day, the one of the coffee shop? I'm anxious to see it."

"Patience. You just got here, are you that excited to leave already?"

"No, not at all!"

"I'm kidding, but I was thinking about ordering some food first, I'm starving. Do you like Chinese? There is a great place around the corner that delivers."

"Sounds perfect, I'm in. I'm open to anything, you pick."

As Zander was ordering food, Stef wandered around his apartment taking everything in. She took note of the size of his apartment, it was large for being in the city. Very open and a lot of natural light, it was the perfect art studio. She wondered how Zander afforded it on an artist's salary. There was certainly an element of mystery with Zander; he wasn't quite the open book that Dexter and Dalton seemed to be. She noticed all of the European paintings and mentioned to Zander that she loved Europe. Zander of course said he did too.

"OK, the food should be here in fifteen. Bear with me, I need to clean that table off. You'll have to excuse the mess. The table doubles as my art and dining room table." Zander pointed to the large solid wood table over in the corner that was covered in canvas and paint bottles. "This may surprise you but I don't host a lot of dinner parties here."

Stef liked Zander's sense of humor. He wasn't nearly as charismatic as Dalton, but more of the quiet and gentle type.

The two sat at the table enjoying each other's company as they waited for the food. Stef felt at ease around Zander. He had a calming way about him. It was different hanging around him compared to Dalton or Dexter. They continued talking through dinner, Zander had opened a bottle of wine and Stef was starting to feel the effects of the alcohol. While Zander was cleaning up the leftover food and takeout containers, Stef grabbed a brush that was laying on the side of the table and had been playing with it. Zander noticed her.

"I have an idea, wait right there." Zander walked quickly over to a closet and brought out a matted canvas. He walked over near Stef and propped it up on an easel. He then grabbed a palette and started to put paint on it.

"What are you doing?" Stef was curious.

"You are going to have your first 'lesson by Zander' painting session."

"Oh my gosh no, I'm not going to ruin one of your canvases and use up your paint! That would be a complete waste, I'm an awful artist.

Wait, what am I saying, I'm not an artist!" Stef put the brush down as she was talking and shaking her head.

"Everyone is an artist. It doesn't matter the quality or quantity of the art, or what you decide to make. It's all about creating something, anything. It doesn't matter what it is." Zander believed what he was saying.

"I don't really think this is a good idea. I'm embarrassed, it will be an awful painting."

"Come here." Zander grabbed Stef's hand and walked her over to the easel and the blank canvas. "I'll hold the palette, you paint."

Stef paused for a bit, not knowing what she should try to paint.

"Here, I'll help you." Zander gently took Stef's hand and dipped the brush she was holding into the brown paint. Although Stef was caught a little off guard, she liked Zander's touch. He moved her hand and the brush up the canvas.

"What are we painting?" Stef was intrigued.

"You'll see, just go with me on this."

"I'm not going anywhere." Stef was getting a little flirtatious, their bodies touching as they painted together.

After a few minutes of Zander holding Stef's hand and the brush she now realized what they were painting. It was a picture of Divine Mind, the store that Stef worked at. "Ahhh, that's sweet!"

"I thought you could take it into the store, our little donation."

"I love it, that's very thoughtful Zander." She continued to be overcome by Zander's thoughtfulness. As she turned towards him, they were face to face, very close to each other. Halfway through the painting Zander had put his other arm around Stef's body to hold her. All Stef could think about was how much she wanted to kiss Zander. It felt great to be close to him. Zander didn't move to immediately kiss her, and not wanting to wait any longer she wrapped her arms around him and made the first move. They were now passionately kissing, Zander pushing Stef firmly up against the heavy wood table. Just as the intensity was increasing, Stef's phone started to buzz on the table. It startled them both and they turned to see the word "Dexter" come across the screen.

"I'm sorry, I should have turned that off." Stef felt embarrassed. She knew that Zander had probably seen it was a guy's name on the phone. Although she wanted to go back to kissing Zander, the moment had now passed.

"That's OK, you can answer that if you need to." Zander was curious to gauge her reaction to that statement. He obviously didn't expect her to answer and certainly didn't want her to.

"No, it can go to voicemail. I think I'm going to shut my phone off."

Zander smiled. "We should probably finish our painting. We got a little side-tracked," he smirked. "Although I'm not complaining."

They finished the painting, both of their moods now relaxed, feeling very comfortable around each other. Zander was upset that Dexter had called and interrupted them but part of him felt it may have worked out to his advantage. He didn't want to risk going too far this early. Stef loved the painting of Divine Mind. She promised Zander she was going to take it into the store and hang it up for everyone to see.

"So *now* do I get to see the other painting? You did finish it right, or is that why you haven't shown me yet? You're stalling?"

"Funny, yes I did finish it. I'm a little nervous, I hope you like it. I feel like the expectations are pretty high."

"I'm sure it looks great." Stef followed Zander over to the corner of his apartment. There was a painting on an easel that was covered up.

"Are you ready?" Zander put his hand on the cloth that had been covering the painting, and with a quick swoosh, he drew it away, revealing the finished product.

Stef's eyes immediately focused on the painting, studying every part of it. She then noticed on the corner of the street Zander had painted two people, one of them appeared to be standing in front of an easel painting, and another behind him watching. "It's us!" Her eyes lit up enthusiastically.

"Do you like it? I thought you may find it a little cheesy."

"I love it, it's perfect."

"Good, although I've never seen your apartment I'm hoping it will look good there."

"What do you mean?"

"It's yours, I painted it for you. Don't feel obligated to hang it up. I won't be offended if you just throw it in your closet."

"Are you kidding? I can't accept this. I mean it is gorgeous and I would absolutely hang it in my apartment, but I can't accept it."

"You have to. After all, you were the inspiration that got me back into painting. If not for you, this painting wouldn't even exist."

"At least let me pay for it, I'll buy it from you." Stef loved the painting and wanted to hang it in her apartment, but she felt bad. She didn't think Zander had much money, and painting was how he earned what little she thought he had. The large loft apartment however made her think maybe his art business was better than most.

"I won't accept anything. It's yours." Zander found it funny that she wanted to pay him for the painting—a bit ironic given the reality of the situation and his intentions.

"Are you sure? I'm sure you could sell it for a lot of money."

"First off, thank you, I'm flattered you think I could sell it for a lot of money. Second, I'm positive. If I come over to your apartment and see it hanging up that will make me happier than any amount of money."

Stef was blushing. She was starting to believe that Zander was one of the kindest people she had ever met. Nobody had ever given her a handmade painting. "You are so sweet. Thank you very much, I guarantee you will see it hanging in my apartment...hopefully soon."

Zander had a huge smile. He doubted Dexter and Dalton had this successful of a first date; it wasn't possible.

Stef looked at her watch. Although she didn't want to leave it was already almost eleven p.m., and she had a Pilates class with Amy at six a.m. *Ugh*, she thought, *that was early*. "I hate to do this but I have a very early Pilates class with my friend Amy tomorrow morning, I should probably get going."

"No worries, I understand. I can give you a ride home?"

"That's OK, I'll just grab an Uber."

They sat and chatted a little while longer, and Zander wrapped up her paintings in paper so they wouldn't get ruined on the ride. The Uber arrived a few minutes later, and they closed the night off with another kiss, albeit a little less intense than the first one. As Stef was riding home, she could feel the wine starting to wear off. What a fantastic night. Zander seemed like an amazing guy, and she loved the painting. It couldn't have gone much better. She still couldn't believe she had three guys pursuing her at once, and they all seemed great. The dates with Dalton and Zander were fantastic, and although the Dexter date wasn't ideal, she was still intrigued. It was then that she remembered Dexter had called so she turned her phone on and listened to the voicemail. As she suspected, he was just calling to touch base after their date ended awkwardly. In the voicemail, he said that he had found out through an acquaintance of his that it was his ex-girlfriend Angela who tried to sabotage their date. In his voicemail he apologized again, asking for another chance. Stef reflected a bit on that point, unsure if she would.

Back at Zander's apartment, he was quietly celebrating the

successful date with Stef. Although he knew he was still far off from a marriage proposal, tonight made him even more confident it could work. He thought about whether or not he should rub it in to Dexter that he was making out with Stef when he called.

Although part of him wanted to piss the muscle-head off, he knew the smart play was to be as tight-lipped as possible about what happened. He felt both Dexter and Dalton viewed him as the long-shot underdog, and as a result they would probably focus more on competing with each other. The situation was perfect. Dexter and Dalton would use all of their energy to try and take the other out.

CHAPTER 17

The First Debrief

Several days had passed from her dates, and it was clear Stef was enjoying her newfound stardom. The affection and attention seemed to only intensify. Dexter had recovered from his episode at the park by getting a female friend to call Stef impersonating his ex-girlfriend Angela and apologize. She said Dexter was a great guy and she had taken the breakup really hard. She told Stef to do whatever she could to hang onto him, he was one of the good ones. Dexter knew it was risky. The chances of a girl calling to apologize seemed remote, particularly if she was insane enough to arrange what she did. Hopefully they never ran into the real Angela, although Dexter thought the chances were slim. Dalton had tagged pictures of Stef and him on Facebook at his uncle's restaurant that his aunt had taken. Dalton knew that would accomplish a couple things. First it would make his relationship with Stef much more public, something the stereotypical player avoids at all cost. Second, he knew it would really piss Dexter and Zander off because they would no doubt see the pictures. On both counts he succeeded, Stef was surprised about the pictures since she questioned Dalton's monogamous intentions. While Zander didn't seem overly concerned about the pictures, they put Dexter in a rage.

He had convinced himself over the last few days that it must have been Dalton that set him up. He was already plotting his heinous revenge, he would pull out all the stops. Zander continued to work the angle that seemed to work well for him, he invited Stef to join him next week at an art exhibit that showcased artists who focused on the European Renaissance era. Stef was excited to go. The guys continued to work every angle possible pursuing Stef.

The time had now come for the first check-in meeting with Mark. All the guys would come together in just a few minutes at the Liquid Cougar warehouse. Mark's friends were also joining for the meeting. They had all arrived at the warehouse, just waiting for the three guys to arrive.

"Well Ronald, you clearly proved me wrong. I did not think you'd be able to shotgun six Liquid Cougars in under two minutes." Christian knew that Ronald was a sucker for his dares; he almost never turned them down.

"Shit Ronald, do you have any idea what that's going to do to you? That's equivalent to ten cups of coffee." Steve seemed genuinely concerned.

"Please, I've had more chemicals running through these veins on any given day than most people do in a lifetime. This stuff is like apple juice." Ronald smiled at the guys, smacking his lips loudly.

Mark, who had been laughing, interjected. "Tony told me that some frat kid in Florida died after chugging ten of them. His body overheated, then he went temporarily insane. He apparently broke into the zoo, climbed the ten-foot fence and jumped onto a gorilla. He bit the gorilla in the ear Mike Tyson-style and started punching him from behind. The gorilla threw him across the pen but the kid was still juiced on adrenaline from Liquid Cougar. He got up and tried to swan kick the gorilla as it was charging him. The gorilla hit him so

The First Debrief | 153

hard that it shattered most of the bones in his face, but the kid still didn't give up. They ended up tranqing both the gorilla and the kid, even had to hit the kid twice before he finally went down. It was quite the story. Liquid Cougar faced some legal issues but ended up settling out of court as the kid was hopped up on other substances, and it was difficult to pinpoint exactly what triggered the meltdown. You may want to quit at six, Ronald."

Ronald smiled, pleased at his accomplishment. "My record is fifteen. Some weak-ass Florida frat kid is not a challenge."

Just as the guys continued to laugh, Dexter walked into the warehouse. He had a stone cold look on his face, as if he was ready to go Rambo on someone. Ronald even took a couple steps away from Dexter as he approached the group, presumably he was still uncomfortable around him. Shortly after that Dalton and Zander both arrived. All the guys were there and Mark wanted to get started. Dexter said he had to use the bathroom before they got started, Mark pointed him in the direction and he was back in a couple minutes, now they were all ready. Although Mark had already been briefed that morning from the PI he had tailing Stef, he was anxious to get the guys' side of the story. He had seen what happened at the park with Dexter and thought it was hilarious. Although he couldn't confirm Dalton was behind it, he was pretty sure it was all orchestrated by him. So far Mark was impressed at the guys' abilities. They had managed to exceed even Mark's lofty goals this early in the project. All of this instilled more confidence to Mark that his plan would work: Stef would marry one of these three guys within six months.

They proceeded to give their updates on how things were progressing. Mark didn't want any of them to know he was having Stef tailed. He thought it was going to be interesting to see how close their stories would match up with reality. As expected, Zander was modest in his description of how things were going. He explained he thought he was making progress but unsure of what Stef thought of him, even commenting that she seemed pretty happy in the pictures with Dalton on Facebook. He knew the Dalton type very well, and would exploit his character weaknesses. Build up his inflated ego, he would get a false sense of security. Dalton of course acted as if this was all a bit beneath him. There was no competition in his mind.

It came time for Dexter to give his update and he proceeded to talk about the kick-boxing session and subsequently meeting Stef for a picnic. Dalton gave a smart-ass smirk when Dexter mentioned the picnic.

"That sounds sweet; I bet she loved it." Dalton's comment dripped with sarcasm.

"She did." Dexter's jaw clenched as he looked at Dalton.

"That was a cute picnic basket you carried there, well played." Dalton's grin grew even wider. At this point the guys were looking back and forth between Dalton and Dexter, knowing something was going on.

"Mother fucker!" Dexter grabbed Dalton by the shirt and shoved him up against the cases of Liquid Cougar surrounding them. All of the guys jumped up, including Ronald who let out a loud "Hiiiii-yaaaaa," crouching down in a karate pose next to them. Clearly the Liquid Cougar was setting in.

"Easy gents, put that energy into the mission." Mark knew he couldn't have a fight break out, Dexter would be impossible to contain. All the guys got into the middle of them and finally split them up before they started swinging. "Remember, if this gets too out of hand and you *all* lose, *nobody* gets the money."

Once everyone settled down, Mark asked if there were any questions.

Dexter stepped forward, calmer after the incident. "How do you suggest we handle Amy, Stef's friend? She's an obstacle. Stef seems to be heavily influenced by her."

This was a question that Mark had been pondering. The problem was that he didn't have a plausible solution yet. Stef would likely fall for one of the guys, but Amy would do everything in her power to talk Stef out of getting into a serious relationship. Marriage would be a high hurdle. Amy would go ballistic. "I have some ideas, but for now just focus on getting to Stef. That's your mission, get her to fall in love with you. If you succeed, it will all work out." Mark didn't entirely believe his words, but he knew at this point he needed the guys to believe. He hadn't figured out how to get Amy out of the equation, but it was a problem he knew he would eventually have to conquer.

None of the other guys had questions, so they agreed on the next meeting time and adjourned. Mark and his friends were walking out of the warehouse, when they all looked over to Dalton who had been walking in front of them to his black BMW and had yelled "What the fuck!"

All of Dalton's tires were flat; someone had slashed them.

"Bad neighborhood." Dexter looked at Dalton with a grin. "I would give you a ride but you know that Mark said we can't be seen together. Sorry buddy."

"You fucker." None of the guys had seen Dalton rattled up to this point, but this clearly hit him where it hurts. His face was flush red, the Italian blood was boiling. Despite being furious, he knew he couldn't do anything about it right there. Aside from the fact it wasn't the time or place, he was also probably no match for Dexter in a brawl.

Ronald who had been fidgety the entire time and clearly hopped up on caffeine looked confused. "That's weird Dalton, I wonder why your tires were the only ones slashed. Strange."

Mark glanced over at Ronald, shaking his head, subtly telling him to shut the fuck up. Ronald still looked confused, not understanding what was obvious to everyone else.

"What Mark, don't you think it is strange? Look, your tires are fine, so are everyone else's. It's almost as if Dalton was targeted." Ronald apparently wasn't getting the message.

"Ronald. I think we all get that. I think Mark is saying that you don't need to point that out further." Christian was laughing but loved Ronald's completely naïve tendencies; he was clueless sometimes.

Dalton was glaring at Dexter.

"Don't look at me dude," Dexter asserted, shrugging his shoulders. "I got here before you. Maybe you picked up a few nails on the road?" Dexter's comments dripped with sarcasm, clearly trying to agitate Dalton into throwing a punch.

The guys were all on edge waiting for the next move, unsure of what Dalton would do. It was true that Dexter arrived before Dalton, but Dexter slipped away to the bathroom shortly thereafter.

"Dalton, let me call a friend of mine who owns a car shop. He'll come out and get you squared away. I'll make sure he takes care of you." Mark jumped in, knowing he needed to quickly diffuse the situation. Tension between the guys was expected and healthy, but if it boiled over it would derail his entire plan. He'd be back to square one. The biggest risks to his plan were the guys turning too much against each other or Stef finding out. Mark grabbed his cell phone and urgently dialed his friend. "He'll be here in ten."

Dexter had already hopped in his car and left, as did Zander. Dalton said he was fine so Mark and the other guys hopped in their cars. They were all going to grab dinner at the North Shore Tavern, one of their favorite hangouts and where this plan had originated. What Mark didn't know was that his friends had arranged a surprise party for him of sorts, or at least a surprise outing. Mark thought it was just a normal dinner, but they had a few events in mind for the night. Mark had been divorced for months now. Between work and trying to plot a strategy to get Stef married, he had not really taken much of an opportunity for himself. The guys all thought a crazy night on the town for Mark was long overdue. They had even invited Tony out for the occasion. None of the other guys knew Tony all that well but figured Mark would enjoy it, and they knew Tony had connections that would come in handy for a night in the city.

"We just need to get you laid, Mark. How about this, I know some professional ladies who work for an entertainment company that Liquid Cougar hired last month. I'll call them up, I promise, you won't regret it. They are bat-shit crazy. It's time to release you back into the wild, like a lion with a wounded penis that is now fully healed," said Tony in his ever creative and gross metaphors.

"I'm in. I feel like I have a fully healed lion penis." Ronald suddenly sat up straight and continued to stare at Tony. He had heard a lot about the guy but hadn't spent much time with him. Every time they were together Ronald would get awkward and nervous, saying strange things. He viewed Tony as immortal. Whenever Mark would tell the guys stories, Ronald would be in awe.

"See, Raymond is game for it, what do you other guys think?" Despite the fact that Tony would always get Ronald's name wrong, nobody would correct him. The guys all thought it was funny and Ronald was presumably in too much awe to even care. He just smiled and nodded his head. They weren't even sure if he realized Tony didn't get his name right.

"Is it written somewhere in the divorce recovery manual that you should forego all morals to get your life back in order? You should launch a support group, Tony. Forget about all of that spiritual well-being shit and finding yourself. Although that sounds fun and I'm sure the girls are indeed hot, I suggest we take a little tamer approach to the night." Mark was used to dealing with Tony's bizarre suggestions.

"You're so predictable, Mark. You have a good friend who is offering his support and you turn him down. That's rude. Not only to yourself but you ruin it for the rest of us." Christian grinned at Mark, he loved hanging out with Tony, the two were alike in many regards, just different generations.

"Hey guys, Mark's right, Jenny would kill me even if she overheard this conversation."

"Steve, you would jizz in your pants if we were in the same room as these girls and someone said the word gang-bang. Your pants would explode." It was pretty much written in the friend code that Christian would slam Steve every chance he got. No opportunity went unnoticed.

"Fine," said Tony. "I have a solid plan B. Ludacris is playing over at Bling. It will be off the hook. Plus most of the guys that hang out over there are douchebags, so we won't even have to try to get laid, the women will be all over us." Bling was one of Tony's favorite clubs as of late with Liquid Cougar getting into the mainstream at clubs he was even more plugged in than he used to be.

"It's eight p.m., and we didn't buy tickets Tony, how will we get in?"

"Sometimes I feel like you don't even know me." Tony raised his fingers, and a brunette waitress came running with his check. He commanded attention everywhere he went.

Tony had arranged for his driver to pick them up, and about fifteen minutes and two bottles of Cristal later, he dropped them off at the front door of Bling. Although the line wrapped around the block, the bouncer saw Tony and immediately slapped his hand and gave him a man-hug. He unhooked the velvet rope and let them right through. Ronald was mesmerized on the ride over. He kept asking who the guy driving was and looked confused that Tony had his own personal driver and car.

Christian was the only one who had been in Bling besides Tony.

When they got inside they realized Tony was treated like he owned the place. The guy worked the room like he was royalty, and women half his age would immediately stop talking to whatever guy they happened to be with at the time to come over and flirt with him. It was entertaining to watch. Even Christian was a little jealous. Tony waived them over to the stairs. They were going up to one of the private VIP rooms that overlooked the dance floor and stage. The room was already stocked with bottles, Liquid Cougar, and of course women waiting for Tony to arrive.

"Mark, let me introduce you." Tony waved Mark over to the girls he was talking to. "Ladies, this is probably the smartest man you'll ever meet, he's like a brother to me. If it wasn't for Mark, I'd probably only be worth $20 million, but thanks to him I'm worth about fifty times that. He's the brains behind my success."

Typical, Mark thought, Tony would give you a compliment but only if it made him look even more amazing. Feeling somewhat embarrassed at the intro, he continued to laugh and quietly said hi to the six amazingly gorgeous women who were standing in front of him. The other guys were just watching, Christian eagerly waiting to be introduced and Ronald slamming Liquid Cougar vodkas, working hard to look cool in front of Tony. Steve was his normal self, fairly quiet and out of place in the scene.

Tony then whispered into the girls' ears and they all looked at Mark longingly with puppy dog eyes, each coming over to him. One on each side grabbing his arm and the others crowding around him. Mark went with it, but had a slight look of concern on his face, curious what the hell Tony had told the women.

"What did you tell them?" Christian walked over to Tony with a curious look.

"I told them that Mark had been engaged about a year ago when his fiancé was out walking his dog and both were killed after being run over by a drunk garbage truck driver. He sued the city for hundreds of millions but only recently started to get his life back in order. He just got a really cute puppy and is thinking about starting to date again."

"Hopefully Mark doesn't screw it up. He might be too honest to keep a great story like that up." Christian was beaming with amazement. Although he had heard the Tony stories, he hadn't experienced many of them firsthand.

The guys continued to enjoy all that was to be had in the VIP room. Not surprisingly, Christian and Tony ended up hitting it off well. Their ridiculous stories only seemed to escalate, one feeding off of the other. It turned into a challenge to see what they could get women to believe. Since many of them knew Tony, Christian would change up his character with every new woman they met. In one case they actually convinced a group of girls that Christian was an astronaut and scheduled to leave on the Space Shuttle "Desire" next Sunday. He was going to be the first human to ever visit Pluto, and he would be there for ten years. After he realized they were buying all of it, he kept pushing the envelope just to see how much he could get them to believe. He said today was the last and final day that NASA would let him have sex.

They looked confused, but then he explained that he was specifically selected for this mission because his testosterone was abnormally high. Ten times the normal level of a thirty-five-year-old male. He went on to say the only living animal that has a testosterone level higher than him are male bull sharks, known for their aggressive tendencies. Christian was spewing out statistics like he was a biologist. He declared that high testosterone offsets the negative effects of space travel, and it allows him to handle G-forces better than the average human. The story rolled off Christian's tongue. He was straight-faced to make it believable. As the three girls listened in awe, they started to fight over who was going home with him.

While all the guys were busy in their own respective worlds, Mark made a clean getaway from the VIP room to wander around the club. He could only take so much of Tony in this setting, and the combination of Tony and Christian was proving to be too much. Despite the fact that he was now newly single and at some point surely would get back into the dating world, the club scene wasn't entirely second nature to him. He was curious however to wander the club and check Bling out, he had heard a lot from Tony. As he walked around the bar he noticed all of the Liquid Cougar branding, they practically had a shrine built. The more he learned about the Liquid Cougar enterprise, the more impressed he was. This could be bigger financially for Tony than Kilimanjaro.

As he rounded the bar, trying to push his way through the crowds of pretty people trying to get laid, he had to take a double take thinking he recognized someone. Sure enough, he did—Katie from the Dog Den was at the other side of the bar. Their eyes met briefly, then she waved him over.

"There you are, where did you disappear to?" Katie looked at Mark and her eyes suggested to say please just go along with this. "I thought you were only going to be gone for a few minutes, I missed you."

For a split-second Mark was confused, but then grinned, realizing the guy at the bar who had been talking to her was not a friend. "Sorry beautiful, you wouldn't believe the line to the men's room. Besides, I thought we were meeting in the VIP room, why are you lingering out here with all the common folk?" Mark spoke loudly, knowing the guy was still turned a bit towards Katie and could overhear. He threw in the common folk line for effect.

Katie grinned. "Ah yes, the VIP room. I was headed there, but got sidetracked, I was talking to…ummm, I'm sorry, what was your name again?"

"Larry, my name is Larry." The guy turned and looked at both Mark and Katie, the tone of his voice was condescending, and he started to turn away.

"Hi Gary, I'm Mark." Realizing he was being mocked, Larry quickly turned and walked away. "Aren't you going to join us in the VIP room, Gary?" Mark hollered as Larry kept walking.

"That was rude, why did your boyfriend Gary just walk away after I invited him into our VIP room? Was it something I said?" Mark grinned at Katie.

"I have to admit, well played Mr. Coughlan. I always had a hunch you were good at thinking on your feet. Thanks for saving me." Katie seemed genuinely appreciative.

"My pleasure. Hi, by the way. I was surprised to see you here! Who are you here with and why were you hanging out at the bar with Larry?"

"First off, I don't know Larry, other than to say that he's like most of the other guys here playing the law of large numbers trying to get lucky. Second, I came here with friends, I think they are still around here somewhere, but I came over to the bar to get another drink. That's when I met our friend Larry, and he wouldn't leave me alone."

"Can't fault old Larry for trying. You were hanging out by yourself at the bar, seems like an open invitation."

"So what's this about the VIP room, is that true?"

"It is. I'm here with friends," Mark said. "At least I hope they are still here. I got a little bored and decided to wander around the club. My plan was to find lonely girls to prey on at the bar, and lucky me, I didn't have to go far!"

"Funny. Well I can let you get back to your friends. I should probably find my friends too."

"Actually I'm debating if I should make a run for it. My friends are all pre-occupied, and I'm feeling like I've had enough of Bling for one night."

"Well in that case, I have an idea. You want to leave, I want to leave, why don't we leave together?"

Mark paused, not exactly sure what "leave together" meant in Katie's mind. Although they had been flirting a bit and the two had spent time together, he didn't know if he should read into that comment. "Sure, I'm in. Did you want to let Lar-Gar know? He strikes me as the possessive type."

Katie just shook her head and laughed. "C'mon, let's go. I'm going to text my friends to tell them I'm headed out. You should do the same."

Mark paused. He felt a little bad that he was just leaving, but he knew his friends wouldn't care, and he saw Steve leave a little while ago.

As they left the club and started walking down the street, there was an awkward silence. After a few moments Katie jumped in, "Are you hungry? There is a great diner down the street, perfect after-club diner type place." She smiled and then said, "Larry recommended it!"

Mark laughed, and they walked down to the diner to grab the last table available. There didn't seem to be any more awkward silences, Mark and Katie covered a wide range of topics and really enjoyed each other's company. Although they hadn't known each other long, Mark felt like he could trust Katie. They ended up talking for two hours, laughing, telling stories, reminiscing about how similar their childhoods were. They lost track of time, practically shutting the place down—then realizing they should get home. After all they both had dogs that would be quite anxious to be let out. It was a little awkward in terms of goodbyes, but they ended up hugging before each grabbing an Uber to go home, heading out in opposite directions.

During the ride home Mark was reflecting on the night, and

most of all his run-in with Katie. He really liked hanging out with her, but he didn't know what his own intentions were, much less hers. He thought why force it, just see where it goes. By the time Mark got home Tyson was thrilled as usual to see his best friend. It didn't matter how long Mark was gone or what time he got home, Tyson was always there happy to see him. *Too bad human relationships weren't as simple* Mark thought.

CHAPTER 18

Amy, Amy, and More Amy

The next afternoon Zander had arrived at the European Renaissance art exhibit about thirty minutes early. He knew the curator and had planned for them to get a private tour of the restoration workshop. They would even get a personal tour of the exhibits from the gallery owner who was an expert in European art. As Zander sat on a bench outside the gallery waiting for Stef, his mind started to wander about how his life would change if he married Stef. He knew he didn't have much time, even less time than what Mark had given them.

Stef arrived and looked great. Although she was never in bad shape, the last few months of working out with Amy were showing. Pilates, kick-boxing, and Zumba classes were paying off.

"You do know that people are supposed to pay attention to the art, right? You look amazing."

Stef blushed; she was not used to compliments like that. "I doubt that's true, but thank you. I'm excited about this. I haven't been to many art exhibits!"

"Well, I have good news, I called in some favors so you'll get to experience it right the first time. To start, we are going to get a private tour of their restoration workshop, then the gallery owner will give us a personal tour. He's an expert in European art, and a friend."

"That sounds amazing, I was excited to just walk around the art gallery with you, the rest is a bonus." Everything about Zander seemed to intrigue Stef. She loved that he was an artist, a great example of someone who stayed true to themselves.

They finished the private tour and spent some time walking through the gallery. All of a sudden, they got to a painting and Zander stopped cold. Stef looked over and a tear was appearing in Zander's eye.

"Zander, what's wrong, are you OK?"

"Yeah, I'm sorry. It's nothing."

"What's wrong?" Stef's tone was of genuine concern.

"It's silly, I shouldn't let it upset me anymore."

"Let what upset you? Please tell me."

"It's the painting. This was my grandma's favorite, and I'll never forget how she used to bring me to art galleries as a boy and point this one out to me." The painting showed a little girl and boy running through a European countryside chasing sheep and an older lady looking on from afar. "I miss her."

"Zander, I'm sorry, I had no idea." Stef stepped closer to Zander, touching his hand trying to comfort him. "The painting is beautiful, and your grandma will always be with you. She would be so proud of you, and no doubt she is comforted right now by the fact you carry on the wonderful memory."

Zander leaned in towards Stef, pulling her hand and body closer. Although the painting was one that he and his grandma had viewed as a child, his reaction was a ruse. "I wish you could have met her." Zander turned and looked into Stef's eyes as he spoke.

"Me too, very much. Thank you for sharing the story with me, it means a lot." Stef smiled warmly back at Zander. She continued to appreciate how open he was and in touch with his emotions. He was different from Dexter and Dalton. He was actually different from any other guy she had been with.

As they continued to walk through the gallery, their bodies became closer. Stef felt a strong emotional connection with Zander, and although his intentions were not pure, he couldn't disregard a connection as well. That made the situation a bit more appealing, although he would have married any girl no matter how hideous or bitchy she was to get what he wanted, he would obviously rather marry someone that he actually enjoyed hanging around.

"I have a surprise for you. I know we didn't make plans for after the art gallery, but I was hoping you could come over to my place?" Stef's voice sounded a little nervous, like she had been debating whether or not to invite Zander over.

Jackpot, Zander thought. He privately celebrated the win, knowing that Stef probably hadn't invited many guys over to her place. He could tell by her voice that she was a bit nervous. There was no way he would turn this down. "There aren't many things in life I would leave an art gallery for, but I think you just discovered one."

Stef blushed a bit, not sure if Zander was talking about just going to her place or something more, but either way she seemed pleased with his answer. "Hmmm, now you have me curious. What other things in life would you leave an art gallery for? Also, what if the surprise is something terrible?"

"I'll take my chances on the surprise, and you'll just have to use your imagination on the other things." Zander was starting to get a little more forward with his flirting, taking some risk.

Stef was still blushing. She didn't mind his comments at all. They walked out of the gallery and hopped in a cab headed to Stef's place; it was only five minutes away. Zander was anxious to see it, imagining it was nice given how much Mark was on the alimony hook for. After a few minutes their car pulled up to the front of the Winston, Stef and Zander both jumped out and were immediately greeted by the doorman. Just what Zander imagined, nice but not over the top.

"Great place, I've never been in this building before but have always wanted to check it out." Zander looked up at the towering skyscraper.

"It's probably a little more upscale than I need. My friend Amy helped pick it out." Stef felt a little embarrassed. The building seemed pretentious compared to the more hipster place where Zander lived. She privately wondered what he really thought about it. She even thought twice about inviting him over, worried he would be turned off.

"It's great, your friend Amy has excellent taste." Zander knew all too well about Amy, and although they hadn't met, it seemed like a good idea to start out complimenting her. Like Dexter pointed out at the warehouse, all the guys knew Amy was going to be an obstacle.

As they walked inside and took the elevator up to Stef's condo, there was an awkward silence. The elevator stopped on the forty-ninth floor and they both stepped out, walking towards her unit. As Stef unlocked the door, they both stepped inside and Zander walked over to the floor to ceiling windows. They had a fantastic view of the city.

"Wow, this is an amazing view. I knew it would be good, but this is breathtaking. You don't even need art with a view like this."

"Come here, I want to show you something even better." Stef grabbed Zander's hand and took him down the hall. "I disagree, I do need art." Stef pointed to the painting on the wall in the hallway. It was the one that Zander had given her.

"I'm flattered, and while I'm very biased, I think it looks perfect here."

Stef smiled back at Zander. "I agree, it is perfect. Thank you again."

Zander thought now was as good of time as any to make a move, so he leaned in to give Stef a kiss. Just as their lips touched, Stef's phone rang. *What the fuck*, Zander thought, if this was Dexter again he was going to kill someone. Twice in a row, what are the odds.

Stef seemed embarrassed again, grabbing her phone, not sure what to expect. She was privately hoping it wasn't one of the other guys either. *What terrible timing*, she thought. As she looked at her phone, she noticed it was the front doorman. "Hello." There was a short pause, and Stef's look turned from flustered to frustration. "OK, yes that's fine, she can come up." She hung up the phone, visibly angry.

"Everything OK?" Zander wasn't sure what was going on either.

"I apologize, I wasn't expecting anyone, but my friend Amy has this really bad habit of popping in. The good news, you'll get a chance to meet her." Stef was cringing inside knowing that Zander's nice-guy persona was no match for Amy, she was going to tear him apart. This might be worse than having it be one of the guys calling.

A few moments later Amy walked in. "What a surprise Amy, I didn't know you'd be stopping by." Although Stef was normally subordinate and submissive to Amy, her comments made it clear that Amy didn't have an open invite.

Amy disregarded Stef's comments entirely, focusing on the man in the room and wondering who he was. "I didn't realize the cable guy was here."

"Hi, I'm Zander. I'm Stef's friend, but no worries about the confusion. I've been referred to as worse things than the cable guy." Zander reached out to shake her hand.

"Are you suggesting it is bad to be a cable guy? I have friends who work in the cable industry, what the fuck are you saying?" Stef cringed at Amy's comments, she seemed to be in an extra terse mood today.

Although Zander knew Amy was a bitch, he was still a little taken aback by her immediate abrasiveness. He didn't know what to say, but after a short pause managed to get out the first thing he could think of. "I'm sorry, I wasn't suggesting it at all. I didn't mean anything offensive by it."

"Great, now that we cleared up that you didn't *intend* to be offensive. I'm sure the hundreds of thousands of people in the cable industry will feel much better that you didn't *intend* to offend them. I know I feel better. That usually makes it all better when you make disparaging remarks about someone and then explain to them how you didn't intend it, and they should feel the way you do."

"So, Amy, did you stop by for a reason?" Stef was cringe-worthy embarrassed by Amy's comments. She couldn't have come at a worse time with Zander there.

"Yeah. I want to try out a new class tomorrow night and was hoping you'd join me. It's called Krav Maga, supposed to be a fantastic workout. Even better than kick-boxing. I also wanted to see if you were up for Indian food tonight."

Stef was frustrated that Amy couldn't have just called her or sent a text; she clearly didn't have to stop over. "I might be able to come to the class but not sure." Stef was a little uncertain what to say. Dexter had mentioned getting together tomorrow night, but they hadn't firmed anything up. "As for Indian tonight, I have plans with Zander."

"Zander, you like Indian food?" Amy looked directly at Zander, not even giving Stef a chance to provide a response. "You look like one of those vegan leafy tree huggers."

Zander wasn't sure what to say. He wanted to hang out with Stef just the two of them, but it was fairly clear at this point that Amy wasn't going to let that happen. After pausing a moment, he said that he did, but he also didn't want to interfere if they wanted some girl-talking time.

"Girl-talking time? What exactly do you think girl-talking time is Zander?"

"I don't know. I just meant it as an expression." Zander was fumbling over his words, knowing it was going from bad to worse quickly with Amy.

"Right. I swear you guys just think women sit around talking about babies, birth control, and menstruation. Is that what you call girl-talk?"

"I didn't say that." Zander interrupted Amy who was clearly ready to go on a rant. "That's a good idea, let's order Indian, my treat." Zander knew that at some point he was going to have to figure out a way to get on Amy's good side, tonight was as good as any to start.

As they waited for the Indian food to arrive, the three sat down in the living room in what was still an awkward situation. Amy had asked what Zander does for a living.

"So you're a graphic artist? Do you work for one of the big ad agencies or marketing firms?"

"I am an artist but not the graphic type, and I don't work for a company. I mainly just do paintings on my own and sell them directly to the public, occasionally to galleries." Zander wasn't sure why Amy thought he was a graphic artist. He had just said artist.

"Isn't that what people say when they can't find a real job?" Amy laughed at her own comments.

"Amy, be nice. Zander is a great artist." Stef felt compelled to stand up for Zander. She didn't want to mention the painting in the hallway, that would just subject Zander to more torture.

"It's OK, it's not the first time I've heard comments like that. I'm not extremely successful commercially yet, but I hope to have more success someday. More than that I just want to do what I love."

"Stef's ex-husband was a very successful executive. I should warn you that's normally her type: guys who are very successful." Amy threw the comment out there again without any regard for Zander's feelings.

"Amy! Stop it!" Even Stef was taken aback by the comment. It was going from bad to worse to outright intolerable.

At this point Zander was growing less and less confident he would be able to win Amy over, it certainly wasn't going to happen that night. The cutting comments continued through the duration of dinner, and Zander was just doing the best he could to stay polite which was increasingly hard to do. He decided it was probably best to make a quick exit after eating, since there was no real upside for him to stay and continue the pummeling. He mentioned he was going to call it a night and Stef started walking him to the door. They walked outside into the hallway to get a little privacy away from Amy.

"I'm sorry, she really isn't that bad of a person, she's just opinionated." Although Stef sincerely felt horrible, it sounded as if she was just making excuses for her friend.

"Is there anything I could have said or done differently? It seemed as if everything I said was wrong. She's relentless; she wouldn't stop." Zander was more upset about Amy than he led on, but also knew the dynamics between her and Stef. He didn't want to push his luck, Stef could quickly turn against him if his comments sounded offensive or degrading towards Amy, despite her being blatantly rude.

"No, I don't think so. That's just how she is. She's very protective of me, she just doesn't want me to be hurt again. On top of that she's independent, and subscribes to the strong belief of women not needing men. I'm sorry, I should probably get back in there, before she comes out here."

Zander could see just how challenging it was going to be to get Stef away from Amy's grip. It was even more pronounced than Mark had described it. Presumably it had strengthened since the divorce as the two of them had been spending more time together. Zander and Stef said their goodbyes and exchanged a fairly unromantic kiss. Although Zander was confident their relationship hadn't taken a step back, it ended up being a disappointing evening. At least now he knew what he was up against.

Stef walked back into her apartment, dreading the inevitable interaction with Amy.

"Well. It's a good thing I stopped over. I saved you from a couple more hours of boredom with that loser. He's even worse than Dextron, and I didn't think that was possible."

"Amy, you haven't even met Dalton yet, and Dexter is a separate person. Zander is a nice guy...you are wrong about him."

"If by nice you mean pathetic, then yes, he's exceptionally nice. I don't get it. You leave Mark for a life of independence and now you are involved in some kind of sad love triangle. Dextron or Zander, either way you lose. I'm disappointed in you Stef."

The words hung on Stef's soul. Although Stef liked all three of the guys, she was consistently torn in her feelings when she was around Amy. Stef just couldn't handle Amy's overpowering personality. After a brief pause, Stef finally responded and told Amy that maybe she is moving too fast. She tried to allay Amy's concerns by suggesting she was just playing around—they were only dates. It was all harmless, she told Amy.

Deep down Stef felt even more torn than ever. She was really starting to fall for all three of the guys, although she still had questions about Dexter and the park incident. Dalton was amazingly good looking and every girl's dream. Dexter was the ultimate protector, the rugged manly man who would carry his girl over the threshold and make her feel as if nothing bad could ever happen to her. Zander didn't have any of those qualities, but he was possibly the most thoughtful guy she knew. On top of that, they all seemed to have taken an intense interest in her, and surprisingly she had a lot in common with all of them. It still amazed her how the guys seemed to know just what to say and do around her. All that being said, she couldn't turn her back on her one friend who has been with her through thick and thin. If it wasn't for Amy's push to divorce Mark, she wouldn't have even had this chance to date the three guys. After Amy left, Stef was alone in her apartment, lying in bed and pondering the situation. Although she wasn't making any decisions right now, she was starting to wonder that maybe she should just dump all three of the guys and go back to her life of hanging out with Amy. She knew that she wasn't going to just give up on her friendship with Amy, she could never do that. She just wasn't sure how Amy would ever come around to accepting any of these guys.

The next day Stef woke up, continuing to stress over the situation. Dexter had called early that morning to see if they could get together. Damn, she told Amy last night she could probably go to Krav Maga just to placate her, but she had also told Dexter that they might be able to get together. She suggested the two of them get together another time, and then casually threw out an invitation to join her and Amy at Krav Maga. Stef still didn't really know what it was and figured Dexter would surely say no after the last kick-boxing class episode with Amy. To Stef's surprise, Dexter said he would go to Krav Maga, joking that he needed to get redemption against Amy. Although this wasn't what Dexter had in mind as a date, he felt as if he couldn't turn down any offer to hang out with her. He was still working to regain her trust after the picnic episode.

Dexter showed up at the Shock and Awe Gladiator Dome later that afternoon. He had never heard of Krav Maga or the Gladiator Dome, but he was a little intrigued to find out what it was. Looking around the room he saw a couple tables set up with fake rubber knives, guns, and several urethane kick-boxing dummies. Perfect he thought to himself, this was exactly the type of class an ex-Navy SEAL should excel at. A few minutes later both Stef and Amy walked in. Stef had told Amy that Dexter was joining them, and after a few minutes of being lectured again about dating, Amy finally accepted that Dexter was joining and joked that it was going to be fun to beat up on the jarhead again.

"Back for more I see? You military guys were never too smart, never know when to give up?" Amy made a quick motion stepping forward to Dexter, pretending she was going to punch him. Dexter actually flinched a little and then laughed. Part of him wished it wasn't considered rude to hit a girl.

Just as Dexter was laughing, the instructor walked to the front of the room. There were about twenty people in the class, only four girls including Stef and Amy. The instructor looked like Dwayne Johnson. He actually made Dexter look small and scrawny, which was not easy to do. He had a steely glare as he walked to the front of the room.

"Look around the room. Not all of you will make it through this class. In fact, by the looks of it I bet most of you won't. You may think you're bad-ass, that you're in shape and know how to fight. Well I have news for you, unless you've been to one of my Krav Maga classes you don't know shit about what it takes to be a fighter. Krav Maga is a form of Israeli street fighting. It is used in situations where death is a likely outcome." The entire class was silent, his words hung over the room. The instructor continued to walk in front of all the students, glaring at them. "For you sissies in the room who don't want to get your asses kicked, I suggest you sit on your thumbs and watch, this isn't the class for you. Save yourself the embarrassment. If the thought of getting punched in the throat, getting your eyes gouged, or—for the boys in the room—getting kicked in the groin over and over until you piss and vomit blood for a week scares you, the door is right there. The front desk will even refund your money. My name is Vince. My friends call me Steel Roundhouse, but you can call me Mr. Vince. I'm your instructor for the class, and after today, I'm also the guy you're going to have nightmares about for the next month. Now that I've introduced myself and given you an idea about what to expect, I'm going to go put my nut cup in while most of you morons collect your things to leave. For the few of you wannabes who still think you want to give it a try, start stretching. I'll be back in two minutes and we'll get started." Everyone at this point started looking around at each other. Normally they would have thought he was joking, but it was clear by Vince's tone that he probably didn't joke often, or ever.

"Wow!" Amy was grinning.

"Let's leave," Stef immediately responded. Kick-boxing seemed like child's play compared to this. There was no way she wanted to stay.

"Are you kidding? This sounds fantastic! I wish I had known about this class sooner." Amy was enthusiastic.

Dexter and Stef just stared at Amy, raising their eyebrows at her words. Although Dexter was as bad-ass as they came and Vince didn't do much to scare him, he could have thought of better things to do on his date with Stef. His definition of date normally didn't include getting kicked in the groin repeatedly until vomiting blood.

"I'm for sure out. You guys can do it, but I'm going to watch on the side." Stef looked at Dexter, thinking he needed to decide what he was going to do.

Dexter paused, knowing he had to decide. On one hand he clearly would rather sit on the sidelines with Stef and watch, which seemed like an easy decision. On the other hand, he knew if he did that he would be ridiculed endlessly by Amy. Although he could deal with that, what message would it send to Stef? He's an ex-Navy SEAL. If he backed down from this, he worried it would make him look like less of a man to Stef. He knew he was already treading on thin ice after their last date. Playing all of those factors out as fast as he could in his head he knew he couldn't ponder it much longer.

"Maybe they'll have a powder puff class you can join next week. Something more your speed?" Amy laughed, taunting Dexter.

"I'm in. I agree it sounds great, like a scaled back version of Navy SEAL training for civilians. A weekend warrior class for people who aren't in great shape." Dexter looked condescendingly at Amy. There was no way he would back down now after that comment; Dexter was too competitive. Stef walked off to the side. She was bummed Dexter hadn't joined her but figured being an ex-Navy SEAL this would be right up his alley.

Vince walked back into the room, there were only eight people left in the class. Stef was watching from the side and all the others had left. As he walked towards the class he walked by one of the punching dummies and let out a thunderous "*Hiyaa!*" and with the velocity of a cannon he hammer-fisted the dummy so hard it knocked it over entirely. The class jumped, and one guy even let out a loud yelp. "It's go time!" Vince shouted with the intensity of a drill sergeant on a 'roid rage, glaring straight into the eyes of the eight remaining students. The only one at this point who was smiling was Amy. Even Dexter was curious about what to expect. What are the odds: his first date ends with a black eye, he gets set up by Dalton on the second date, and now the third date was shaping up to be similar to something out of the movie Fight Club. If he didn't have bad luck, he would have no luck at all.

Vince told everyone to pair up; they were ready to get started. Amy immediately motioned to Dexter, asked him if he was ready for a rematch, and told him, "I hope you wore a titanium cup." Dexter laughed nervously, knowing Amy wasn't kidding. Although Dexter was protected down there, he still didn't feel excited about testing the boundaries of the ten-dollar piece of plastic.

Surprisingly, the intensity and pure testosterone rage from Vince seemed to only escalate once they started the actual class. If he wasn't shouting disparaging remarks at them for being a lazy, out-of-shape piece of shit, he was using them as a guinea pig to show the next move. For some reason much to Dexter's dismay, Vince chose to pick on him the most. The basic principle of Krav Maga was to end any fight as quickly and efficiently as possible, so the most vulnerable parts of the body are targeted.

One move that Vince illustrated on Dexter was a defense to someone trying to choke you. It was simple: Dexter reached for Vince's throat and three moves quickly followed from Vince. The first step was to gouge the attacker's eyes with your thumbs, this would throw your attacker off and they would loosen their grip. Next, you'd follow the eye gouge with repeated knees to the groin. As soon as the attacker fell to the ground from the knees to the groin, you "stomped the shit out of their head." Normally for purposes of sparring, you'd intentionally let up a bit and tried not to hurt your sparring partner, but Vince felt otherwise. He said, "The four gang-bangers in the bar who want to take your money and sodomize you with a pool cue aren't going to just go through the motions. They will bring the heat, so pretend that's the situation in class." While Vince was illustrating the moves on Dexter, Amy continued to raise her hand, asking Vince to repeat certain steps. She first asked him to show her again what he meant by "stomp the shit out of Dexter's head."

"It's like *this!*" Vince shouted as his shoe repeatedly bounced off of the back of Dexter's head, who was laying on the foam mat trying to flex his neck muscles as much as he could to withstand the blows. He glared at Amy who was off to the side watching and quietly giggling at Dexter's head bouncing up and down.

After Vince illustrated the move a couple of more times on Dexter's skull, Amy nodded and then raised her hand, "That helps with the head stomp, but what about the repeated knee to the groin. Can you show us again?" Dexter was fuming inside, although he politely smiled and tried as best as he could to control his temper. Amy was clearly enjoying the sight of Dexter being used as Vince's personal punching bag. He couldn't wait to return the favor on Amy. She would get what's coming to her he thought to himself shortly before getting another punishing blow to his nut cup from Vince's oversized knee.

After Vince illustrated it a few more times, he told the students to pair back up and try it on their sparring partners. *Perfect*, Dexter thought, revenge was going to be sweet.

Amy hopped up to her feet and moved in front of Dexter. "I'll go first, I want to do it while it is fresh in my mind."

Dexter reluctantly agreed, knowing he would get his time sooner or later. As Amy started through the moves, it was clear she was not holding back. The eye gouge, knees to the groin, and head stomping were coming with ferocious intensity. It was like she had been doing this forever. Although Dexter could take the punishment, every move made him more and more anxious to get his chance against her. Amy was clearly strong, stronger than most men. After several rounds of Amy's punishing blows to his groin and head, it was finally his turn. Although Dexter would be the last guy to ever resort to hitting a girl, this was a different situation.

Amy reached up to grab Dexter's neck in a strangle-hold, and Dexter immediately responded by jabbing his thumbs into her eye sockets. Although he was not going to let up much, the one thing that Vince did stress is that the eye gouge should be light. Although

Steel Roundhouse didn't seem to care too much about anyone getting hurt, he drew the line at losing an eye. Probably a good idea. As Dexter reached over to gently place his thumbs near Amy's eyes, she let out a loud scream and fell to the ground. Dexter was stunned; he had no idea what happened. The entire class including Vince came over, Stef also came running onto the mat. Amy had her hands over her face.

"What happened? Are you OK?" Vince had dropped to the floor and placed his hand on Amy's back.

"The bastard jabbed his thumbs deep into my eyes. I thought we were only supposed to lightly do that part?" Amy was crying, or at least appeared to be as she held her face.

Everyone turned to look at Dexter. He was dumbfounded. He hardly touched her eyes, what the hell was she talking about. "Ahhhh, I don't know what she's talking about, I just lightly touched her eyes." Dexter put up his arms in a sign of confusion.

"Can you see, look at me?" Vince asked Amy to move her hands so he could see her face. Amy obliged, moving her hands away and looking at everyone. The students all gasped when they saw Amy's face, her left eye was red and the corner of her socket was bleeding.

As Vince called the onsite medic over to look at her eye everyone turned to look at Dexter, including Stef. Dexter was completely baffled. He had no idea how her eye could have been injured like that. He'd hardly touched her. Stef ran over to be with Amy, and at this point the entire class was sharing time between consoling Amy and giving death stares to Dexter, who was still confused. "I'm sorry, I really didn't think I pushed that hard." Dexter was searching for an explanation.

"Clearly that isn't true, look at her eye." Stef shot a look of disgust at Dexter.

Dexter didn't know what to say. He was speechless, unsure of how to respond. He felt like crawling in a hole, the entire class kept glaring at him.

After a couple of minutes, the medic concluded it wasn't anything serious, a minor flesh wound and abrasion. It would likely clear up in a week or so. Dexter still had no idea what happened, but at this point he was being shunned by the entire class. Stef continued to give him glares and hadn't said a word to him since her earlier comment. The class was ready to get started again, and Amy told everyone to continue without her. Dexter was going to follow suit. He obviously didn't want to continue the class after what happened. Amy walked over to get her bag that was off to the side of the mat, Dexter followed her. It was just the two of them in the corner.

"I'm really sorry, I have no idea what happened. I thought I hardly touched you, but clearly that wasn't the case. I'm so sorry Amy." Dexter was still confused but at this point felt awful, it was as if the entire class hated him. He placed his hand on her shoulder, Amy turned partially towards him and had a big grin on her face.

"Haha, got you jarhead." Amy was whispering, just loud enough for Dexter to hear her, but out of earshot from everyone else. "I did this to myself, figured it would be enough to scare Stef off if she thinks you're a lunatic psycho."

Dexter's mouth dropped open. He was speechless as he absorbed the words that just came out of Amy's mouth. In his mind he was trying to piece it all together. He hadn't done that to Amy's eye after all, so how did she get it to be inflamed and bleeding? Then it occurred to him: she'd dropped to the floor and covered her eyes, and that must have been when she gouged her own eye.

"The stupid dipshit look on your face was hilarious," Amy whispered, then walked away to where Stef was.

Dexter stood in the corner motionless, still in disbelief. Clearly it took someone psychotic and pathological to hurt themselves as a way of making someone else look bad. He was playing through the options in his head. He could tell Stef what really happened, but she would never believe him over her friend. It was too bizarre of a story and Amy obviously knew that—it was all part of her plan. Dexter slowly walked over to Stef, who had now been joined by Amy. He had no idea what to say.

"I'm sorry again Amy, let me try to make it up to you, how about I buy both of you dinner?" Dexter knew it was a stretch but at this point he had nothing to lose. Inside he was irate and wanted to go off on Amy and tell Stef the truth, but he knew that wouldn't work.

"I think I'm going to pass, but you guys go ahead, you should go out. I should probably go home and shut my eyes for awhile." The comment was incredibly out of character for Amy, no slams or disparaging remarks, which was her plan of playing the victim. She was no doubt a good attorney, a master at manipulation.

"No way you are going home alone Amy, I'm coming with you. You need someone to take care of you tonight." Stef put her arm around Amy.

"Thanks Stef, you're a great friend."

That was pretty much it. There was no way the date was going to go any further tonight. In a last-ditch effort, Dexter suggested that he come over and make dinner for both of them, but Amy said she really just wanted to rest her eye. The medic had given her an ice pack and she had placed it over her eye. Dexter knew there wasn't anything else he could do at this point. He would probably try to send both of them flowers the next day as an apology. Although he was furious at Amy, he didn't want to give up on the money, and more than that he was hyper-competitive. Just like he was trained in the Navy, he needed to complete the mission. In a move of desperation, something popped into his mind. It was something he had planned for later in the night but now seemed as good of a time as any. He thought it might help take some of the hatred away from him.

"My cousin is having a party this week to celebrate being done with med school. You guys should both come. He's having it at some Italian restaurant on the east side. I've never been before, but it's called Trattoria Matera. Apparently he's friends with the owner's family." Dexter threw the invite out casually, he couldn't make it sound too obvious. Dexter had seen the pictures on Facebook, and although they hadn't checked-in with the name of the place, he had done a little recon work to figure out the restaurant and connection to Dalton.

Stef stopped cold, immediately recognizing the name as the Italian restaurant Dalton's uncle and aunt owned. She turned to look at Dexter. "What did you say the name of the restaurant was?"

"Trattoria Matera. Why, have you been there? I hadn't heard of it before, but my cousin has a friend of a friend who apparently has connections with it. It is supposed to be one of the better, more authentic Italian places in the city.

Stef paused, not sure how to answer. "It sounds familiar, but maybe I'm thinking of something else." She was sure it was the same place, but obviously didn't want to tell the story about how she had been there.

"Based on what my cousin said, you would probably remember if you had been there. The food is amazing and it's run by an older couple who immigrated here from Italy. My cousin has a friend who knows one of their relatives, some dude named Dalton. You should both definitely come, it's Friday night."

Stef was in shock. She couldn't believe what she was hearing. By some freak coincidence, Dexter's cousin was having his med school graduation party at Dalton's family restaurant. Finally after a lengthy pause, Stef figured she needed to say something. "I don't think we can make it but appreciate the invite. Congrats to your cousin. You said the guy's name is Dalton? That's an unusual name." *What the hell*, she thought to herself. 'That's an unusual name'? Why did she say that? She was kicking herself for the idiotic comment.

"I think that's his name. I don't know, my cousin was telling me about him. Some bigwig politician or lobbyist…something like that. You know the type, probably drives a fancy car, always has a different woman by his side telling them what they want to hear. He's apparently a pretty smooth guy, a real ladies' man. He brings a different girl by the restaurant each week. Kind of a jerk from what I hear, but his uncle and aunt run a great restaurant."

Stef's mouth dropped. Dalton had told her that he never brings girls by the restaurant. Could Dexter be making this story up? There was no way, Stef convinced herself. Dalton and Dexter knew nothing about each other. There were the pictures posted on Facebook, but she wasn't Facebook friends with Dexter yet so he probably wouldn't have seen them. This had to be a legitimate story. Unfortunately for Stef it was certainly more believable that Dalton indeed brought girls to the restaurant, not so much that Dexter was concocting this entire story and had somehow tracked down her relationship with Dalton. She shouldn't be surprised, she'd had a hunch all along. Stef had spaced out for a while thinking how stupid she'd been to fall for Dalton's lines. She had almost forgotten about what happened to Amy and her eye, exactly as Dexter hoped. The news on Dalton completely threw her off. Amy was a few steps away from both of them on her phone, and she didn't hear any of the conversation, which was probably best for Dexter. As Amy and Stef left the Gladiator Dome, Dexter walked into the locker room to get his things. He still didn't consider it even between him and Dalton, but he was getting there. He figured it would be an all-out brawl till the end between the two of them, but Dexter was confident he would still be standing. He was laughing out loud in the locker room as he collected his things. The look on Stef's face had been priceless. He couldn't wait to hear how she confronted poor old Dalton with the accusations. He may have lost this battle having the date end poorly with Stef, but at least he got a good jab in on Dalton and made progress in winning the war.

CHAPTER 19

Blackmail

Mark was sitting at his computer, staring blankly at the monitor. It had been two and a half months since Dexter and Stef's failed date at the Gladiator Dome. Countless dates, romantic weekends away, and competitive jostling continued. Stef was growing closer to all three. That said, the same obstacle to getting close to a proposal kept rearing its ugly head—Amy. They'd just had their sixth meeting at the Liquid Cougar warehouse the night before, and although Ronald didn't overdose on cougar juice and no tires were slashed, the time was spent talking about the overarching theme.

The guys were unanimous: Amy had to go. Stef had developed feelings for all three of them, but each would take a step back after Amy unleashed her influence on Stef. The time had come to do something about it, the question was, what would work best. As Mark was staring off into space trying to come up with a solution, Tony barged into his office.

"Are you surfing leprechaun porn again? I can leave you alone for some private Mark time if that's the case...just clean up after you're finished."

"You're gross. What is leprechaun porn? Forget that, I don't want to know. Sorry, just deep in thought. I'm running into a snag and I don't know how to fix it."

"What's the problem?"

"One word...Amy. She's hell bent on Stef being single, and it seems she'll stop at nothing to make sure it happens."

"Maybe she just needs to get laid. I can help her with that."

"Good luck. There is a rumor she eats her partners after sex."

"That isn't a deterrent," Tony said straight faced.

Mark proceeded to share with Tony everything that had been going on, all based on the reports he had been receiving. Over the past few weeks, Amy had become increasingly clingy to Stef, continuing to "coincidentally" crash many of their dates. Although Stef seemed to be falling for the guys, Amy was a barrier and Mark wasn't confident it would resolve itself on its own. Aside from the obstacle Amy was presenting, Mark thought the leaderboard was starting to unfold. Dexter had been struggling to overcome the early setbacks, although there were things that Stef definitely liked about him. He was likely in third place at this point to Dalton and Zander. She hadn't dumped him, but Dexter was sensing that things weren't going his way and had kicked his efforts into high gear. Dalton on the other hand had recovered nicely from every revenge plot that Dexter threw at him. It was difficult not to believe Dalton. On top of his charismatic charm and princely good looks, there was something about his steely blue eyes that made women want to obey his every wish. Mark started to explain in detail the type of guy Dalton was because he knew the stories would resonate with Tony. Realizing he had gotten off topic, he shifted the conversation back to Amy.

"It's oddly predictable. Amy was the person responsible for Stef pulling the trigger on my divorce, and now she's the person standing in the way of getting out of my alimony payments. I need to get her out of the picture, but I don't know how to do that. I've even considered trying to have Dexter date her since he seems more of a match for her versus Stef, but I doubt it will work to find Amy a boyfriend. She hates all men! In the time I've known her, I don't know that she has ever had or even wanted a boyfriend." Mark looked at Tony. "Outside of hiring a hitman, I have no idea what to do," he said jokingly.

"If you need a hitman Mark I can give you several recommendations…"

Mark laughed, but part of him knew there was at least a tinge of sincerity in Tony's comment.

"Actually, I might have an idea. It's crazy, but worth a shot. Can you send me her contact info and a picture? I feel partially responsible for what happened with the judge, it's the least I can do."

"Although I would love a solution, I'm not sure I'm comfortable with whatever you are talking about. Why do you want her picture and contact information?" Mark was puzzled. He had no idea what Tony was up to, but knew him well enough to suspect it wasn't good.

"Don't worry Mark, it will be a win-win. Everyone will get what they want if it works. Nobody gets hurt, it might even be good for Amy." Tony had an uncharacteristic serious look on his face.

"What are you going to do?"

"It's better if you don't know for now. I'll clue you in if and when the plan works. I don't want to get your hopes up."

Mark paused, unsure of what Tony was talking about and even more unsure why he wouldn't just tell him.

"Mark, trust me, I'm not going to do anything you disapprove of—I promise. Nothing remotely illegal." Tony's words came across as being sincere, and his facial expression confirmed he was being serious. No wisecrack remarks and no smirking. Mark didn't see this side of Tony often, but he knew he could ultimately trust him to look out for his best interests. "You know I could get the info myself, but would rather have your blessing. Just get me her picture and her contact info."

"OK, but promise me this won't jeopardize the overall plan. I can't risk Stef finding out, then I'll have no chance whatsoever in getting her married off." Mark was still a little uneasy about Tony getting involved, but he believed he was being sincere for a change. Mark also felt he didn't have much of a choice at this point—the Amy situation wasn't going away and he couldn't think of any other viable solutions.

"Done, you have my word. If my actions result in Stef finding out, I'll personally pay half of your alimony. Like I always tell strippers, I'll put my money where my mouth is."

Mark laughed, but knew Tony meant it, even the part about paying half his alimony.

"I doubt it is going to work so don't get your hopes up. What I have in mind is a long shot," Tony said as he walked out of Mark's office.

Mark continued to ponder the Amy situation, and although he was optimistic for Tony's help, he knew he couldn't put all his eggs in one basket. Amy was a deal-breaker to his overall plan and her continued presence meant Mark would have to pay alimony. Although he had seriously considered diverting Dexter's efforts onto Amy, he was not convinced it was even worth the effort. At this juncture, he felt like he had to give it a shot. There wasn't much to lose, or so he thought. Mark sent Dexter a text and asked to meet at the warehouse tonight after work. He wasn't going to let any stone go unturned and time was of the essence.

Later that night Mark met up with Dexter at the warehouse. He had thought through the offer: Dexter would steer his efforts away from Stef and towards Amy in an effort to deter her. Dexter would only get a third of the money he originally wanted, but he was already a distant third in his pursuit of Stef and considering he didn't have to marry anyone, it should have been a no-brainer. Some money was better than nothing, was the way that Mark was presenting the offer. All he had to do was distract Amy. It would be a good way to keep Dexter involved and the additional investment from Mark was worth it on both sides—both for Dexter and for Mark.

Dexter listened as Mark explained the concept. Although he was self-aware enough to understand he was in last place, he didn't expect Mark to be giving up on his chances. Mark continued to explain every detail, Dexter would divert his efforts to keeping Amy busy, and if he was successful in doing so he would get one-third of the money. He didn't even have to date Amy (which seemed impossible), he just had to keep her occupied enough so the other guys would have a clear path to Stef. Although Mark explained it was a long shot, it was worth a chance and this would keep Dexter in the game. Dexter hadn't said a word at this point, just listened quietly to Mark.

"What do you think?" Mark looked at Dexter anxiously, knowing there was a chance he could react negatively to the proposition.

"I have a better idea." Dexter had a cold look on his face, staring directly at Mark with intensity. He paused momentarily, letting Mark hang on his words with curiosity. "How about you pay me the full amount I asked for and I won't tell Stef what you are up to? Regardless of whether or not I help you with Amy, you'll pay me the full amount in exchange for my silence." Dexter leaned back in his chair, continuing to stare at Mark. Although he had hoped it wouldn't come to this, he knew all along it would be his exit strategy if his chances of winning the money became grim. Going to Stef would destroy Mark's entire plan, in Dexter's mind it was an offer Mark couldn't refuse. Dexter wasn't going to settle for one-third of the money. He was in it for everything and was certainly not going to willingly walk away with the consolation prize.

Mark sat motionless for a moment, not yet responding to Dexter. This was a scenario he had expected from at least one of the guys. In typical Mark fashion, he had a carefully planned counterattack. "You do realize you signed a contract, right?" Mark thought he'd play along with Dexter's little game for a couple minutes. *This will be fun*, he thought.

"Oh right, I'll be breaching a contract that entitles me to money if I secretly marry your ex-wife, so you can get out of paying alimony. I'm sure the courts will appreciate your argument. I'll take my chances, you can sue me." Dexter's tone had changed from confidence to arrogance.

"You might be right, but I'm asking you nicely not to tell Stef. Don't you think that's part of the guy code? How would you like it if you were in my shoes and someone was doing this to you?" Mark continued to play along. He wasn't quite ready to let Dexter in on his other secret just yet. He pretended to squirm a bit in his chair, just for effect.

"Your problem, not mine. Maybe you should have thought of all this before you concocted this plan or married the gold digger who took you for everything. Aside from all that, go ahead and sue me. In case you hadn't noticed, I don't have much to lose. You are the one that has everything at stake, not me. I rent my apartment and drive a used Honda. You likely have more money in your checking account than I have in my 401k." At this point Dexter was very sure of himself.

"You really have me. I suppose I have no choice but to pay you." Mark shrugged his shoulders, there was a twinge of sarcasm in his voice.

Dexter's face turned to surprise. He hadn't expected Mark to roll that easily. "I'm glad you see it that way. You seem like a good guy and while I think I'm entitled to the money, I was hoping it wouldn't have to get ugly. I hope you know this isn't personal against you. It's really just about the money."

Mark paused. Now was as good of time as any. "Talking about

getting ugly, I heard a funny story about you and a SEAL mission to Bahrain. When was it again that you went on that mission? Was it early 2007?"

Dexter's look of shock turned to slight confusion, although in typical Dexter fashion he did his best to maintain his game face. He glared at Mark, unsure of what to say. "What do you mean? I don't know what you're talking about." It was the only thing Dexter could think of without letting Mark know the comment caught him by surprise.

"Well, I can't be certain of all the details, but rumor has it you and some of your Navy SEAL buddies got involved in a few extracurricular activities. Something crazy about underage girls in a prostitution ring and shooting up a village of innocent civilians. You probably know more about it than I do, I'm just going off of what I heard. Does any of that ring a bell Dex?" Mark leaned in towards Dexter, resting his chin on his hand. Although subtle, Dexter's face began to show signs of discomfort and embarrassment. Exactly what Mark was waiting for, ready to pounce at the first sign Dexter was cracking.

"Um, I don't know what you're talking about," Dexter said, stammering slightly. "I don't think the person you heard that from knows what they are talking about."

"You're probably right, after all he did say the State department closed the investigation after someone with a high rank called in a favor. The copy of the classified report I have at home suggests there was evidence found supporting the involvement of your SEAL team, but I'm sure they would take your word if that report just happened to leak to the media and the story made headlines. I doubt my friend at the *New York Times* would even be interested in the story. Prostitution, government cover-ups, foreign relations with the Middle East, corrupt Navy SEALs...none of that stuff would attract readers." The sarcasm was dripping from Mark's voice. "Who knows though, in the unlikely event that kind of stuff interested readers it could cause real problems for you. Remember that Army platoon that hit the newswires a couple of years ago for raiding that village in Jordan, killing innocent children? I heard they were all dishonorably discharged, losing all of their pay, benefits, and pension. They claimed to be innocent, but the US government couldn't really sit by and do nothing. They almost had no choice but to take action. I can't imagine how difficult it would be to rebuild your credibility after being linked to something like that. Shit like that lives on forever." Mark paused momentarily, letting the words continue to sink in for Dexter. "I'm sorry, I digress. I think we got a little off-topic, how rude of me. You were just explaining how you were going to blackmail me into giving you all of the money..."

The veins in Dexter's neck and forehead were now protruding. Although he was doing his best to retain his composure, this had clearly caught him off guard. His cocky demeanor was now gone as he sat motionless, unsure of what to say. He briefly thought of strangling Mark and dumping his body in the water. "That wasn't me, I wasn't involved in any of that. I tried to stop it, but they wouldn't listen to me. Aside from that, you wouldn't dare release that to the media, it has implications well beyond just me. Other lives will be impacted, not to mention it will cause unrest between the US and Middle East. You have no idea what and who you will be messing with. You will literally be picking a fight with the entire US Navy and some committee-level senators. The case was closed for a reason."

Mark laughed, still smiling at Dexter. "C'mon Dexter, you know how those things work. Shit rolls downhill. The high-ranking senators will immediately claim they have no knowledge of the allegations and say the behavior is morally reprehensible. I'm not going to be anywhere near it. I'll be the anonymous source. I can almost read the prepared statement: 'The individuals responsible for this will be held accountable, every action will be taken.' You and the handful of Navy SEALs that were on the mission will be made an example of. It's an election year, the President certainly doesn't want anything like this hanging over his campaign. Aside from that, you're the one in control here Dexter. You are still calling the shots. You can choose to blackmail me knowing the disruption this will cause not only in your life but countless others, or we can go back to talking about your plan to distract Amy while Dalton and Zander pursue Stef. Still your choice, you have options."

Dexter's jaw was now clenched, the benefit of keeping his cool had passed, and it didn't matter if Mark knew he was upset. The truth was that he was raging inside. Although he had only jokingly thought to himself about killing Mark and dumping his body in the water, it now seemed like a more viable option. It wouldn't be the first time he had killed someone with his bare hands, although this was a little different than his targets in the Navy. Murdering a civilian came with complications he wasn't ready to embrace. Plus he knew Mark was a smart and calculated guy who undoubtedly had taken steps to cover his tracks. If he died, it would likely set off a chain of events that would oust Dexter anyway. He had tracked down all of the intel on Dexter and he wasn't sure how he did it since the information was classified. "So how do you propose I try to distract Amy? Did you forget that I'm trying to date her best friend, and that she hates men? If I agree to this I want 50 percent. I think that's more than fair given the challenge with Amy."

"For starters I think you can use all of the energy and anger you feel towards me and divert it to trying to distract Amy. I agree there are some challenges involved with the idea, but if we put our heads together we can come up with a plan. You aren't that close to Stef yet. She is clearly more interested in Dalton and Zander. You should be able to let the breakup naturally run its course. Just quit calling her, it will die off. As for Amy, focus on the exercise and workout angle. You both love to do that, and that's when you can also expect to get her away from Stef. Try to engage her in conversation on topics that she can control, one idea is legal advice. Make up some kind of situation that you need her advice for and strike up a conversation that way. She always likes to be in control, and my advice is to work on exploiting that."

"Maybe I can ask her how to legally blackmail someone or get away with murder?" Although the comment was intended to be sarcastic, Dexter sat stone-faced. There was an element of sincerity in his tone.

Mark smiled, although he too knew that Dexter was not a guy you wanted to cross too often. He was thankful the dirt he had on him was devastating, still giving Mark the upper hand. Once he'd narrowed it down to the final three guys, he secretly had a thorough background check done on each of them. He wanted to be sure the guys weren't complete con artists or lunatics, and just as important he needed some kind of dirt on each of them, for this exact type of situation. Mark knew the type of person signing up for this would also try to double-cross him at any opportunity.

"You could try that angle," Mark said, playing along. "Most women would be scared away by those questions, but as you know Amy is not most women. Murder and blackmail would likely be a turn-on for her, particularly if she knew I was the target." Mark's smirk grew wider as he finished the sentence. "Kidding aside, I do want to make sure you and I are still on the same team. I don't need to like you, you don't need to like me. I'm fairly certain you probably won't, but we still have the same goal. You want money, and I want Stef to get married. I could have easily cut you out entirely after you tried to blackmail me, but your secrets are safe with me so long as you hold up your end of the deal. Given what we know about each other, we make much better friends than enemies. Tell you what, as a show of good faith I will agree to pay you 50 percent, like you're asking, if you're successful."

Dexter nodded reluctantly, still steaming from the position he was in and walked away without saying a word.

As Mark drove away from the warehouse he was pleased with the outcome. Although putting Dexter on assignment with Amy was a long shot, there wasn't much downside.

Romantic Weekends

Once the news broke to Dalton and Zander that Dexter was essentially out of the mix, the competition for Stef's hand in a sham marriage grew even stronger. Over the next few weeks Dalton's arrogance also grew. He felt he was single-handedly responsible for Dexter's demise and still wasn't convinced Zander was legitimate competition. Dalton showered her with gifts, even springing for a trip to Italy with her in a couple of months. Capitalizing on the fact he had to be in London for work, he invited Stef to join him. Following his work assignment, they would leave London and spend a few days in a chateau in the foothills of the Italian Alps. Although the expense would off-set the $300,000 he expected to receive after winning, it was a small investment, and no doubt would be fun. In Italy he would tell Stef of his desire to "spend the rest of their lives together," and he had even worked it out with the chateau to handle the formal nuptials if she accepted. Italian wine, great food, and fantastic sex in one of the most romantic spots in the world—most women would give their ovaries to take a trip like this with Dalton. He was convinced there was no way Stef would refuse him. Stef was falling for him, but what woman wouldn't.

While Dalton was wooing Stef with gifts and European trips, Zander was scheming a plan that had equal parts offense and defense. From an offensive perspective, Zander had spent much of his time focused on very personal details—all things he knew about Stef from the playbook but led her to believe he was just interested and wanting to know. One example was Stef's family and her late parents. He wanted to know every detail as if he knew what it would have been like to meet them. From a defensive perspective, he never missed an opportunity to lay doubt in Stef's mind about men who were perceived players. Zander had built himself up to be the complete opposite of a player—loyal, unassuming, and genuine. It was a plan that was going to play itself out even more in the hours to come.

As Stef stepped out of her car and started walking through the dew-filled grass of the cemetery, she noticed a person kneeling in the exact spot she was headed. *That's odd*, she thought. She very rarely ran into anyone here. It had been over eight years since her parent's death, and it always made Stef sad to know the visits from others dropped off with each year that passed. She was happy to see someone else there and curious who it was. She picked up her pace. It was a route she knew well and had traveled countless times over the last eight years. As she grew closer, she could tell it was a man, someone by himself. Once she was within ten feet or so, the man heard footsteps and turned his head, making eye contact with Stef. Stef stopped cold upon recognizing who it was.

"Zander?" Stef said surprised, barely getting the words out.

"Hi Stef." Zander stood up, showing a faint smile. Although he was happy to see her, he needed to be respectful of the situation.

"What…what are you doing here?" Stef was still surprised, absorbing the encounter.

"I'm sorry, maybe I shouldn't have come. I'll go now and give you some time alone." Zander knew there was a chance his plan could backfire and Stef would view this as a violation of her privacy. His comment would help diffuse the chance of that happening.

"No, I mean I'm just surprised to see you here, I didn't mean you should go. I just didn't expect to see you. I noticed someone kneeling by the tombstone from a distance, but I figured it was one of my parent's friends."

"I wanted to pay my respects. I remembered today was your parent's anniversary. Even though we never had the fortune to meet, I feel like I know them."

Stef body tingled listening to Zander's words. She had been coming to visit her parents every day on their anniversary since their passing. There were only two people in the entire world she had ever told: Amy and of course Mark. Emotion started to overtake her, tears welling up in her eyes.

"I'm sorry Zander," Stef said as she wiped the tears away. "That's very touching, I'm a little overcome with emotion." Zander stood up and hugged Stef, locking her in a long embrace.

Stef and Zander spent the next forty-five minutes kneeling near the tombstone, with Stef passing the time by telling stories about her parents. Zander had listened to stories about her family before, but today was particularly emotional. She told stories about how her dad used to read to her before bed when she was a little girl and how the three of them used to pick out pumpkins at the corn maze every year for Halloween. Stef loved how Zander listened to her and seemed genuinely interested. It was as if nothing or nobody else existed to him when they were together.

After Stef finished the corn maze story, there was a lull in the conversation, it was the opening that Zander had been waiting for. "As much as I don't want to, I should go. I want to give you some time alone with your parents, Stef. I appreciate you sharing the memories and moments with me, and I'm glad you weren't upset that I was here. I didn't expect to run into you." Obviously, Zander knew she would be there, and he knew how important it was for her to visit on their anniversary. He also knew she had only told Mark and Amy about it. It couldn't have gone any better or been planned more perfect. Although Zander was still motivated by the money, with each passing week he had grown closer and closer to Stef. While he forced himself to not get emotionally attached, it was getting more difficult.

Stef didn't want Zander to go. It was nice to have someone there to share the moment with. "You can stay Zander, you don't need to go."

Zander paused. "No, you need this time alone. It's important to have that." Zander didn't say it but he didn't need to, Stef knew he was referring to his visits to his grandma's grave. He would routinely go, and both he and Stef had talked about how important those things in life are.

Stef smiled, hugging Zander and kissing him before he turned and walked away slowly. As Stef watched him, her mind wandered about how great of a man Zander was. Not many guys would do that. In fact she didn't know of anyone who would. Zander continued to raise the bar when it came to sensitivity and thoughtfulness. Ever since their first encounter in her store and his painting, he always seemed to do something that surpassed even the lofty expectations he had set. It didn't seem to be a passing fad with Zander. It had been several months and Zander had yet to show any signs of tiring in his ambition. She really felt like she was falling in love with him. Once he was well off in the distance, Stef kneeled down again at the tombstone. She thought she would place the flowers she brought at the base of the tombstone, and do the same with the flowers Zander had placed on the ground. As she reached to pick them up, she noticed a small card attached to his flowers. Stef took the card thinking it was one that had mistakenly been placed in the bunch of flowers. Seeing it was sealed, her curiosity got the best of her and she decided to open it. Slowly pulling the card from the envelope, she read the note—it was a thank-you card.

> *Unfortunately we never had the chance to meet, but if we had I would have reserved this day to not only wish you a happy anniversary but also to say thank you. Your wedding day was not only a special day in which the two of you shared your love for each other, but it was also the day that made possible for me to meet your beautiful and amazing daughter. It's clear from the many stories Stef has shared with me that your marriage was filled with countless happy memories and love—and one of the greatest accomplishments was bringing your daughter into the world. You have my word, I will be there for her and support her every way that I can.*
> *With love,*
> *Zander*

Tears started to stream down her face. She read the note over and over, absorbing every word, each time more overcome with emotion. It was as if it was ripped from a romance novel. Nobody had ever said anything so heartfelt and kind about her before. Stef stayed kneeling by the gravesite for another fifteen minutes, her mind racing with emotion, reading the note over and over. She never felt a stronger feeling of emotional attachment or love than she did at that very moment with Zander.

Off in the distance Zander peered through his binoculars wanting to make sure Stef saw the note. Originally he thought she might see it right away and ask. Although reading it in front of him would have worked, he preferred to witness her reaction from afar. This way it was pure and uninhibited. It also showed again that he was selfless; he didn't write it to impress. *Certainly not a quality that Dalton possessed*, he thought.

Everything was going as planned. Although he wasn't concerned about playboy Dalton, he knew Dalton was going to move fast. He had heard about the Italy trip and suspected it was part of Dalton's grand plan—the proposal. Zander still liked his chances and was confident he would win, but he also couldn't underestimate the "in the moment" power of Dalton's charm, his good looks, and a romantic Italian villa. Stef was easily influenced, and any girl could fall for that and have a hard time saying no to fairy-tale type of life. He was going to stay the course, trying to defeat Dalton with his Achilles heel—could he be trusted or would he eventually just revert to his playboy ways? Zander would do everything in his power to convince Stef it was the latter, and he had a few tricks up his sleeve yet that would help ensure that was the case.

Poker Night

The guys arrived at Mark's house promptly at seven p.m.; poker night was long overdue. Between Mark's work schedule and managing the Megslist Husband project, he hadn't been able to keep up with his social calendar as much as he would have liked. Tyson was excited too. He had been spending more than his fair share of time at the Dog Den. Although the catalyst for getting together was poker, the guys were anxious to get an update from Mark on what had been transpiring with Stef. He had kept them up to speed a bit by email but there was a lot to talk about. He wanted and needed their advice on getting rid of Amy.

"Are those hickeys, Ronald?" Steve was sitting down at the poker table and happened to notice large and apparent bruises peppering his neck.

"Hell yeah…aren't they awesome? It took long enough for you to notice! I was interviewing a girl for a job at the theater last week and things went well. *Really* well, if you know what I mean." Ronald was smiling and giggling excitedly like a schoolgirl, using air quotes when he said "if you know what I mean."

The guys all stared at Ronald, giving him the same look they always did when something ridiculous came out of his mouth. Steve finally broke the silence. "Ronald, Ronald, Ronald. For starters, how many times do we have to explain the proper use of air quotes to you? When will you learn?" Ronald was always using air quotes in situations when they weren't called for and it didn't make sense. He also would use the phrase "no pun intended" often, but never in situations when there was an actual pun. He seemed to think every phrase qualified as a pun. For example he would say "speak now or forever hold your peace, no pun intended." The air quotes and no pun intended had become a standing joke for the guys, not that Ronald needed more help. "Aside from that, I shouldn't be surprised by this either but do you really think hooking up with a girl you are interviewing for a job is a good idea?"

"I know what you're thinking Steve, and I agree. I told her that if she's hired she could only give me hickeys in areas where the other theater girls couldn't see them, to avoid jealous coworkers. Like the one she gave me here…" Ronald stood up and started to undo his belt and unbutton his pants.

"Whoa!" Christian shouted, starting to laugh as Mark and Steve turned away, groaning Ronald's name in disgust. "Easy Peter Pan, we'll just take your word for it!" Christian was laughing as he successfully convinced Ronald to sit back down and keep his pants on.

"Sorry guys, aren't they super cool though? Check them out." Ronald was grinning from ear to ear as he pointed to his neck that was two-thirds covered in black and blue golf-ball size hickeys.

"No Ronald, hickeys were cool when we were in high school, maybe. You missed the window by about fifteen years. Now they are trashy and just weird. Plus your theory on why it was OK to hook up with the girl you interviewed is absurd. Haven't you ever heard of sexual harassment?"

"That only applies if you don't wear a condom. I remember that from the HR video we had to watch." Ronald looked smugly at Steve, crossing his arms as if he had just made a game winning chess move.

Christian just sat back in his chair smirking the entire time, although normally he has the wise cracks, he was just enjoying the banter between Steve and Ronald. Steve paused for a moment, just shaking his head in disbelief. "Let me get this straight, you think it is OK to hook up with a girl you interviewed for a job as long as, if she's hired, she only gives you hickeys in places where the other girls can't see them... in addition the law will protect you if she files a sexual harassment claim against you so long as you wear a condom?"

"Yes Steve, that's how it works in the corporate world. It's probably different since you're a teacher. You can just freely go nailing your students, but we have strict laws in the business world that we have to adhere to."

"Wait, so now you're saying this is the law for corporations, and teachers can just do whatever they want and won't be held responsible for harassment ever?"

"He does have a point Steve. I nailed several of my teachers in high school and college...they didn't seem to mind. In fact I think they talked pretty freely to each other about me." Christian couldn't resist interjecting on that one. Mark was still silent, just enjoying the discussion.

"Shut up Christian. Ronald, that's absurd—on every level. I'm not sure where to start. For one, it's sexist. Second, you could get sued. I'm worried about you."

"I think we should just agree to disagree Steve, no pun intended." Ronald looked over at Christian for affirmation, and Christian responded with a wink and nod, using air quotes. Ronald beamed with excitement. In his mind, he'd just won the chess match.

"OK guys, now that we have that settled, let's regroup and start playing cards. Plus, I need to get your advice on the Stef situation." Mark started dealing, but he was anxious to get their perspective, particularly on Amy. Nothing seemed to be working and he was increasingly worried a solution wasn't anywhere on the horizon.

Mark gave them a thumbnail sketch of where things stood. Both Zander and Dalton were making impressive strides with Stef and it was difficult to know at this point who had the upper hand. He talked about the lavish Italy trip that Dalton was planning, and how Zander continued down the path of being the "sensitive and caring one." From that perspective, the plan couldn't have been working better. Jason, the private eye he had trailing them, had very positive reports on their progress. He was optimistic. The hang-up was almost solely with Amy.

Although Dexter had been reassigned to try and consume some of her time, that plan didn't have a strong chance at succeeding. Mark had learned that Dexter couldn't just ask Amy out, so he'd tried the fitness angle, pushing her to be his workout partner on a regular basis. So far not only had the plan failed, but Dexter was tired of the continuous beatings he would take in the gym. Amy's intensity only seemed to increase in terms of the type of activities she was interested in. Dexter was forced to attend daily sessions of Muay Thai, jujitsu, Krav Maga, and even some bizarre fighting methods he hadn't heard of. While Dexter would never admit it, Mark had the impression that Dexter was tired of taking a beating, and his ego and self-esteem were wavering. Apparently even Navy SEALs had their limits. Mark had considered offering Dexter a little more money to stay in the game with Amy but thought it might be pouring money on a lost cause. The guys all listened quietly to Mark, even Tyson was tuning into the story and predicament. Mark still had confidence in the other part of the plan. Zander and Dalton were extremely close to Stef, and he knew she was falling for both. His concern was that as they grew closer to proposing, Amy would turn it into an eleventh-hour stalemate. Finally, Mark took a breath and asked for the guys' opinions.

Steve had concerns it wasn't a great idea from the beginning, so maybe this was a sign. He didn't have any solutions for the Amy issue. Christian thought it was going great and just said full steam ahead, but he offered no real solution for getting rid of Amy. Ronald seemed to still be too focused on his hickeys to provide any kind of meaningful input. The game continued into the late-night hours. Although Mark had a great time, he unfortunately wasn't getting any input on what to do.

The game didn't wrap up until two a.m., and after Mark took Tyson out, he was back in the apartment continuing to obsess over his situation. Although he didn't think Steve was right, he was frustrated and unsure of what his next move should be. He wasn't a quitter, but he clearly needed a new strategy for Amy. He didn't sleep much that night, his mind racing.

The next morning Mark had been in his office for a couple hours, still trying to wake up from the late-night poker episode when he noticed an email come through, it was from Dexter:

> *Mark,*
> *This just isn't going to work with Amy. I'm out.*
> *Dex*

Mark stared at the email, the words weighing heavily on his already beaten-down spirit. Although it had seemed inevitable that Dexter wasn't going to be successful, the actual email was just another nail in the coffin. Although Dexter asked him to not try and talk him out of it, Mark knew he had to at least try. He knew the chances were slim but he sent Dexter an email back asking to meet at the warehouse to discuss face to face, Mark expressed confidence to Dexter they could figure something out. It was a long shot but Mark felt he had no choice. He had spent most of the night thinking about the years of expensive alimony payments, and it was increasingly seeming like he was stuck. Although he hadn't forgotten about the discussion he had with Tony, it had been several weeks and Tony hadn't said anything more about it. It was probably another one of his crazy ideas, and Mark was foolish for getting his hopes up.

The next day Dexter never showed up at the warehouse. Although he hadn't replied to the email, Mark had still held out hope—only to be stood up. Alone at the warehouse and realizing Dexter wasn't coming, Mark decided to take a walk and clear his mind. He hadn't slept much the night before and was starting to question the entire mission of getting Stef married. His confidence was shaken, he felt up against the ropes. He tried to pump himself up a bit. Although the alimony payments were burying him, it wasn't as if he was dying. He still had plenty to be grateful for—a great job, fun friends, Tyson, and unlimited possibilities now that he was single. Most people would kill for a life like his. Perhaps he did start to obsess over the alimony issue too much. Although he got screwed by the judge, everything happened for a reason—even when you have no idea at the time what the reason could be. Maybe it was time to let the entire situation go. At the very least he had some amazing stories. Maybe he could write a book or sell the movie rights? Mark joked to himself as he got into his car and drove back to his office. *What an emotional rollercoaster*, he thought.

Later that night Mark was at home enjoying a quiet night with Tyson when his cell buzzed. He let it go the first time, knowing it was late, and whatever it was it could wait until the morning. The phone buzzed a second time, Mark again decided to ignore it. After a third time Mark got up and walked over to get his phone, at least he thought he should check to see who it is. He saw that it was Tony. Although Tony would call him at all hours, his topics ranged from the latest girl he just hooked up with to prank phone calls. Normal things for a fifty-plus-year-old! That said, it was unusual for him to call three times. Just as he was about to dial Tony, the phone rang again.

"Hey Tony, is everything OK?"

"Can you meet me in twenty minutes for a drink? I have something to show you." Tony sounded enthusiastic but serious at the same time.

"Is everything OK? Can you just tell me about it now?"

"It's better if we meet, you won't regret it. I'll be at the Silver Dollar bar, on the corner of Third and Franklin."

Mark was annoyed, but at the same time intrigued—it must be important. Mark confirmed it wasn't some stupid prank to hook him up with a girl or another one of Tony's antics. "OK, I'll be right there, give me thirty minutes."

As Mark drove to the bar, his mind was racing with what it could be. *Show you something*, he thought, why couldn't Tony just tell him? He was going to be so pissed if Tony got a tattoo or something ridiculous and had dragged him away from a quiet night at home just to show it off.

Mark showed up at the bar, spotting Tony with a hot brunette cocktail waitress. She was sitting on his lap laughing. Tony flagged Mark over.

"Mark, meet my new friend Erica…I was just telling her all about you. Young, successful, single—and about to be even richer thanks to me." Erica was giggling as her eyes homed in on Mark, sizing him up like he was a turkey on Thanksgiving. "Please give us a moment Erica. I need to fill my friend in on some news…but don't go far." They both watched her walk away, wearing a short form-fitting skirt shaped to her body.

"So...you are going to make me rich Tony? I'm all ears, this clearly sounds like it was worth me leaving my house for. Are you resigning and making me CEO?" Mark joked, but was curious.

"Even better." Tony put his hand in his jacket pocket and pulled his phone out. He pulled up an email and set the phone in front of Mark. "Read it."

Liquid Cougar Blazes New Ground, Launches First-Ever Woman vs. Man Mixed Martial Arts Fighting League. Names League Spokeswoman.

Liquid Cougar shocked the sports world today by confirming reports that it is moving forward with a controversial new MMA league, pitting women against men in the octagon. The Nevada fighting commission is said to have conditionally approved the license, but no official statement from the commission has been released. Liquid Cougar has scheduled a press conference today to unveil their new endeavor, but a source close to Liquid Cougar is confirming the report.

It is reported that the "Liquid Cougar League" is set to launch soon, and will showcase their first main event at Caesar's Palace. Relative unknown fighter Amy Brightman is said to be the league president, and also scheduled to fight in the main launch event. At the time of publication, Miss Brightman had not yet replied to our inquiry.

Mark read and re-read the article, unsure if this was a hoax or joke by Tony, finally he asked, "Is this for real?"

"Amy signed a three-year contract. She moves to Vegas in a week." Tony was beaming with excitement. "A reporter is breaking the story tomorrow first thing in the morning and sent me this as a heads up."

"This is crazy…man vs. woman MMA? Amy is the president *and* a fighter?" Are you shitting me?" Mark was still having a hard time comprehending it all. This seemed even far-fetched for Tony.

"I have wanted to tell you for the weeks we had this in the works, but I couldn't. It took forever for the Nevada Fighting Commission to approve it. Those bastards, I even had to use our connections in Mexico and pretend we were going to launch across the border. Finally, when Nevada figured out they may lose the deal to Mexico they caved. It was far too big of an opportunity for them to pass up. As you were telling me about your friend Amy, I thought this may be the perfect way to divert her attention elsewhere. We originally had someone else lined up for the job, but I slow-played the other candidate when you told me about Amy. I should mention, for what it's worth, you did me as big of a favor as I'm doing for you. Amy is bat-shit crazy, she's straight out of some kind of fucked-up fight camp. We had her in the gym last week and she knocked three guys unconscious, the fourth guy refused to fight her. I would have picked her just to help you, but she was clearly made for this. Liquid Cougar's sales growth was starting to slow, the energy drink business has been great, but we needed to diversify. This is going to be huge."

Mark's mind was racing as he was absorbing everything. Although he was thrilled that Amy was going to be out of the picture, the entire situation was still too bizarre to believe. "I don't even know what to say. Was Amy hard to convince?"

"Although convincing women to do things for me is something of a personal expertise…" Tony grinned as he paused for effect, "this took little encouragement on my part." I called her up personally, proposed the idea and before we even got to the numbers and salary, she wanted to sign up. I'm telling you, this chick *loves* to beat the shit out of guys. Although I made her an offer she couldn't refuse, just so she wouldn't back out, she may have done it for free. She just loves beating up dudes, plain and simple."

Mark smiled…the story was starting to sink in. It was still far-fetched and crazy, but everything that took place so far was similar. Amy's bizarre intervention to convince Stef to divorce Mark, Tony sleeping with the judge's daughter, the crazy alimony verdict, the Megslist ad to find a guy to marry Stef, the auditions, the playbook, and now woman vs. man MMA. "I wonder if Stef knows? This is big, I need to get the word out to Dalton and Zander. No doubt their odds just increased by a factor of ten." Mark grinned with excitement. The two toasted their victory and ordered several more rounds, ending up sitting at the bar for two hours.

The next morning Amy stopped by and broke the news to Stef. Although Amy suspected Stef would take the news hard, her emotions were both sadness and relief. While Amy was the only real girlfriend she had, lately her destructive remarks towards Zander and Dalton were too much to handle. Vegas was a flight away, and it was clear to Stef how one-sided the relationship was. Stef felt it would also make things with guys she was dating a bit simpler. After delivering the news, Amy left to attend the Liquid Cougar press conference and prepare for the move. The door closed, and it was clear that Stef would only see Amy a few more times before she left. Knowing how wrapped up Amy would be with her new opportunity, it was going to be even less than she thought.

Although Mark was invited to the press conference, he knew he couldn't risk it. There was a chance Stef would be there and certainly a high likelihood that Amy would see him and start to question his attendance. That said, he couldn't resist watching it online. The event was even more bizarre than he expected. Every major media outlet was there to cover it, and Liquid Cougar stock was skyrocketing as soon as the market opened. The shock value of the story was hard to ignore. Violence and sex attract viewers, and this had elements of both. Several organizations were also there protesting the event. That only added to the attention.

The CEO of Liquid Cougar spoke first, officially announcing the venture. As soon as the CEO was finished, he introduced Amy to say a few words. This was the moment everyone was waiting for—who was Amy? Although the company had certainly coached her what to say, it was predictable that Amy wouldn't take their advice. Her initial remark as she pointed to the protesters was, "Hey, 1985 called and they want their signs back." She then proceeded to deliver a very passionate and articulate speech about why this was actually positive for everyone—most of all women. "This puts women on equal footing," she explained. "We don't need our own league or any special treatment." To Amy's way of thinking, the support groups, the protestors, and many of the 'women power' talks all just supported the false notion that they were inferior. Although Amy started out being a frequent supporter of those groups, over time she began to feel they were part of the problem. She applauded Liquid Cougar for being a progressive organization, and of course closed her speech off by delivering a challenge to all male MMA fighters. If they didn't embrace the Liquid Cougar League, they were cowards, afraid of losing.

Before taking questions from reporters, Liquid Cougar played a trailer to introduce the new league. To say the trailer was over the top was an understatement. It showed Amy beating the shit out of guys while sparring in the gym, and also real-life *National Geographic* videos of cougars in the wild violently mauling their prey. It was a bizarre montage that as much stunned the crowd as it did get them fired up about the new league. They even brought in caged cougars to pose with Amy. Reporters were aggressively raising their hands to get their questions answered. This was by far the biggest story of the day and probably the biggest entertainment story of the month. Everyone wanted to know more about Amy: who was she, had she been fighting long, why hadn't anyone heard of her before? Amy was in her element, verbally pouncing on reporters that were challenging the league.

The press conference concluded; it was a clear success. Liquid Cougar was the number one trending hashtag on Twitter and journalists were feverishly typing away to get their stories online. The stock was up another 10 percent after the press conference, now over 50 percent for the day. Analysts were revising their earnings estimates, quantifying what the new league meant economically. Mark was still slightly shocked by everything, but the pragmatic side of him started to kick in. The next step was alerting Zander and Dalton to the news, in case they didn't already know. This was huge, and no doubt Stef knew by now. Likely a bit distraught, and still trying to grasp the fact that her best and really only female friend was moving to Vegas.

Unfortunately for Zander he was going to miss the first-mover advantage getting to Stef. In a stroke of luck, Dalton already had plans to meet Stef for lunch. As he walked into the restaurant, he noticed Stef sitting at the table, a somber look on her face. Dalton had not heard the news.

"Hey gorgeous, is this seat taken?" Dalton's signature grin shined.

"Hi," Stef said, working to eke out a half-smile. She thought about canceling the lunch but figured it would be rude, and quite frankly she needed someone to talk to.

"What's wrong?" Dalton quickly picked up Stef was not her normal self.

"You probably don't want to hear about my problems…" Stef was a little concerned that Dalton would see it as a sign of weakness that she was taking the Amy news hard. *This was a good test*, she thought.

She knew how Zander would respond but less certain how empathic Dalton would be.

"Of course I do, I'm here to help you. I hope you know that Stef. If you don't, then I'll just have to keep reminding you," Dalton smirked. "No matter what it is, I always want to know. A bad day with you is much better than a good day anywhere else." As usual, Dalton had a way with words.

Stef was blushing. Not only did Dalton know exactly what to say, but he was so damn good looking. It wasn't lost on Stef that most of the women nearby had been checking him out ever since he arrived. "Amy is moving to Las Vegas. She just took a new job and will leave in a few weeks."

"Oh my gosh, I'm so sorry, I had no idea. Did you just find out?"

Stef walked through the entire situation with Dalton, explaining the Liquid Cougar League and her conversation this morning. Dalton was surprised, but immediately recognized the huge opportunity this presented. He understood how it changed the game, and was curious if it was somehow Mark's doing. Although on the outside, he was projecting empathy and concern, on the inside he was thinking how perfect it was, timed incredibly well for their Italy trip. He found it difficult to contain his excitement.

After Stef explained the situation and Dalton empathetically listened, he asked "What are you doing this afternoon?"

"No plans, I don't work today. I was supposed to work out with Amy, but I don't think that's happening now, she's busy...with her new 'situation.'"

"Perfect. I'm going to take the rest of the afternoon off. I only have a few meetings, but I'll have my admin reschedule. I have an idea." Dalton took out his phone, emailing his admin to reschedule the meetings.

Stef was a little taken aback. She didn't expect Dalton to be quite so empathetic. "Are you sure? You don't need to do that, Dalton."

"Not even a question, it's already done." He smiled as he just hit the send button on the email to his admin. "Now just one more phone call to make and our afternoon will be set."

"Eduardo, hey buddy, it's Dalton. I need a favor. I'm coming over with Stef in about an hour, can you take care of us?" Eduardo was indeed a friend of Dalton's, and he was the general manager of the Four Seasons Spa. It just opened a few months ago and was difficult to get into, not to mention expensive. Dalton remained cryptic on the call, he could tell Stef's curiosity was piqued. She didn't know Eduardo and was even shocked that Dalton used her name in the discussion. Dalton confirmed everything and hung up, saying nothing to Stef verbally, but his grin said it all.

"What are we doing?" Stef was now smiling, anxious to hear more.

Dalton debated keeping her in suspense but decided to fill her in. He explained the spa and what they had planned for the afternoon. "Massages, pedicures, facials...whatever you want, Eduardo's team is at our disposal."

Stef was beaming. Not only did she love going to spas, but she had been excited to see the new Four Seasons. In addition, she was more than touched that Dalton was taking the afternoon off and had spontaneously set this up just for her. He really cared about her feelings.

They hurried through lunch, anxious for the spa adventure to start. Dalton as usual was oozing with confidence. He knew he had scored major points in the race to Stef's heart. "This will help prepare us for those Italian spas in a few weeks!" Dalton let the words hang, subtly reminding Stef they would be in Italy together soon. For now, Stef had forgotten about the Amy news, her mind racing, thinking about how sexy Dalton was and their day together at the spa.

When they arrived, Eduardo greeted them. He advised they could choose any variety of spa services they wanted, and he had even hooked them up with a room for the night—no charge. Dalton hadn't been expecting that; it caught him off guard. He had been extra cautious to slow play the physical aspect of their relationship. Although they had certainly messed around, they hadn't had sex yet, and he knew it was a fine line to balance. He had a reputation as a player—the last thing he wanted to do was scare her off. He took the key, but indicated they weren't going to stay the night. That said, it might be nice to have access to a room and Eduardo said it had a fantastic view. At the very least they could check it out. Dalton watched Stef's body language closely, she didn't seem to show that she was concerned.

The afternoon couldn't have been better, for over four hours they worked their way through everything the spa had to offer, even a couples massage. Although Stef had seen Dalton with his shirt off a couple of times before, it had always been dark. She never had a full appreciation for his ripped body. She felt her face turn red and her body warm when Dalton walked into the massage room with nothing but a towel on. Seriously she thought to herself, is there anything about him that wasn't amazing? Not only was he tall, dark, and handsome, but he had perfect hair, teeth, and said all the right things. Now she could add a ripped body to the list of reasons why any woman would kill to be with him. At the end of the day, Eduardo gave them access to a private hot tub. It felt like they were in the middle of a tropical oasis, steam was rising off the water and the smell of eucalyptus permeated the room. The setting was romantic, and at this point Stef was completely relaxed and inching closer and closer to Dalton. Their legs and feet touching underwater, their bodies getting closer each minute. The sexual tension was starting to rise. For the next half hour, not many words were shared, but they weren't necessary.

After spending too long in the hot tub, they both went to their respective locker rooms. As Stef was showering, she closed her eyes. Starting to imagine what Dalton's body looked like in the steamy shower with hot water and soap dripping off it. *Too bad the showers aren't co-ed*, she thought.

They met in the lobby. When Stef came out, Dalton was already talking to Eduardo. "I have good news and bad news." Dalton looked at Stef with a sarcastic look on his face. "Eduardo is going above and beyond. We can stay for dinner and he'll comp our meal. The bad news: you have to spend more time with me."

Although Stef hadn't intended to spend the entire day with Dalton, it was an offer she'd be crazy to refuse. She really had no reason to go home yet, and it was a great diversion not to think about the Amy news.

"Eduardo said we could probably still catch the sunset from the room he got for us if we want to check it out before dinner. It's on the fifty-fifth floor and has some of the best views in the city." Dalton wasn't sure when to play the room card; it was a little risky. That said, he thought this was as innocent as possible. Stef accepted the invite.

As they arrived in the room, the sexual tension that had started in the hot tub continued to elevate. Although Dalton's mind was focused on his end goal, he couldn't help but be sexually attracted to her. It was an unusual situation for him. Normally he would have slept with Stef a long time ago or discarded her. The fact that he had to hold off made it even more tempting. Eduardo was right, the view was amazing—the floor-to-ceiling windows couldn't have captured a better picture of the sunset. They stood close to each other watching the horizon. Dalton thought this was as good of a time as any to move in for a kiss. He gently touched her hand, lightly pulling her close to him. With his other hand, he slowly caressed her cheek, pausing momentarily before kissing her. Their lips touched, gently at first, then becoming more passionate. Dalton was cautious, but he could tell Stef wanted him. Their hands started to move up and down each other's body, Stef pulled Dalton's T-shirt over his head.

After seeing Dalton in the spa and fantasizing about his wet body, Stef could hardly wait to run her hands all over his chest. Pressed against the window, Dalton picked Stef up and took her over to the bed. The sexual energy that had been building up throughout the day was now exploding. Dalton knew this was game time, and he didn't lack the confidence needed. He would show Stef things she had never experienced before, certainly nothing she would experience with Zander. After teasing Stef to the point just before orgasm several times, he could tell Stef was ready to burst. When he finally entered her, she let out a primal scream, her eyes rolling back into her head. This was the first time Stef had been with anyone since Mark, and Dalton was hitting all the right buttons. After rolling around in bed for a couple hours, both passed out from exhaustion. After joking about completely blowing off the dinner reservation, they were famished and ordered room service. They ended up spending the night together at the Four Seasons after all.

From Stef's perspective, two things were clear that night: not much sleeping occurred and Dalton's machismo and sex-appeal catapulted him into first place. Zander still had part of Stef's heart, but the rest of her body was owned by Dalton. This was particularly true since Stef was in a weakened emotional position on the heels of the Amy news earlier that day.

Several times throughout the evening, Stef's phone would buzz. Dalton laughed to himself, thinking it was probably Zander, trying to talk with Stef about the Amy news. As Dalton pressed up against Stef's naked body in a Four Seasons suite fifty-five floors above the city, Zander was going to voicemail.

After a brief period of sleep and a morning romp in the shower, Dalton and Stef went their separate ways. Stef was beaming, like she had just landed the prom king she had been pining after since freshman year. Since they had to go in separate directions, Stef hopped in an Uber to head home. She had intentionally not looked at her phone since arriving at the Four Seasons, and feeling a twinge of guilt she looked to find three missed calls and four text messages from Zander. Although she was still warm from the inside out after the night of ecstasy with Dalton, she couldn't help but feel bad for what happened. How was she supposed to turn down Dalton? Although she ran through all of the justifications in her mind, she couldn't help but feel bad. Zander was such a great guy—trusting, loyal, and loving. What he did at the cemetery was probably the most genuine show of affection she had ever experienced. All that said, Zander didn't make her body feel the same way that Dalton did.

She had almost forgotten about Amy's decision to join the Liquid Cougar League and move to Las Vegas. It was difficult to know what her life would be like without Amy. Although most people would think Amy was a terrible friend, it was that unusual magnetic Stockholm Syndrome pull that Stef always felt towards her. Deep down, there was an appeal towards Amy's unwavering confidence and dogmatic "take shit from nobody" approach to life, something Stef didn't possess. It still didn't feel real yet, that she would be leaving. As the Uber sped through the busy city streets, the news started to sink in more and more for Stef. She needed someone to talk to, and while it wasn't appropriate on many levels after what just happened the night before, she knew Zander would be an understanding ear. He was a great listener, and hopefully he wouldn't question her on why she didn't respond last night. Given the news maybe he had assumed she was with Amy. As Stef was typing a text to Zander, she didn't realize what would have been obvious to everyone else. Her dependency was already starting to shift—and with Amy out of the way, Mark had just taken one very large step closer to accomplishing what seemed unachievable just a week ago.

As Dalton handed the ticket to the parking valet, he had an impossible to contain smirk. He felt legendary, even more than usual. He was certain Stef never had a night like that before. He should be etched permanently in her mind. At one point when he was penetrating Stef from behind with her hands pressed up against the floor to ceiling window, he actually thought he should make a living out of this. There have to be other guys like Mark out there who need his help. *Everyone has a gift*, he'd thought as he stared out the window looking over Stef's tousled hair. This was his. The trip to Italy was probably overkill at this point, but no harm in sealing the deal he thought to himself. Plus the travel was for work anyway, the trip was basically paid for.

Zander received the first text from Stef and pondered his response. Although he suspected that Stef had spent the night with Dalton and the thought of that infuriated him, he knew the best thing to do was stay focused on his strategy. There was no upside in pressing Stef or even asking her where she was last night. He already knew the answer, and there was upside in making Stef feel bad. He had to be the guy who was always there for her. The caring listener, the rock, the person she could rely on. Although the strategy was already proving to be effective, it was even more critical once he played his final, and likely fatal, card against Dalton.

The next day Mark was still in disbelief over what transpired. He had spent the night at home celebrating the Amy news. He was anxiously awaiting the report back from Jason who had already let Mark know that Stef and Dalton arrived at the Four Seasons yesterday around noon, and he did not see them leave at any point before two a.m., when he finally left. *Fantastic news*, thought Mark. He actually laughed to himself a little bit, how crazy was it that he was happy to hear his ex-wife was holed up in a penthouse suite with a hot Italian getting laid out like she was Sunday's ironing. Knowing Stef as well as he did, he was confident that her world had been turned upside down yesterday. She likely threw herself at Dalton faster than a knife fight in a phone booth. He was curious what would happen now. Tony said that Amy would be overwhelmed for the next few weeks with her newfound celebrity status, and she needed to be fully moved to Vegas before the end of the month. Stef would hardly even see her before she left. The situation couldn't have been better, and Mark knew he had to focus on making sure nothing happened in the coming weeks which could derail his plan. He thought about asking Dalton and Zander to meet up with him at the warehouse but decided against it. Time was too precious right now to waste it meeting at the warehouse.

Later that evening, Stef showed up at Zander's place. They were going to get take-out and hopefully take Stef's mind off of the Amy news.

"Hey cutie, did you miss me," Zander smiled a bit, leaning in and embracing Stef in a tight hug. He could feel the stress in her touch.

Stef didn't say anything, but she didn't need to. Her grip around Zander was getting tighter, partially because of the Amy news but also because she still felt bad that only a few hours ago she was in the shower with Dalton.

They spent the next few hours sitting on the couch together, facing each other with their legs intertwined. Jazz music was playing in the background. Stef did most of the talking while Zander listened and added supportive comments. Zander's loft was very tranquil and peaceful. It was the perfect place for Stef to feel relaxed.

Not surprisingly, Zander already knew most of what Stef was talking about. Much of the history between Stef and Amy meeting at self-defense class and how she had influenced Stef to hate on men was in the playbook, and he had read it numerous times. He often had to catch himself from not finishing her sentence or leading onto the fact that he knew exactly what she was talking about. He slipped up early on letting her know he knew her manager was named Savannah and couldn't let a slip up like that happen again. Since it was getting late, Zander knew he had to act while the time was right. He had a proposition for Stef. A proposition she hopefully would not turn down.

"I know you have a lot going on right now and understand if you say no, but I wanted to ask you something." Zander's voice came across as slightly nervous, but serious. That was the tone he was trying for. He was the antithesis to Dalton and needed to keep the act up. He was the peaceful and somewhat shy artist, and always a gentleman.

"Of course Zander, what is it?" Stef didn't know whether to be excited or concerned given Zander's tone.

"My family has a cottage in Cape Cod. It's been in the family for generations and nobody will be using it this weekend. I was thinking about heading up there this weekend and was hoping you would join me." It was a fairly big step given how slow he had taken things, but he knew the timing was right. Particularly after what happened last night with Dalton, and their Italy trip only a little over a week away.

Stef paused, not because she was taken aback by the proposition but because Zander's family had a cottage in Cape Cod. Zander hadn't mentioned that before and it sparked more mystery about him. He actually didn't talk about his family much, except for his grandma. Stef had never asked him about the loft, but now it was starting to make sense. *Maybe he has family money*, she thought. After pausing a bit, contemplating the money question, she finally told Zander she would love to go. They ended up falling asleep together on the couch that night. Stef fell asleep shortly after the discussion, undoubtedly tired from not sleeping much last night and Zander laid awake for a bit plotting his next moves. This was working perfectly—in a few days they would be in Cape Cod and he would be one step closer to accomplishing the mission.

In the days leading up to the weekend, events unfolded as one might have predicted. Dalton and Zander both pursued Stef aggressively in the wake of the Amy news, and it seemed to be working. That said, Stef's twinge of guilt for sleeping with Dalton was apparently not enough to stop her from doing it again. She actually hadn't slept at home since the Amy news, literally splitting her nights between Dalton and Zander's places. It was actually getting quite complicated. She had never mentioned to either of them she was dating another person, and she assumed they knew nothing about each other. It was unchartered territory for her, learning to balance it along the way. She and Zander still hadn't had sex, but they were building up to it. The sexual tension between them was rising as the weekend in the Cape approached.

Separately, Stef's curiosity finally got the best of her and she started researching Zander's family. She had always wondered since he only talked about his grandma, but up until this point had respected his privacy. The cottage on Cape Cod piqued her curiosity. She was still trying to piece it together and confirm everything, but she was starting to wonder if Zander's parents owned a string of banks along the East Coast.

Douglass Capital was the holding company for several regional banks that were scattered up and down the coast between Florida and Maine. Zander's last name was Douglass, and Max and Jane Douglass were listed as co-CEOs of the "family owned financial services holding company."

Zander had never talked much about his parents with Stef, only that he had a falling out with them several years ago and since then only spoke when they had to. He had actually never mentioned them by name, but the Douglass Capital website indicated that Max and Jane lived in the town that Zander had said he grew up in. She couldn't find the mention of a son's name, only one newspaper article that referenced one child. She also knew Zander had no siblings, or at least that's what he had told her. The banks were privately held and solely owned by Max and Jane, estimates of their wealth was in the billions.

Although some of the facts lined up—same hometown, only one child, and the appearance that Zander must have money from somewhere—the entire idea that Zander was an heir apparent to a billion-dollar fortune still seemed far-fetched. Outside of the loft, it appeared that Zander lived frugally. Could he really be the sole heir to a billion-dollar fortune? Stef found herself obsessing over it, but wasn't sure what to do. She didn't want to pry and come across like she was interested in the money. Maybe she would see how this weekend would go. If the opportunity presented itself she could ask him questions about his family.

Friday arrived and Stef was scrambling to get ready for Zander to pick her up for their weekend getaway. Once again, Stef fell prey to Dalton's womanizing dominance last night and had spent the night at his place. The sex seemed to get even better, something she didn't think was possible. Fortunately for Stef, Dalton had to work Friday and that helped create an opportunity for her to leave in time to get out of his place, but she was still cutting it close. She made up a story for Dalton that she was going to a women's retreat for the weekend, something that she originally planned with Amy, but now she was going by herself.

Zander beamed as Stef got into the car he had rented for the weekend. Stef leaned in, giving Zander a kiss as she hopped in. Aside from the obvious reason for him to be excited to make up some of the ground he'd lost to Dalton, he thought the weekend was going to be fun. He was starting to like Stef more and more, and genuinely enjoyed spending time together. They had a five-hour drive ahead of them, so plenty of time to talk and for Zander to continue to move ahead with his aggressive plans. Dalton was putting all his chips on the Italy trip, but if Zander had his way, that trip was not going to happen.

Stef was also excited for the weekend, and a little nervous as well. She had been very physical with Dalton, but sex hadn't happened yet with Zander and she figured a weekend away was the likely time. Part of her was concerned, whatever happened between the two of them would likely not compare to the physical feats she had experienced with Dalton. As the two spent the first hour of the drive getting out of the city, they both started to unwind and enjoy each other's company. Now that they were starting to relax, Stef thought it was the perfect time to start asking more questions about his family.

"So, this is a family vacation home? Did your grandma own it?" Stef was growing curious. Was he really the heir to the banking empire she had read about? She was doubtful but still curious.

"It is a family vacation home for the past couple of generations. My parents are the owners." Zander was expecting the line of questions and had been thinking through how he would explain the situation.

Stef paused, hoping Zander would share more, using silence to draw it out of him. Zander didn't say anything else so finally Stef interjected again. "I see. Do your parents live there part of the year? You haven't said much about your parents, are you close with them?"

Zander paused, turning to Stef briefly with a grin. "I feel like this is one of those situations where the appropriate answer is, 'it's complicated.'" Although Zander already had a script in his mind of what he was going to share with Stef, he thought it was fun to make her work for it a bit.

Stef took the cue that it was a sensitive subject was prepared to tread delicately. "It's a five-hour drive, so we have time for 'it's complicated.'" Stef smiled back at Zander.

"In all honesty there is part of me that feels a little bad talking about it with you. It's true, I unfortunately have a less than perfect relationship with my parents. When I've thought about talking through it with you, it just makes me think more about how much you loved your parents, and tragically lost them in an accident. I feel guilty and selfish. Maybe I should do a better job of looking past the reasons we don't get along." Zander used this as an opportunity to solidify Stef's perception of him as a kind and compassionate guy.

"Zander, that's terrible! You can always talk with me about anything, and you don't have to worry about me judging you. I don't know your parents, but I obviously know you to be a very caring person. I'm not sure how anyone couldn't get along with you." Stef continued to fall into Zander's trap; that's exactly how he hoped she would respond.

Zander smiled. "Maybe you can convince my parents of that, the part about how everyone should get along with me."

"Why don't you get along?"

"We've just always lived different lives, had different priorities." Zander was continuing down the path of making Stef work for it.

"In what ways, how so?" Stef was intrigued. She really couldn't imagine someone not liking or getting along with Zander. Unbeknownst to Stef there was a side to Zander she didn't know.

"We have different ideals." Zander paused, and then continued. "My dad is a very successful businessman, a banker. My great-grand-father started a small bank about a decade ago, my grandfather took that over and then ultimately passed it on to my dad. My dad had different ambitions and grew the bank into a large banking conglom-erate, buying up every small bank he could up and down the East Coast. He's very driven by money. He especially took advantage of small banks during the credit crisis, buying up banks for pennies on the dollar. He bought up small community banks, closed branches and fired long-time employees. I don't think it's what my grandpa or great-grandpa would have had in mind." Zander shook his head, a look of frustration passed over his face.

The news shocked Stef; it turned out that Max and Jane of Douglass Capital were Zander's parents. She privately wondered if he was the heir to the fortune. Not sure what to say next, she asked if he still talked with them.

"We talk occasionally. I realize everyone has a different goal in life, and I'm not judging my dad's decisions. I just struggle with knowing that my grandparents probably wouldn't agree with it. I think what troubles me the most is that I've never been good enough for my parents, no matter what I do I can't live up to their expectations."

"What do you mean? How do you not live up to their expectations?"

"It's more that I can't live up to their expectations if I live the life I choose to live. They would be happy if I followed in my dad's footsteps and became a banker, but that's not what I want to do. I have always wanted to be an artist and they can't seem to accept or respect that. They want to control my life." Zander was trying to hold back his anger as he spoke because he didn't want to show Stef how upset he was, and of course didn't want her to realize what he was truly upset about, this was only part of it.

"They must think you are a very talented artist?" Stef was starting to understand the issues between Zander and his parents. "Is it more your dad, or your mom too?"

"Neither of them respect my art, nor do they support it. My dad thinks my pursuit of art is a waste of time and I'll never be successful. He doesn't understand why I would want to do that when I could help him at the bank. He claims most kids would kill for that type of opportunity, and it's embarrassing that I choose to be a 'starving artist.' I've begged and pleaded with them to not judge me based on what I want to do, but it's pointless. It's been like this for years. My mom is a little more understanding, but in the end she listens to what my dad says." Zander realized his anger was starting to show though, intentionally trying to inject more calm in his voice.

"Wow, that's awful Zander. I'm so sorry, I don't know what to say."

After a couple more hours of driving and Zander strategically sharing more tidbits about his family, they arrived at the home.

"When you said 'cottage,' I was expecting something a little more on the modest side," Stef said jokingly as her eyes danced across the expansive estate. The Douglass eight-bedroom mansion sprawled across the three-acre private waterfront lot. A rock cliff lined the back of the yard with stairs leading down to a private beach. "This is amazing!"

"The property has been in my family for two generations, although my parents rebuilt the home a couple of years ago and expanded it significantly. It's certainly excess for my taste, but that's how my parents live their lives." Zander wanted to continue to drop hints about his aversion to money or at least let Stef believe that.

After Zander gave Stef the full tour of the estate and grounds, they decided to head into the village for dinner. It was a great start to the weekend, and there was one primary goal Zander had before they left. It was not sex, although that finally happened shortly after they came back home after dinner and went to bed. While it didn't quite reach the levels of Dalton in terms of intensity, it exceeded Stef's expectations.

The next morning, Zander and Stef slowly woke up as the sunrise was just coming over the coast. Their bedroom overlooked the ocean, the sounds of waves and seagulls created the perfect atmosphere to wake up, relaxed and recharged. Zander told Stef he would pop downstairs and make coffee and breakfast, and bring it up to her. "Just sit tight, I'll be right back. Oh and by the way, I made plans for the day. Pack your boat gear, we're going sailing! I have a friend who owns a rental company. He's providing the boat and will be our personal captain as well."

As Zander was making coffee downstairs, he secretly unpacked some documents from his backpack. He placed the envelope marked Private and Confidential in big bright red letters on the kitchen table, in plain sight for Stef to see later.

The sailboat was a massive hit; Stef loved it. Their captain was a longtime friend of Zander's, and he also brought his wife. They ended up sailing to Nantucket for the day, taking in the shops, eating fresh seafood, and drinking rosé. It couldn't have been more perfect, and while Zander felt it was important to keep up his "money isn't important" message, he also wanted to show Stef what life could be like with him.

They arrived back home early that evening, fairly wiped out from a long day. They decided to just stay in and order pizza. Zander strategically set the pizza box next to the papers he left in the envelope on the table. He noticed Stef's eyes catch it, locking in on the envelope. "Oh sorry, stupid papers I need to sign this weekend for my parents, I'll move those," Zander said with an intentionally long sigh.

"Is everything OK?" Stef asked both curiously and empathetically. She could tell Zander seemed troubled by it.

"It is, it is," Zander said, somewhat unconvincingly. "I mean it is what it is at this point. I'm kind of resigned to that."

Stef paused, very curious but unsure if she should press Zander. "I'm here to talk about it, if you'd like to."

"I don't want to bore you with family drama."

"You aren't boring me at all!" Stef said. "We both know I've shared a lot of drama with you, and because of that I feel very close to you."

Zander paused, giving the appearance he was deliberating what he would say. "They are updated family trust documents, which my parent's attorney annoyingly wants me to sign. I've been procrastinating and wanted to read through them another time. I'll probably sign, I'm just not happy about it. It's yet *another* example of how my grandparents are rolling over in their grave right now at the actions of my parents."

"What are they doing now?" Stef continued to be very curious about Zander's family dynamics.

"It's mainly my father. He knows I disagree with how he is carrying forward my grandfather's legacy, and he also disagrees with how I want to make art my profession. That has come to a head now. The trust has a strange provision that he's using against me, and I feel as if I have no choice but to agree to his demands. If I'm not married by the time I'm thirty-five—so in just a few weeks—he gets full control of the trust. The intention was to protect my future wife and marriage because my grandparents assumed I'd be married by the time I was thirty-five, but it was worded poorly and he's now using that against me. My dad has the ability to waive it, but of course he will only do it if I agree to giving up any future control I have over the bank, including a board seat and any voting rights my shares have. He knows that means more to me than the money. It's really upsetting, although entirely predictable. I should have known he would do this." Zander paused. That was a lot for Stef to take in.

Stef was stunned, processing all the information that Zander just shared. The biggest shock was that he needed to get married in a few weeks in order to resolve the trust issues and carry forward his grandpa's legacy. She hadn't thought about marriage with anyone since Mark, so this was an unexpected twist.

After a short awkward silence that Zander anticipated, he broke the ice. "Anyway, we don't need to focus on that, we came here to have fun and enjoy the weekend, don't let my family drama get in the way. Oh and by the way, hopefully it's obvious, I'm not going to do anything crazy and marry someone else in a few weeks! You are stuck with me." Zander smirked. He was very pleased with how the message was delivered.

The remainder of their weekend was great, exactly as Zander had planned. He tactfully continued to drop wedding jokes along the way, and also more subtle points about how his grandparents would be so disappointed in his father. He knew how to play with Stef's emotions, and the trust marriage story was just crazy enough to work. Everything was falling into place.

MMA

The big night was here. It was the debut of the new Liquid Cougar MMA League. While Stef had a ringside seat reserved for her, courtesy of Amy, she debated whether or not she should go. Amy would only give her one ticket, knowing Stef would just invite either Dalton or Zander, and she (Amy) didn't want either to attend. Stef relented, deciding to attend despite not being able to take either guy. In reality it was probably a fitting final sort of get together for the two, now that Amy was a celebrity and had been devoting all of her attention to the league. Stef had been devoting all of her attention to the guys.

As Stef was getting a ringside attendant to escort her to her seat, she noticed Mark, directly opposite of her on the other side of the ring. The two hadn't seen each other since the court hearing, and the visual of him caught her off guard. She knew Mark's boss had some involvement with Liquid Cougar but hadn't thought much about the connection. She immediately recognized Ronald, Steve, and Christian, but not the two girls with their group. One appeared to be with Christian, which wasn't at all a surprise given his track record. The other was standing next to Mark. From a distance it looked like one of the girls from the doggy daycare place they where they'd taken Tyson.

Mark had expected Stef to be there, or at a minimum he knew through Tony that Amy had used one of her free ringside tickets for her. While Liquid Cougar wasn't part of his original plan, he had to admit it couldn't have been working out better. Not only did it come in handy for getting rid of Amy, but he thought bringing Katie to the event may also be helpful. Not that Stef would be jealous, but seeing your ex with someone else can create a little more incentive to move on, just out of spite. Even better, Mark could now see that Stef was attending solo, without Zander or Dalton. He was careful not to make eye contact with Amy as she made her way through the crowd.

"Hey guys, I think I dated her!" Ronald excitedly pointed to one of the girls in the ring, an undercard fighter named Anna "Sandblast" Wallace. "Hey Anna, remember me? Kick his ass!" Ronald was blowing her kisses and pointing at his bicep simultaneously.

"Did your friend really date her?" Katie leaned over to ask Mark with a confused and amused look on her face.

"It's hard to say for sure. With Ronald it's 90 percent bullshit, but there is 10 percent that turns out to be true—and it's usually the most unbelievable parts. He's like the Most Interesting Man in the World but for all the wrong reasons."

"He's very funny! It's nice to meet your friends, they all seem *interesting*." Katie had a tinge of sarcasm in her voice.

"*Interesting* is a great way to describe them." Mark smirked. He wanted to be sure Stef noticed he was having a good time. "I'm excited they're getting a chance to meet you, I just hope they don't scare you off." Mark smiled, putting his arm around Katie.

On the other side of the ring, Stef had found her seat and had indeed been watching Mark and his friends. She now for sure recognized Katie from doggy daycare. Even though Stef was the one who ended things with Mark, it still bothered her to see him happy with someone else. She wondered if there had been something going on with them the entire time, even when they were married. Stef found herself spending more time watching the two of them than she did paying attention to action in the octagon.

The event center was electric and bursting with energy. It was more than Tony ever hoped for. They could have sold out ten times over. In the weeks leading up to the event, Amy was a constant fixture in the sports world, making almost daily media appearances. Videos of her training, trash talking her opponent, and overall just forecasting the demise of all-male MMA fights permeated the internet. With the advice and encouragement of Liquid Cougar's PR team, she had started to tweak her narrative a bit. She came across a bit less crazy and more focused. They were trying to mold her into more of a role model for women as opposed to just a man-hating anger machine. She was still angry and crazy but would now consciously sprinkle in more supportive comments towards women's achievements and overall equality.

The undercards were wrapping up, and it was time for the main event. Stef had found herself increasingly fixated on Mark and Katie. Things always worked out for Mark she thought to herself. This of course was playing right into Mark's plan. He had been ignoring the guys and making it clear that his attention was being devoted to Katie.

"I'm pretty sure I could take her," Ronald shouted towards his friends as Amy was getting in the ring.

"In a hot dog eating contest you would crush her!" Christian retorted, eliciting a laugh from everyone. Ronald looked on with a face that was split between confusion and pride, then just smiled and nodded his head.

The crowd was on their feet, this is the moment everyone had been waiting for. Despite the fact that Amy was fighting a relatively low-ranked flyweight named Bob "Sundown" Miller, the place was erupting as the fighters tapped gloves. Although she wanted to immediately fight the champ, she finally relented and agreed to start with "the loser with a boring ass name," as she called Bob.

As the bell rang, Bob immediately came out and charged towards Amy. He was reluctant to take this fight, but Liquid Cougar made it financially too good to turn down. That said, he knew his job as a fighter was likely on the line if he lost. He didn't have much to gain by winning but everything to lose.

Everyone in the arena was on their feet, including Stef, who was still paying more attention to Mark and Katie. As Bob was charging Amy, she took one step forward, waited for the right time and then launched into a forward somersault thunder kick, dropping her heel right onto the side of Bob's head. A cracking sound loud enough to be heard several rows back was followed by a momentary hush over the audience. Bob fell to the canvas like a sack of water, and the crowd erupted with screams of applause. Just like that, Amy was not only the first female MMA fighter to take on a man but also the first to score a knockout within seconds of the match starting. Amy had found her calling, and Bob was likely going to be pivoting into a car sales career in a few weeks.

After the crowd calmed a bit and the medics were able to get Bob back up to his feet, Tony came into the ring. He gave a short speech about how Amy's victory not only would forever change the world of MMA, but it also would be an inspiration. "Women everywhere should move forward boldly and take charge," Tony expressed excitedly. While Tony wasn't an example of someone who should be giving advice on equality, his words sounded believable. He was also just ecstatic, knowing at that moment Amy would continue to take Liquid Cougar to new heights. This was only the beginning.

Meanwhile, Stef had been continuing to watch Mark and Katie

while also listening to Tony's words. *Move forward boldly and take charge,* Stef thought. The words echoed in her head as she thought about Mark clearly moving on with Katie. She shouldn't let that get her down, she was also moving on with her life. She had two great guys vying for her attention: Dalton and Zander. *She would show Mark,* she thought.

Little did Mark know, Amy winning and Tony's speech were like the icing on the cake for what was already an effective night of steering Stef towards marriage. Stef didn't wait around to see Amy after the event, Mark saw her walking up the stairs toward the exit after Tony's speech. Mark ended the night with a renewed feeling of confidence. Not only did he have a great time with Katie and his friends, but he thought the night played out even better than expected with Stef. He had been getting daily updates from Jason, his PI. The Cape Cod trip had been a success, and he knew Dalton had planned Italy out to every last detail—including a proposal. It's hard to believe he could be just days away from taking a big step towards solving his alimony issue. This all might just work he thought to himself.

CHAPTER 21

TSA

In the days leading up to the Italy trip, Stef continued to bounce back and forth between Zander and Dalton like a metronome. She was truly torn, and the guys weren't making it any easier. They knew some sort of decision was imminent, and it was increasingly looking like Stef was going to actually agree to get married. Stef also felt the pressure, trying to juggle both guys and running out of excuses for the excursions, especially with the recent trip to Cape Cod and the imminent and extended trip to Italy.

"Ciao bellissima, come stai?" Dalton gave Stef his trademark grin as he held her hand in the back of the town car he hired to take them to the airport.

"I'm not sure what that means, but I still can't help but blush," Stef said with a big smile on her face.

"Did you know Italian is thought to be one of the most romantic languages in the world? Many consider it to be the language of love." At this point the town car driver glanced back and was doing all he could to hold back rolling his eyes, Dalton was laying it on pretty thick to Stef.

"Well, I'm lucky to be able to experience that over the next few days, and hopefully you can teach me a few words." Stef was beaming at this point.

"Oh, I'll teach you a few words alright…"

"And here we are!" The driver said loudly as he pulled up to the international terminal, anxious to interrupt Dalton's theater-level flirting. "I'll get your bags if you folks just want to sit tight for a moment, and you can be off for your *language of love* vacation." Dalton shot a look at the driver, not appreciating the subtle mocking.

As they walked through the airport to security, Dalton had his trademark swagger in overdrive. He oozed confidence, and anyone around him could see and feel that. Stef always felt like she was a princess, Dalton had this air of royalty about him.

"Passports and boarding passes please," the TSA agent stated plainly and matter of factly, eyeing up the couple. Scanning both of their passports into the reader, the TSA agent paused and raised an eyebrow after the second beep. "I'm sorry, I think there is something wrong, let me scan those again."

Stef and Dalton were looking at each other, not paying close attention to the TSA agent. After a second scan, the TSA agent called two more TSA agents over for a consult, looking at their computer screen. They backed away slightly, talking quietly to each other so they wouldn't be heard.

At this point both Dalton and Stef caught on to something being up. "Is something wrong?" Dalton asked the TSA agents.

"Sir, ma'am, we'll need you to come with us." At this point the TSA agents seemed serious, and they had all moved very close to Stef and Dalton.

"We have a plane to catch, we can't be late. What is this about?" Dalton was annoyed and confused.

Without further discussion, the agents guided both Stef and Dalton around security and into a long hallway, one of the other agents was quickly walking ahead of them and communicating on a walkie-talkie.

Stef looked at Dalton at this point, confused and a little concerned. "What's going on, where are we going?" she whispered to him. "Wait, is this part of your plan? You're always scheming on something..." Stef was still confused but starting to think Dalton had arranged this.

Dalton had a blank look on his face, which was a rare occurrence. "No idea, this isn't anything I planned," he said.

"Sir, if you can step into this room, and ma'am please follow us down this hallway a little further." There were two more TSA agents in the room they pointed Dalton towards.

"Hold on, wait a minute. What is this all about? Why do we have to go into these rooms, and be separated? We're traveling together, we have a flight to catch, I don't understand what this is all about!" Dalton's normal confidence took a dramatic turn. He had real concern and anger in his voice.

"Please have a seat here and I'm sure we can clear this up so you can get on your flight," the TSA agent in the room said to Dalton.

Dalton reluctantly went into the room, and Stef followed the other TSA agents down the hall, before going into a room of her own. She was asked to sit at a small table, across from a female agent. The door shut behind her, so it was just the two of them in the room.

"What is going on? Am I in some sort of trouble?" Stef was confused and worried at this point.

"No ma'am, you aren't in any trouble at all. I just need to ask you a few questions, clear a couple things up. What is your relationship with the person you're traveling with today?"

"Dalton? My relationship with him?"

"Correct."

"Well, I guess you could say he's my boyfriend. We've been seeing each other for a while. Is he in some sort of trouble?" Stef was increasingly confused at this point.

"What was the nature of your travels with him to Europe?" The TSA agent ignored Stef's question about Dalton being in trouble and was taking notes as she asked the question.

"It's a fun trip. He invited me to spend a few days in Italy with him. He needs to go to London for work, but we'll be extending it to Italy and spending time together when he's not working."

"Exactly what will he be doing for work over there?" The TSA agent continued to take notes and run through her questions.

"I don't know, meetings I suppose. You'd have to ask him exactly. What is this about?" Stef was getting annoyed.

"Do you work with him?"

"No, I just told you, we are seeing each other!" Stef's voice jumped with anxiety.

"So, you're going on this trip willingly, voluntarily, as his girlfriend?"

"Yes, of course! Why won't you tell me what this is about?"

"Do you travel with him a lot internationally?" The TSA agent wasn't budging, continuing to ignore Stef's questions and taking notes.

"No, this is the first trip. You saw my passport, you can literally see exactly where I traveled to. Do I need an attorney or something? We're going to miss our flight!" Stef was fed up at this point, getting close to shutting down without having more answers.

The TSA agent continued to take notes, then stopped, looking up at Stef. She paused for a few seconds continuing to study her, then said, "OK, I don't have any additional questions for you at this time. I'm going to need you to wait here for a few minutes. I'll be back. There is another agent waiting outside the door, just knock if you need anything."

The TSA agent left, and Stef immediately pulled out her phone to find there was no service. She couldn't text Dalton, or anyone for that matter. A million things were racing through her head. Was Dalton in some sort of trouble? Why were they asking questions about them working together? It didn't make any sense.

Five minutes turned into ten, and ten minutes turned into twenty. Finally, thirty-two minutes later the door opened and the agent came back into the room.

"I apologize for the wait ma'am, we just had a few things to clear up. I appreciate your patience."

"Am I free to go now? Our flight leaves in twenty-five minutes, we need to get to the gate!" At this point Stef was a bundle of anxiety.

"Yes, you are free to go. That said, I'm not sure you'll be catching your flight. Your travel partner, Mr. Russo, is still being held. He will likely be detained for quite a while."

Stef sat back in her chair, shocked and unsure of what to say. "What? I don't get it. Why is he being held? Is he in trouble?" Her voice stammered as she was trying to find the words.

The TSA agent looked back at Stef, pausing, unsure what to say. "Look. I'm not able to share all details with you about why Mr. Russo is being held, but you seem like a sweet and innocent person who should have some answers." The agent paused again, searching for what she could and couldn't say. "There are allegations and some evidence that Mr. Russo has been involved in trafficking people out of Europe and into the US— namely, underage girls."

Stef was in shock, completely speechless and stunned.

"I told you more than I should have, but it's for your own protection. If I were in your shoes I'd want to know," the TSA agent said with genuine sincerity.

Stef, still stunned, trying to absorb the words. "I don't get it, that can't be. It must be some mistake. Dalton, trafficking girls?"

"I'm sure it's a lot to process and seems unbelievable. It usually is in these types of situations, I've seen a lot of them. You'd be surprised. His name came up on an alert that had been set up by law enforcement. Right now, Mr. Russo is in FBI custody, being transported to their offices for additional questioning and detention. Do you have anyone you can call, perhaps a friend? It might be good for you to talk through this and be with someone right now."

Stef paused on the question. She was starting to appreciate the gravity of the situation and felt like the agent's words were good advice. In the past she would have called Amy in a situation like this, but she wasn't talking to her much anymore and knew what Amy would say anyway.

All she thought about was Zander; he was the person she now turned to when she has to talk about something, but how would she talk about this to him? He didn't know Dalton existed, or that she was traveling to Italy with him. What would she say? "Yes, I do have someone I can call," Stef finally said after a long pause of thinking through the options.

As Stef left the airport, her head continued to spin. She was in a state of bewilderment as she pulled out her phone and noticed she had a text from Zander:

Hey love, have a great time in Italy, I'll miss you!

Stef had told Zander she was going to Italy, but obviously left out all the details. She paused, thinking about what to text him, deciding to keep it simple.

Hi there! So, a slight change in plans. I'm no longer going to Italy, and could use someone to talk to, if you're available? No worries if not, I know it's last minute.

As soon as she sent the text she could see Zander typing back, and he wrote:

I'd love to see you, come on over!

Stef said she was going to stop home to drop her things off, then come to his place. She would come over right after that.

Zander's Plan

As Stef was heading home and on her way to see Zander, he was celebrating that he somehow managed to pull off the airport prank with Dalton. Who knows where that would go, although Zander didn't care. At a minimum it would scare Stef away. Maybe Dalton would end up in jail, who knew. None of that mattered to Zander.

While it had cost him a little money and he had to call in several favors from family friends in high places, it was worth it. Dalton was in FBI custody now, and it would be extremely difficult for him to win Stef back after this. To set it all up, Zander had someone call in an anonymous tip. That tip led to an interview of someone who claimed to be in possession of evidence that a man matching Dalton's name and description was involved in human trafficking. He had a family friend of a friend who worked for border patrol pull Dalton's passport travel history for the past two years. He linked those dates to the dates of the anonymous tip and what the interview subject said, so the story all lined up. The timing was incredibly challenging to pull off. He'd started the anonymous tip the day before they left for Italy, trying to perfectly time it for when they were both at the airport. This was much better than just being arrested at his home without Stef, it would make it that much more real. He would later find out that Dalton literally went postal at the airport, and then later in FBI custody. He was obviously innocent, and after while realized this must have been a set up by Zander, but he couldn't talk his way out of it. If only Zander could have been a fly on the wall to see all of it. Now that the first part of his endgame plan fell into place, he had to execute the second part.

By the time Stef had dropped her stuff off and was pulling up to Zander's place, she had regained her composure and had a narrative for what she would tell him. She felt like their relationship had always hinged on honesty (or so she thought), so she would tell him the truth, leaving out some details. That it was actually a trip to Italy with another guy.

"I have a confession." Stef had a somber and serious look on her face as she observed Zander. "I feel like I should tell you, but I'm afraid you'll be upset with me and I don't want to lose you."

"I promise you won't lose me, I can guarantee that." Zander reached out to hold Stef's hand as they sat on the couch.

"I wouldn't be so sure. You don't even know what I'm going to tell you." Stef paused, still unsure this was the right decision but was won over by Zander's trusting eyes. "I actually was going to Italy with a guy, someone I had been dating. He turned out to be not who I thought he was, and after one of the most embarrassing moments of my life, the trip is off. Even though I was dating someone else, it in no way impacts how I feel about you. If anything, the incident made me realize who really matters, and what I really want—and that's you." Stef took a deep breath, her stomach churning with anxiety now waiting to hear what Zander would say.

"First off, thank you for telling me. I know that must have been difficult. Second, I was right —you didn't and won't lose me. You never told me it wasn't a guy you were traveling to Italy with, and we had not talked about being exclusive yet either. You didn't do anything wrong. I'm sorry the guy ended up not being who you thought he was…well I guess I mean I'm *not* sorry about that, but I'm sorry you were hurt in the process. For what it's worth, the guy is a complete fool for upsetting you. His loss is my gain!" Zander squeezed Stef's hand, smiling warmly.

Stef's stomach of nerves immediately turned into a rush of warmth throughout her body. She really needed support at that moment and was relieved beyond belief to hear his words. "It means everything to hear you say that. I'm sorry I wasn't more up front with you. I definitely learned my lesson." He was always there for her, literally. The moment reminded her of what he'd said to her at the cemetery, and how caring he was. At that moment she also felt incredibly stupid for trusting Dalton, especially after ignoring red flags.

Zander paused, smiling at Stef. "I think everything happens for a reason. Think back on how we met. What are the odds I would wander into Divine Mind and meet you, or that I'd see you again when I was painting in the park? It all leads to something, even small things that you don't expect to have a big impact on your life. It sounds like whatever happened at the airport, while painful, was also meant to be." Zander knew the spiritual narrative always landed well with Stef.

"That's true." The comment made Stef pause and think more deeply about what happened, her relationship with Zander, and her future. Her emotions at that moment were overflowing with all of the great memories she built with him over the past several months.

After a long pause, finally Zander interjected. "You must be starving. You were at the airport for hours, then went home to unpack, and now over here. I'm guessing you didn't eat at all today, have you?"

"Just a bagel early this morning." Stef was still pondering what Zander said, and she was relieved they had moved on so quickly from talking about the airport incident. In her mind she had distanced herself from Dalton and just wanted to move forward. *Typical Zander,* she thought, *concerned about how she was doing and putting himself second.*

"I'll order food. You should just relax. You've been through a lot today, let me take care of you."

Stef relaxed on the couch while Zander ordered food. She found herself exhausted from the crazy day. Instead of being in Italy with Dalton, she had almost been arrested and was now not going to Italy or likely (hopefully) seeing Dalton again, and instead with Zander. She was continuing to ponder what he said about everything happening for a reason, and her life in general. The divorce, Mark moving on, Amy's new life, and Stef's own relationships. As she was relaxing and thinking, she noticed what looked like the trust papers on the coffee table in front of her. She recalled their discussion in Cape Cod. Zander hadn't said much about it and he hadn't said anything since, but now she felt selfish seeing the papers. She hadn't asked. She had been so consumed with her own issues and dating multiple guys, she forgot that Zander was struggling with his own challenges. Yet in true Zander form, he didn't bring that up to her. That's one of the reasons she was falling more in love with him; he was so selfless. She hadn't realized that Zander had left those papers out intentionally, a subtle reminder for Stef.

The food arrived and Zander joined Stef in the living room. "I ordered your favorite, General Tso's chicken!"

"You're too kind, Zander."

"Ha, well I like it too, so it's not purely selfless." Zander laughed a bit at his own joke.

As Stef was dishing up her food, she thought his comment was the perfect opening. "Talking about selfless, I haven't really asked you anything more about your trust. I know it's not any of my business, but I noticed it on the table. Has anything new happened with that? Any breakthroughs with your parents?"

"Ha, nothing new. My dad being obstinate and stubborn doesn't really qualify as a 'breakthrough.' The situation won't really change, he won't give in. I think it just is what it is."

"Well, someone wise once told me that everything happens for a reason," Stef said with a smirk.

"Well played, I suppose that's fair." Zander was hiding his enthusiasm that the topic came up naturally. As expected, this was playing right into his hands. "I need to sign it, it's not like I'm going to get married in the next week. I've just been procrastinating. I hate giving him what he wants, especially when it feels like he's just betraying my grandparents wishes. I lose sleep at night thinking about that." In reality, Zander did lose sleep, but it was about the money more so than his grandparent's legacy.

"Even though I've never met your dad, I really don't like him. I hate to see you so upset."

Zander had played this scenario out in his mind a million times. It was the perfect opportunity in some ways. He could propose to Stef and profess his love for her, but how would that come across…insincere since she could think he had an ulterior motive? He could bring it up with the ulterior motive in mind, a sort of 'well we could get married and show them' proposal? Or he could also just wait, keep sitting out on the direct question and play coy in hopes that she brought it up. Each had their own risks and potential rewards. His gut told him to continue with the last approach, just wait. "Sure, I'm upset at him, but it's more that I'm disappointed. If I zoom out and think about what really matters in life, then I'm not upset at all. Relationships with people you care the most about are what really matters in life, and for that reason I feel like the luckiest person alive."

Stef beamed, at that moment she also felt extremely lucky. Even though earlier that day she had been planning to go to Italy, only to have that end in embarrassment and disappointment. In that moment she had forgotten all about Dalton, what he did, or what happened just hours ago.

CHAPTER 23

Nuptials??

Stef woke up the next morning in Zander's bed, but he wasn't there. *He must have left to make coffee*, Stef thought. She could smell it. They had a great night, and she felt like she never wanted to leave. They ended up talking for hours and making love. Everything that happened the past few days has given her perspective. She loved Zander, and he was the one for her. He's always there for her, no matter what. Other people like Mark were moving on with their lives, and the speech from Tony continued to ring in her mind. Would it really be that crazy to marry Zander? It would help him with his family situation, and they clearly love each other. She was going to bring it up to him. Before running out to the kitchen she grabbed her phone and noticed seven missed calls and twelve text messages from Dalton. She glanced through the texts, profusely apologetic. He said they got it wrong, it was a big mistake, and she should give him another chance. She paused a bit as she read them, realizing the bizarre reality of her rushing out to tell Zander she wants to marry him while getting love-crazed texts from Dalton. Even if Dalton was telling the truth, in her mind it didn't change anything. She could marry Zander, whom she had true feelings for, and he would be able to carry forward his grandparent's wishes. Stef tapped on Dalton's name in her contacts, hitting the 'block number' then 'delete contact' buttons. *Take charge*, she thought. Just like that, Dalton was gone.

"I have an idea!" Stef was enthusiastically running into the kitchen.

"Ok, good morning by the way!" Zander smiled, Stef catching him off guard.

"Let's get married. You can carry on your grandparent's legacy, and most importantly, I love you! It sounds crazy, but I learned a lot the past few days, and I'm not going to wait on life. I'm taking charge." Stef paused, realizing she actually said it all out loud. She was excited and nervous, unsure how Zander would react.

Zander of course had also played this moment out in his mind a million times. The script he had written in his mind was finally coming to life. He looked into Stef's eyes, playing the part like a Hollywood actor auditioning for the leading role in the next blockbuster. "Stef, I can't believe you're saying this," allowing his voice to crack a bit for dramatic purposes. "I'd love nothing more than to spend the rest of my life with you. From the moment I met you, I knew we had a deep connection. As we grew closer, I realized you were the only one for me. I didn't say anything because I was worried the news about the trust would make you feel as if I was doing it for the wrong reasons. That's the last thing I wanted. I wanted to propose, but I was going to wait until after the weird trust issue lapsed, so you didn't think I was doing it for the wrong reasons."

Stef ran over to hug Zander, both of them letting out a bit of an excited scream. "You're not doing it for the wrong reason, Zander. Let's do it today. Let's get married, like right now!"

"Are you sure, Stef? Today? I mean I'd love to, but are you sure that's what you want?" At this point Zander felt like it was shooting fish in a barrel, but he continued to play the coy angle.

"Yes, 100 percent. Let's go to the courthouse right now."

"Well, we should maybe shower first. I feel like the judge would appreciate that." Zander grinned as he joked with Stef.

"Yes, of course. Ahhhhh!!" Stef was giddy with excitement.

They quickly showered and got ready, Zander reminding Stef to take her passport since she still had that from the trip and would now need it for documentation. He of course was very clear-headed at this point, thinking of his inheritance, not only collecting what Mark promised him, but more importantly, the scam he was running within a scam. He'd take control of the family banking empire, his inheritance, getting back at his dad. He was literally hours away now, and he had to be sure nothing got in the way.

As they left Zander's loft, a car pulled up behind them and followed from a safe distance. Neither saw the vehicle, but it was Mark's PI, Jason. He had heard about what happened at the airport, and updated Mark. Mark had done a little intel digging on his own through various sources and heard that Dalton had been in FBI custody overnight but was finally let go early this morning. He didn't know exactly how it happened, but assumed that it was all Zander's doing; that he set Dalton up. He had thorough background checks performed on all of the guys and nothing like that had come up on Dalton. The airport incident and what Zander did was a complete surprise to Mark, he didn't expect it but was impressed. Mark knew things were getting serious now, but had no idea what just happened at Zander's place or where they were going. Jason just told him they left the loft and he was tailing them. Mark told him he wanted real time updates because he thought this could be it and was obviously hoping it was. Everything was riding on Zander at this point.

As they pulled up to the courthouse, both Stef and Zander were still giddy. Zander had been playing through in his mind what could go wrong at this point and the obstacles were narrowing. He was hoping they could actually get in today for a wedding and that the paperwork wouldn't take forever. Knowing this could be a potential outcome he had planned ahead. He purchased an old ring at a thrift store, but told Stef it was his grandma's. Everything was set, or so he thought. He wasn't worried about Stef changing her mind at this point, she seemed uncharacteristically decisive.

The PI saw their car pull up at the courthouse, and immediately called Mark.

"The courthouse, really?" Mark was surprised, despite knowing this is what he wanted. It was crazy to think this could actually work. He was about to orchestrate a wedding just so he could get out of paying Stef. "OK, well I want real time updates, let me know what happens. Get in there, but don't get caught. Be extra careful. Everything is on the line."

As Stef and Zander got inside, they fortunately found out there was one opening for a ceremony that morning. They just needed to finish the paperwork, which they were told would take thirty minutes. Witnesses were always around and oftentimes people would just be in the courtroom watching weddings. Zander thought to himself, this is it—less than an hour away. He was doing everything to keep his cool and subtly looking around for anything that could throw a wrench into his plan. One wrinkle was a pre-nup, or lack of one in this case. This was something that Zander had thought about extensively and had consulted with his attorney. The state they lived in was what was called equitable distribution, meaning property would be separated by the spouse who earned it. He likely didn't plan to stay married to Stef long, but he couldn't get the marriage annulled because that would mean that it legally never happened, and it wouldn't trigger the trust provision. Because of that he'd have to end the marriage in divorce, but he would likely do that quickly, and the fact that it was equitable distribution meant the risk was extremely low that Stef would get any assets from his inheritance. While Zander didn't love this risk, he had thought it through, and it was the best approach. *A prenup was too risky*, he thought.

The paperwork went well, everything was taken care of and the court administrator escorted Stef and Zander into the room where the ceremony would be performed. Another ceremony was wrapping up, and there were people inside the room watching. They didn't notice him at the time, but Jason the PI was off in the corner and had been texting Mark real-time updates. He just told him that Stef and Zander were now in the courtroom. Mark was literally jumping out of his seat. He couldn't really believe what was about to happen. He so badly wanted to be there. The next few minutes would decide Mark's fate, or so he thought.

The clerk motioned it was time for Zander and Stef to make their way to the front. The both bounced out of their seats near the back and smiled widely as they walked to the front. *Courthouse weddings are quick*, Zander thought, *this could literally be official in less than ten minutes.* They told the judge they didn't have any friends or family present, so the judge asked for two volunteer witnesses who would be needed to sign the marriage certificate. A young couple sitting in the front said they would. Every second that ticked by was like a minute for Zander, and for that matter, for Mark in his office. The judge who appeared to be in his eighties was casually making jokes that weren't funny and talking rather slow, drawing the tension out for Zander. Stef of course was oblivious to any of that.

After the judge walked through the procedural part of the ceremony, he asked Zander and Stef to repeat their vows.

"Stef, do you solemnly swear to take Zander as your husband, till death do you part, in sickness and in health?" The judge looked warmly at Stef.

It was a surreal moment for Stef, hitting her that yesterday at this time she was supposed to be leaving for Italy with Dalton, and now she was in a courthouse marrying Zander. She paused, a bit longer than expected and looked down, as if she was pondering what to say. Zander felt like he had stopped breathing for a moment as Stef took the question in. The PI in the back was glued to Stef, curious why she wasn't answering right away. "I do, yes, of course!" The few observers in the courtroom chuckled a bit, including the judge. Zander took a breath and raised his eyes a bit, as if to say 'whew that was close.'

Just as the judge asked for the rings and Zander put his hand in his pocket to get them, the door to the courthouse swung open. It hit the back of the wall with a loud crack, everyone immediately turned to look and even the bailiff seemed to jump as if someone was storming the courthouse.

A tall man stood at the back, he was sweating and disheveled, looking like he had just ran a marathon. "This wedding is a sham, that guy is getting paid by her ex-husband to marry him so he doesn't have to pay alimony anymore! It's a trick, and she doesn't know anything about it. I should know, I was going to be paid too."

"Dalton?"

"I'm sorry Stef, you needed to know the truth. You didn't reply to my calls or texts, then blocked my phone, and I worried you were doing something crazy. I still had Find Your Friends installed on my phone and tracked you here. I could see you were about to make a big mistake and came here hoping I would catch you in time. It's Mark, he's paying us off so he doesn't have to pay you anymore. Zander and I were in a competition to marry you, so Mark would be off the hook."

Everyone in the room turned back to look at Stef, and it was clear that in the judge's fifty-plus years of officiating weddings, nothing like this had happened before. He was dumbstruck. Jason, the PI in the back of the room, sunk his head low. It was a knockout blow to the plan.

Stef looked at Zander, her face pale white and a look of confusion and shock. "Zander…is what he's saying, true?"

Good Morning

Mark heard a constant knocking noise; he was slowly starting to wake up. His eyes started to come into focus and he could see Tyson staring at him, his butt wiggling with excitement and hitting the nightstand which was creating a knocking sound. Mark felt like he had been hit by a bus, extremely groggy and disoriented.

"Hey Tyson, what time is it buddy? I feel like it's the middle of the night."

A female voice from outside of the room shouted, "It's about time you woke up. I think Tyson thought you were dead."

Mark hearing the voice quickly jolted, sitting up in the bed to see who it was. "Stef?" he said in a moment of confusion. He didn't have his contacts in, but it looked like her.

"Yeah, of course, were you expecting someone else?" she said laughing.

Mark paused, trying to collect his thoughts and figure out what was going on. Why was Stef in his house?

Stef walked into the room at this point, looking at Mark. Mark stared blankly back at her, still confused. "I'm surprised you are even coherent. I don't know what you did last night, but you could barely talk when you got home. You passed out before even brushing your teeth. Christian is such a bad influence on you, and Ronald too, for that matter. You had *way* too much to drink."

Mark looked back at Stef, his mind slowly starting to wake up and absorb the words. His head was pounding and that could explain what Stef had just said. He was starting to remember now, vaguely. They went out to celebrate Ronald's birthday. But what about the divorce and the Megslist ad, Dalton, Dexter, Zander, MMA, and everything else that had happened. It was vivid in his mind.

"You also did that thing last night when you drunk-talk in your sleep. I have no idea what it meant, something about something called Liquid Cougar, and you were talking about Amy at one point. Then just a lot of mumbling. It was weird, not to mention annoying."

"What day is it?" Mark was still confused but slowly starting to grasp the situation.

"Sheesh, you really don't know? It's Friday, our anniversary weekend. We have dinner reservations tonight. You need to get up, get to work. I also have to get to work. Can you get up and take Tyson out now?"

Mark looked around the room again. He pinched himself, still unsure. Slowly he was starting to realize what had happened. *It had all been a dream*, he thought. Literally everything. He was still married to Stef, didn't get hit with a big alimony judgement, and Dalton didn't just interrupt Stef's marriage to Zander. Liquid Cougar didn't start a man vs. woman MMA League, and Amy was not the lead fighter. *What an absolute crazy dream*, he thought. As relief passed through him, he forgot about the headache and started laughing out loud at how crazy it was.

"Hello...you're looking around like you've never seen our bedroom before. That's your dog, Tyson." Stef said as she watched Mark look around like he was in a fog.

"Sorry, yes, of course. I think you're absolutely right, I did hit it a little hard last night. Sorry about talking in my sleep, I had the *craziest* dream." Mark felt obligated to say something, but he obviously couldn't tell Stef the details. More so he was just relieved, his life hadn't been upended after all. Nothing had changed. He was going to pick up their tickets to Greece later today, and they had dinner reservations at six p.m. At that point he jumped out of bed, temporarily setting aside his raging headache, and gave Stef a big kiss and hug.

"Are you OK? What has gotten into you? And by the way, I'm already showered and ready, so enough hugging me. This is a brand-new dress and you probably had the drunk sweats last night." Stef seemed confused and mildly annoyed.

"Sorry, sorry. Yes, just a crazy dream." Mark was beyond relieved at that point. Both relieved and shocked that it was all a dream.

"I'm leaving now, Mark. I didn't feed Tyson yet, so make sure to do that after you take him out." Just like that she closed the door. Mark sat on the side of the bed, scratching Tyson's head for the next twenty minutes, playing the entire dream back through his head. Nobody would ever believe it.

EPILOGUE

After Mark got ready, his headache slowly started to get better. He couldn't get over the sense of relief he felt, knowing it all had been a dream. He took Tyson to the dog park before leaving for work, laughing out loud several times as he was thinking about everything that happened. So ridiculous, yet it felt so real. The story about Amy becoming an MMA fighter. She did hate men—and Mark—but the crazy stories your subconscious dreams up Mark thought: *Men vs. women MMA*!

On his way to work he stopped by the Dog Den to drop Tyson off and found it awkward to talk with Katie. He just had a crazy relationship with her in his dream, though she did seem nice to him. The last stop before heading into work was the travel agency to pick up their tickets to Greece. Everything was in order, they were all set.

The day at work flew by, especially once Mark's headache went away. Around midday he was texting Christian, Steve, and Ronald to see how they were feeling, and equally important to see if anyone remembered what they drank last night. He so badly wanted to tell them or Tony about the dream.

After work, Mark arrived at the restaurant, a few minutes early for their reservation so Stef wasn't there yet. He had tickets in hand and was ready to tell Stef about the Greece trip. As he sat down, his phone buzzed. It was a text message from Stef:

I'm going to be a little late. Amy and I are shopping after work,

Jimmy Choo has a sale. She's also going to join us at dinner, at least for the first part. We have something to talk with you about.

Mark sat motionless, his mouth dropping to the floor and headache starting to return.

About the Author

CN FARGO is the author behind *Liquid Cougar*. He is an entrepreneur, tech startup investor, dog person, semi-professional youth sheep rider, and writer. After growing up in North Dakota, he moved around - living in Minneapolis, Denver, San Francisco, Madison, Milwaukee, Chicago, and Dublin Ireland. His work on Liquid Cougar was a 10 year journey; the story started out as an idea for a screenplay, and after a six year hiatus to start a company, it turned into a novel.

Printed in Great Britain
by Amazon